Mr. Montgomery

by

Nadlee Thims

This is a work of fiction. Names, characters, places, and incidents are either the product of the author's imagination or are used fictitiously, and any resemblance to actual persons living or dead, business establishments, events, or locales, is entirely coincidental.

Mr. Montgomery

Contact Information: info@thewildrosepress.com

Cover Art by *Diana Carlile*

The Wild Rose Press, Inc.
PO Box 708
Adams Basin, NY 14410-0708

Visit us at www.thewildrosepress.com

Publishing History
First Scarlet Rose Edition, 2020
Print ISBN 978-1-5092-3389-2
Digital ISBN 978-1-5092-3390-8

Published in the United States of America

**Are they mixing business with pleasure...
or pleasure with business?**

"I'm so sorry, Mister Montgomery. I'm so embarrassed."

"Don't apologize to me. It didn't offend me. As I said, I found it rather amusing. I just feel bad for you ladies that have to fake anything." He smirked and shook his head. "I don't mean to get out of line, here, but there are some of us men who would never settle for fake. Women deserve so much better than that."

"Are…we really having this discussion right now?"

"Hey! You started it. I'm just saying not all men buy into the fake it pacification." He pressed his lips together and tilted his head, pivoting it slightly.

Apparently, I forgot myself because I shot back, "So, are you one of those guys? How do you know that women aren't faking it with you? We're good at sparing you guys the embarrassment."

He flashed a devious smile.

"I'm sorry, Mister Montgomery. I really didn't mean to get out of line, either."

"Some things can't be faked, and I can assure you, I do know the difference." He smiled a cocky smile, ignoring my apology.

"Sure! Can you prove this somehow?"

Dedication

This book is dedicated to anyone who enjoys a little extra hotness with their bedtime story.

Chapter One

When he came through the door, I could tell from the look on his face that he was pissed. Jackson Montgomery didn't have much in terms of a temper. Oh, no! He wasn't going to throw punches or scream and yell. Not my boss. He had other "outlets" for his anger.

We had been secretly dating for just over four months. I didn't see an end coming anytime soon. He had been my dream guy for so long that once I had his attention, I intended to keep it. What made him so special? It could've been a few things, or maybe a combination. I just knew I could not stop thinking about him.

The passion that burned within this man made my blood run hot. He had a natural sex appeal that crippled me without requiring any effort on his part. When he lifted his broad shoulders to untuck his button up shirt, I instantly craved him inside me. When I gazed into his beautiful, deep, blue eyes, I felt myself surrender to the inviting warmth of his soul. The wild, messy, devil-may-care hairstyle perfectly fit the bad boy that I had come to know. The diamond shape of his face and the perfect angle of his nose gave him an angelic perfection. Yeah! An angelic image…betrayed by his own sexy, seductive, devilish grin.

Ah, that grin!

I often saw it as his lean, six-foot tall frame drove his thick cock deep inside me like some well-oiled machine. To be honest, it could've been his cocky, no apologies attitude. I couldn't put my finger on it, but he had that "it" factor. Mr. Jackson Montgomery could easily be every woman's wettest dream come true.

As he moved through the office, he flashed a smile at Dena, the accountant. She seemed to want to be everyone's big sister. Jackson's passive smile was convincing enough for her, but I could see behind that fake grin. As he passed one cubicle after the other, smiling and nodding, he got closer to my desk. His beautiful eyes had that savage, ravenous glare in them that invited me in, and dared me with temptation.

We had agreed that no one needed to know we had a "thing" going on the side. Some of my coworkers had to have picked up on the inside jokes and the sultry glances we shared, but today, the devious look in his eyes made me believe he would throw me on the desk, right there in front of everyone and put an end to any questions anyone might have had.

He tilted his head to the side as he stared into me. His chest rose and fell with his heavy breath. He arched his eyebrow and bit his lower lip as a smirk spread across his face. I smiled sweetly and slowly blinked.

"Good morning, Mr. Montgomery."

"Good morning, Elizabeth. How are we doing today?"

"Amazing, as always."

I knew he meant my "condition" after he had spent half of the night before, riding me up and down the walls in my apartment. Jackson was a sexual man, and if he fantasized about it, he didn't shy away from asking… No…demanding! He swore he did it all for me, and to be fair, he gave me the hottest sex I had ever had in my life. For no reason did I plan to let go of that.

After I answered his question, he lowered his head, focusing on his fingers as they traced the edge of my desk. A smile spread across his face, then he shook his head as though he were shaking off the thoughts in his brain. I could see it in his eyes. He had a plan brewing.

With a professional tone, he said, "Do you happen to have the budget report for this next fiscal year?"

"I do, actually. I just finished it. I'll print it out for you."

"Can you bring that into my office, please?"

"Of course." I smiled.

His eyes fixed on mine again. "Thank you!"

Could it be an excuse to get me in his office? Maybe the request was real. Something about the look in his eye made me doubt that he gave a shit about that budget report. However, it would be a bad time to be wrong about my hunch, so if for no other reason than for the sake of all of the other subordinates, I played along.

I gathered my coffee cup, a notepad, and a pen. I attempted to make it look like I *planned* to work. I made my way over to the printer, scooped the papers in my hands, and tiptoed my five-foot four frame into Jackson's office.

When I walked through the door, he stood hunched over a stack of papers on his desk, leafing through a packet of some sort. He lifted his head to look at me. His perfect chin jutted out, motioning toward the door.

"Come on in. Can you catch that door for me, please?" He sounded so official.

As the door latch fell into the hatch, Jackson fell into his seat and locked his fingers behind his head as though waiting to be handcuffed by the police. He drew a deep breath and exhaled as he just stared at me. I smiled and closed the gap between us. I tossed the report on his desk and gripped the armrests of his chair, lowering my mouth to kiss him.

"I'm going to have to fire you."

My tongue traced down his neck. "Mmmhmm! You always say that."

"I want to so we don't have to be a secret anymore, but I like being able to fuck you anytime I want."

"Are you okay today?"

"No! I can't see you without my cock getting hard."

"Come on, I mean it. What got under your skin? I can see it in your eyes. You're angry."

"Mmmhmm! You know me too well." He seemed impressed that I challenged him. He smiled as he slowly blinked with a nod. "That would be Bob and his job site, but I don't want to talk about that. I'd rather bend you over, flip your skirt up, and make you come."

I turned around and wiggled my ass, just for effect.

"You want it?" he said as his eyebrows lifted.

He ran his hands up my skirt and closed his fingers over the waistband of my panties. As if they were on fire, he removed them from my body. He gripped my ass, releasing a soft, throaty moan while squeezing with his greedy, firm hands.

"Fuck! You little cock-tease."

Playfully, I backed up, straddling his legs, wiggling my ass as I moved over him. He never stood from his chair. He just pushed me away and turned me to face him. His hands reached up to my hips, pulling my pussy toward his mouth as his tongue brushed over my sex.

"You're a bad boy."

I brushed my fingers through his hair. He said nothing. He didn't need to. The way he handled me told me he wanted to get a little dirty. He stood and turned me away from him, pushing me to the edge of his desk. He pushed against my back, prompting me to lean forward. He said his approval as his eyes scanned over me. My heart pounded and my chest heaved. I knew what he wanted, so I spread my legs to make it easier for him.

He reached under me, between my legs. I gasped when I felt his hand brush against my swollen lips. His fingers dove inside me, spreading my wetness from my pussy to my clit. Then his fingers traveled past my pussy to my asshole. His touch felt so light that it tickled in an erotic, teasing kind of way. My pussy ached, craving every inch of this man's cock. With each pass, he pressed against my hole, threatening to penetrate me, making me want it. I pressed back against his touch, encouraging him to slide in deeper. Pleased with my response, he pressed against my tight hole and I felt him sink into me. I drew a deep breath as he slowly pushed in deeper. My pussy dripped, aching and ready for him.

He draped his solid body over me, as he slowly fingered my ass. His breath in my ear as his finger pumped in and out of me drove me wild. The soft, throaty moans of approval were sending me over the edge.

"You know what I want?"

"What?" I said as I reached over my shoulder,

cradling his head.

He chuckled a throaty, devious laugh. “I want…” He quickly rammed his finger inside me. “This.”

Oh, fuck! I loved it when he wanted to play rough. It turned me on so much when he dominated me like this. His aggressive, demanding tone was as sexy as hell to me. He knew what I wanted, and he knew what buttons to push to get what he wanted.

The gritty sound of his zipper was music to my ears as he unfastened his pants. Then his cock slapped against my butt cheek. His hands gripped me, squeezing as he parted my cheeks. While his hands massaged my ass, the tip of his erection teased my opening. He guided his cock barely into my pussy, then slamming his hips against me, his thickness penetrated me. This time, he seemed restless, as though he needed something more. His soft breath in my ear became temptation on a brand, new level.

“What do you want?”

“I want you.” I meant it. I wanted him in ways I had never wanted a man before. My voice sounded desperate. I needed him to please me.

His tongue traced my earlobe as his hands slid under my blouse, squeezing my breasts. He massaged them for a few minutes, pumping his hips, driving his cock in and out of me. He slid his fingers inside the edge of the cups of my bra and ripped, tearing the fabric between my tits. His hands squeezed and pulled, sending staggering pulses of desire to my core. He pinched my hard nipples between his fingers as his hand squeezed my breasts, and his teeth bit at my neck. The way his heavy breath rushed over my skin awoke every primal desire I had ever had. I wanted him to make me come.

"You gonna let me?" His soft voice pleaded for something I didn't fully understand.

"Let you?"

"Yeah!"

He withdrew himself and teased my ass with the tip of his erection. The thought of what he was suggesting stirred me up even more, for some reason. I could feel myself getting wetter. My heart pounded, and I could not catch my breath. The thought of our naughty play turned me on yet made me nervous at the same time. My pussy ached, wanting to be filled. This man became the king of every ounce of my sexual satisfaction. He had convinced me to do several things that turned out to be the hottest moments I had ever experienced. The thought of letting him pound my ass was one of the most erotic mental imagines I could envision.

His dick skimmed my asshole, pacing, patiently begging for permission. I turned the idea over in my head.

No! Yes! No. Maybe. Mm! Yes!

I stood up and leaned back against him, resting my back against his chest.

"Can we go slow?"

His hand reached around me, and he began flicking my clit as he smiled down at me. "Yeah! We can see how long that lasts."

****

Maybe before I get too carried away here, I should take you back to how I got to the point of fucking my smoking hot boss. This is a naughty, dirty, wildly sexy story, but if you'll bear with me, I'm sure you'll get just as much enjoyment out of it as we have. We'll come back to this hot little moment in a while. First, I want to share several hot moments that led to this one. Wanna come? I'll take you for a playful little stroll down memory lane. Ready?

Chapter Two

I've worked for Jackson Montgomery for just over two years. When he hired me, he expressed a desire to have someone he felt compatible with to fill the position of his executive assistant. He didn't have time to constantly correct mistakes, and he didn't have the desire to have to change the way he did things to make it easier for his assistant. He needed someone who could catch on quickly and roll with the punches.

When I first met him, I felt an instant attraction to him. He seemed fairly arrogant and cocky. However, to be fair, he *had* left a pretty decent gash in the heart of the construction world, especially for a thirty-five-year-old man. He had a passion for construction. He wanted every job that came up, and he usually got them. His ambition, drive, and energy were infectious. I wanted to be part of that. When the call came, offering me the job, I was over the moon. Jackson Montgomery's velvety voice personally offering me the job didn't hurt either. I'll never forget his words.

"Elizabeth, this is Jackson Montgomery from Montgomery Construction. I wanted to give you a call and see if you're ready to get to work."

The sound of his voice… Oh, hell yeah, I was ready to get to work! I'm not sure we were talking about it in the same way, but whatever it took to get me closer to this man, I wanted to do it.

He was only three years older than me. The day I interviewed, his face looked slightly scruffy, and his sultry, blue eyes stared into me. His wicked, sexy grin summoned me as he asked his interview questions. He looked like the kind of bad boy that you might get to hold, but you were never going to keep. It conflicted with the professional manner in which he conducted himself, "Miss Roundtree" this and "Miss Roundtree" that. His respectful demeanor impressed me, but his eyes portrayed something very different.

I wanted him.

After I started training, I had tried, on several occasions, to gauge the size of the bulge behind his zipper. I felt certain he caught me looking a few times, though he seemed dismissive if he had noticed. That wasn't the same thing as inviting me to stare, however. I did anyway, and one day things became even more fun.

He stepped to the edge of my desk. He held a three-ring binder that contained all of the owner's manuals for every piece of equipment we had installed in one of the buildings. These notebooks were a big deal, since they always marked the close of a project. These books happened to be the last thing we gave the client. It was kind of a parting gift. That manual signified we were officially turning the building over to the owner. This particular notebook happened to be one of the most frustrating books I had ever assembled. I knew Jackson always verified all manuals were present and accounted for before he handed them over to the client. This one made me nervous. The job had so many pieces of equipment, I was sure I had forgotten a manual or two. He turned the pages, leafing through the notebook.

"Elizabeth, is this the book you put together?"

"Uh, yes. Is everything okay?" I asked, accidentally staring at his crotch.

"It's great. I just wanted to tell you that I'm impressed. You were very…" He paused, and my eyes quickly lifted to his, "…thorough," he said with a smirk. He held the notebook out and glanced down the front of his body, then his eyes returned to mine as though he expected some kind of feedback.

He never broke his professional demeanor. But in his eyes, I saw a warning sign… No! I saw a curious dare in his sparkling eyes. He slapped the notebook closed as he held the stare we shared. He pressed his lips together, bobbing his head as he covered his crotch with the binder.

"Thank you," he said with a flirty smile. He turned on his heel and went back to his office.

For the next year and a half, I had numerous sexual fantasies about him. I didn't have them all day, every day, but from time to time, a certain catch in his voice would send my mind barreling right for the gutter. He could've had anyone he wanted, and as hot as he was, I didn't think I stood a chance, in terms of making any of those fantasies a reality, but holy shit! That man was sexy, and I felt certain he knew that.

Mr. Montgomery's exchanges with me were always professional and usually about business. Every now and then, I'd see something playful dwelling in his eyes. I would try to coax that out of him, but he stayed too guarded—too professional.

Part of the sex appeal consisted of Mr. Montgomery's ability to be blunt. His confidence and boldness turned me on. He just had a way of saying whatever he thought. He had gained the respect of others in the field with his sharp tongue, and he never used that sharp tongue on me—though I sometimes wished he would—I respected him for his ability to be direct. I had a feeling that as cocky as he could be, Mr. Montgomery would be hard to handle. I wouldn't mind trying to handle him.

Oh, how I wanted to *handle* him.

The day things started getting really flirty between my boss and I happened when I had forwarded a joke email to one of my co-worker friends, Jan. I pulled up an email she had previously sent me, hit "reply," and copied and pasted the body of the joke into the reply to her original email. Within a short time, people were cackling in their cubicles and wheeling their chairs to where they could look down the aisles to smile at me or give me a thumbs up. I had no clue what in the hell was going on.

Then, I heard Jackson Montgomery's voice from behind me. "Elizabeth, can I speak with you, please?"

His voice had a tone, that sharp-tongued kind of tone. I felt as though I could burst into flames at any moment, and not in a good way. I stood, smoothing my skirt with my hands as I cautiously stepped into his office. I studied his face as he waited for me, leaning against his door, resting his hand on the doorknob. I stepped past him and my stomach sank. He looked irritated. He closed the door behind me and extended his hand, offering me a seat at one of the chairs in front of his desk.

"You should probably have a seat." He pointed to a chair with a sarcastic smirk.

I sat down and patiently waited as my boss sat across from me. He drew a deep breath, held it, and then forced all the air out of his lungs. He pressed his tongue against the inside of his cheek and cocked his head. I felt torn between wanting to rip his clothes off and wanting to hide somewhere…anywhere.

"I need you to know that sexual harassment is not something I can tolerate."

I gasped for breath. This sexy man wanted to discuss sexual harassment with me? Could he read my mind? He lost me at the word, "sexual," to be honest. My mind ran away with that word and my fantasies about him were revved and ready to go.

Right! Focus!

"Excuse me, Mr. Montgomery?"

"I'm referring to that rather salacious email you sent…to everyone in the company. Why would you do that?"

"I wouldn't do something like that! What email? Maybe I got hacked?"

He leaned back in his seat, intertwining his fingers over his belt, blinking slowly as he turned his head, staring at his computer screen. He began reading aloud. My heart stopped. I knew that message all too well. I intended that email to only go to Jan. This was the same Jan who worked in our human resources department, of all things.

Apparently, I had replied to a company-wide message, rather than a private message from Jan. I'd sent her the sexist joke, poking fun at the way some men think they're the king of the bedroom, and how women fake orgasms to protect them. That's the brief version.

Anyway, as Jackson read the words, my mind raced, trying to think of a way to save my ass, as well as Jan's. *He couldn't tolerate sexual harassment.* What did that mean? Would he really shit-can me over a joke?

I sat there sweating as he finished reading with a smirk on his face. His eyes shifted from his computer screen to mine. He seemed to be fighting back a smile. He shook his head and stood. He leaned over his desk, resting on his knuckles, glaring down into my eyes. One of the sexiest men I had ever seen in my life was about to terminate me. I could feel my heart throbbing, crashing against the wall of my chest. As he stood, glaring down at me, his stern face finally broke into a smile as he tilted his head to the side.

"Mister Montgomery, I'm so sorry! I had no idea that went to everyone. I only wanted to send it to Jan, but she's innocent! She knew nothing. This is all my fault!" I rambled, trying to bail Jan and I out before he could say anything.

"As I was saying, I cannot tolerate sexual harassment. I understand that mistakes happen. I got a damn good laugh out of it, but cover your ass and send out an apology, please. I think most people would see the humor, but there's always going to be that one whiner that's going to raise hell and throw a fit. I don't want to deal with whiners today, okay?"

"I'm so sorry, Mister Montgomery. I'm so embarrassed."

"Don't apologize to me. It didn't offend me. As I said, I found it rather amusing. I just feel bad for you ladies that have to fake anything." He smirked and shook his head. "I don't mean to get out of line, here, but there are some of us men who would never settle for *fake*. Women deserve so much better than that."

"Are…we really having this discussion right now?"

"Hey! You started it. I'm just saying not all men buy into the *fake it* pacification." He pressed his lips together and tilted his head, pivoting it slightly.

Apparently, I forgot myself because I shot back, "So, are you one of those guys? How do you know that women aren't faking it with you? We're good at sparing you guys the embarrassment."

He flashed a devious smile.

"I'm sorry, Mister Montgomery. I really didn't mean to get out of line, either."

"Some things can't be faked, and I can assure you, I *do* know the difference." He smiled a cocky smile, ignoring my apology.

"Sure! Can you prove this somehow?"

I couldn't believe the words that were coming out of my mouth. I must have wanted to get my ass fired. F-I-R-E-D! Apparently, it had become my mission for the day.

Jackson cocked his head and gave me a flirty smile. "Proof, huh? I think I'm going to stop pushing my luck. I'll just say that you deserve to feel good. Guys like me wouldn't let you off the hook with that *fake it* bullshit."

"I would love to not have to *fake it.* But, what does that mean? *Guys like you*? I only know you on this side of the sheets, and quite frankly, I'm forced to *fake* a lot for you on this side."

I could have died. Within my head, I screamed, *Shut up, self! Just shut…the…hell…up!*

His tongue pressed against his back teeth as he processed what I had said, then he smiled his sexy smile. It gave me rampaging butterflies in my stomach. Agh! I felt certain he knew what he was doing to me in that moment. He had to! He motioned with his head toward his door.

"Go send your apology before we end up in a bunch of trouble."

"Chicken!" I blurted out. Then I lowered my head in shame. "I'm sorry. I honestly have no idea… Please don't fire me. I don't know what is wrong with me today."

"Probably all that *faking it* you have to do," he said with a flirty grin and a wink.

He turned to walk me to the door, put his hand on the knob, and pulled it open. He passively lowered his head and stared down at me, scoffed, and shook his head.

"Get outta here. Behave yourself, and please, watch who you send those emails to. We can't have that stuff flying around the workplace. Ya know?"

"I'm sorry about that. I'm really embarrassed."

He pressed his lips together and nodded. With playful sarcasm, he said, "Oh! Yeah! I could tell."

He turned and started back toward his desk. I wanted to climb his body from the floor up and claim his magical self for my own. I wanted him so bad.

Instead, I went and wrote a companywide email, explaining my mistake. I sent my sincerest apologies in the event that my email had offended anyone. I promised to watch more closely in the future. I could see the notifications as people read it. I watched for Jackson's notification.

It didn't come. I sent him a private message.

—I apologized. Better?—

A few minutes passed, and then I saw that he had opened my message. Then he opened my apology. He replied to my private message.

—Sounds fake to me.—

In that moment, I made my mind up that I would have that man. No matter what it took, I would have him! I wanted to see how much "faking" I would have to do with him. For someone that cocky, surely sex would be insane. I had to know.

For a couple of days after that, anytime Mr. Montgomery spoke to me, or even looked at me, my clit tingled. I wanted him in the worst possible way. We privately flirted but seemed to be stuck in the flirting stage. I wanted it to be more, then one day, it seemed my wish was granted.

Jackson had gone to lunch. He came back in, smiled as he passed me, and went into his office. I heard the squeak of his chair as he sat down. I heard his keys clicking on his keyboard. Then I heard a grumble, and it didn't sound good. I strolled over to his door and leaned against the doorjamb, staring in at him. He turned his head to look at me.

"Everything okay in here? It sounds a little tense."

He came toward me, his eyes locked on mine as he approached his door. He turned his head and looked out at the office. Without moving his head, his eyes drifted to mine. A wicked grin spread across his face, and his voice became barely a whisper.

"You still want proof?"

"Proof? Proof of what?"

"Shh! Come in here!"

He closed the door behind me. When he turned around, he pushed me against the wall and started kissing me like some fucking porn star. It threw my system into shock. It was a good kind of shock, though. His hand gripped me between my legs, no hesitation, nothing leading up to it. Out of nowhere, he forcefully clenched my mound in his hand.

"Mm! I wanna fuck you."

"Holy shit!"

There I stood, in my boss's office. He rubbed my crotch and kissed my neck, pressing me against the wall with his body. He had just thrown that sexual harassment issue right out the window. His bold, lewd declaration excited me. Actually, everything about him excited me.

I kept thinking he would realize what he was doing, back off, and shamefully apologize.

Not my boss! Not Jackson Montgomery!

As his tongue plunged into my mouth, and he sucked on my lips, I heard the grinding sound of his zipper. His hand fumbled between us as he took his cock out. Surely now he would catch himself and stop. Then, he did stop…for a second.

"I gotta get a rubber. Don't go anywhere."

He put his hand against my stomach, as though he were holding me to the wall. I stared with my eyes wide, my mouth hanging open, and forgetting to breathe. He turned away from me, and I could see from a peripheral perspective as he backed away that he really had unfastened his pants. He went to one of his desk drawers and tore a box open, removing a package from inside. He tore the package open and rolled the condom over his erection.

He put the wrapper on his chair and came at me like a man with a plan, his fierce-looking cock armed and ready. He stopped a couple of feet in front of me and smiled, lifting his shirt a little, permitting me to peek.

"I showed you. Now, you show me," he taunted, staring at me.

"Show you? Show you my crotch? Show you what?"

"Am I making you uncomfortable?"

My heart slammed against my chest wall. "Um, well…"

"Good!" He smirked. "Those panties…they're in my way."

I lifted my skirt on the sides and wiggled out of them. I balled them up in my hand and held them shyly at my side. I still wasn't sure this was really happening. I felt terrified that I had lapsed into a sexual fantasy and was going to snap out of it, finding myself holding my panties, just standing there in my boss's office.

He stepped toward me, closing the gap between us. Oh, my God! His scent washed over me and filled my nose. He smelled so good—a soft hint of his cologne mixed with sweat. Again, he pushed his body against mine, and he stared down into my face. With a devious smile, he lowered his head and kissed me again. His breath rushed past my ear as our tongues caressed each other. He broke the kiss and put his forehead to mine.

"So, how much trouble am I in?"

"Are you really doing this?"

He pulled his head back with a curious look on his face. He scoffed. "If I read you wrong, you should probably speak up now."

"I'm just surprised. I didn't think…"

He licked his lips and he nervously stared at me. "Um, you…didn't think…what?"

"I didn't think this would happen…ever!"

He swallowed hard and bobbed his head as he pursed his lips. "Okay, so criminal charges? Lawsuit? What are we talking?"

I reached between us and gripped his cock. He exhaled a sigh of relief. He smiled and lowered his head to kiss me again. As his lips pressed to mine, he said, "You just scared the hell out of me."

"That's because you're being a bad, bad boy."

"Mmmhmm!" he murmured as his mouth covered mine.

I wrapped my arms around his neck as our kiss became more passionate. I raked my fingers through his hair. His firm hands gripped my ass, massaging my cheeks, kneading harder as his breath quickened and became heavier. His hair dampened with sweat, as our steamy situation only got hotter.

He put his hands on my breasts and began grinding his erection against my crotch. He broke our kiss and looked into my eyes. His eyes scanned my face, and his head pivoted to the side.

"You make my cock so fucking hard."

"It's all about proof." I smiled. "Remember?"

He chuckled. "Now who's being bad?" he asked as he slid his hands down my arms to my hands. "What're you… Are you still holding your panties?" He took them from my hand and tossed them over his shoulder, halfway across the room. "You don't need those."

I giggled, and he put his finger over my lips.

"Sorry!"

"They'll probably want a turn. I can't do this with all of those people," he said as he pointed to the closed door. He flashed me a wink. "This is *our* little secret."

I nodded my head, smiling mischievously.

"No screaming on this ride, okay?"

"You think you're that good?"

He reached down and gripped my thighs as he smiled playfully. "I don't care for your sassy attitude." He ripped my legs up off the floor, forcing himself in between them. I locked my legs around his waist. He reached around my leg and guided his cock back and forth, teasing my pussy, making me want more.

"No noise," he warned, arching his eyebrows.

I inhaled deep as I felt the thickness of his cock penetrate me. I had never been with a man of his size. His girth stretched me, filling me in a way I had never felt before. I felt a slight, sharp, ripping pain, but it felt incredible. I held my breath for a second as I stared into his eyes. He clenched his jaw and delivered a forceful thrust, driving himself in deeper. This time, he slid his hands up my back and folded his hands over my shoulders, pulling down on my body as he thrust his hips upward. His wild eyes stared into mine, and his jaw clenched just before he buried his face against my neck.

"Mm! You're so fucking tight," he muttered as his lips skimmed over my throat. "You doing okay?"

"I love this feeling," I breathed.

He bounced his hips a few times as he watched my face. "Ready to stop faking it?"

"Oh, yeah!"

He slammed his hips into me, driving his cock in deeper. I gasped and ran my hands up my face, my fingers combing into my hair. I heard him softly chuckle as he gripped my hips, pushing me down on him as he thrust his hips upward again.

"That a girl," he said with a smile. "Now we're really getting wet."

He rapidly bumped his hips hard enough that he bounced me like a ball in a child's game. I leaned my head back against the wall as he bumped me up and down. I wrapped my arms around his shoulders, holding onto him as tightly as I could.

"You want more?"

"Yes!"

That son of a bitch pulled his hips back and tore into me with all he had. I gasped and flinched.

"Too much?"

"Maybe we need to do that slowly."

"Sorry!"

He pumped his hips up and down, driving me into the wall. As his hips rocked back and forth, he put his hand between us and moved his thumb in a circle over my clit. As if it were some involuntary reaction, my body started moving with his. He wrapped his arm around my waist and clenched his jaw again, pulling me down on him, as he pressed deeper into me.

As his other hand massaged my clit, I squeezed my arms tighter around his shoulders as the pleasure raced through my body. I had been fucked before, but never like this.

"Help me out for a minute."

"What?"

His tongue brushed over my lips. "Rub your clit for me. I gotta do something for you."

I wasn't sure about touching myself in front of

someone else. It seemed weird. I hesitantly withdrew my arm from around his shoulder. He grabbed my hand in his and shoved it against my clit.

"Rub it. It fucking turns me on," he demanded.

I began rubbing myself as he had told me to do.

"Oh, fuck yeah, baby," he said through his clenched teeth.

He pulled me down on him as he rapidly pumped his hips. Harder. Faster. Deeper. A moan escaped my throat.

"Shh! Our secret."

"I'm trying. You're gonna make me come."

"That's what I want," he said. "Come for me."

He drilled his cock into me so deep and so forcefully, every thrust brought a wave of pleasure. I could feel my body tensing. I had lost all inhibitions about rubbing my clit. I rubbed so hard and so fast it was a miracle I still had one at all. I gasped, feeling that moment coming. A throaty growl slipped out. Jackson covered my mouth with his as he pounded me. I pulled away from his kiss.

"Yes! Oh yes! Ooo!" I said as quietly as I could.

"Hell yeah! Are you going to come for me?"

"Yeees!" I softly squealed.

Then, I drew a deep breath through my mouth as my pussy began milking his cock. His body dripped with sweat as he slammed into me. He began grinding my sex against his body, pulling up and pushing down, forcing my body to move like he wanted it to. I felt consumed by ecstasy. I just wanted him to keep doing everything he was doing to me in that moment. Proof! Boom! Just like that!

"Mm…fuck!"

He thrust into me, driving his cock in deep before his body tensed, and he froze. I felt the thumping as he started to come, then he eased out and slammed into me, again…then again. He repeated the motion until his body relaxed, and he rested his forehead on the wall behind me, both of us panting.

I brushed my fingers through his wet hair as he tried to catch his breath. After a few minutes, he lifted his head and dragged his hand down his face, wiping the beads of sweat away. He smiled at me.

"See? You didn't fake anything that time."

"I didn't want to do that. I didn't want to come. I didn't want to give you the satisfaction, but that…damn!" I softly giggled and bit my lip.

It was a feather in his cap. What the hell? He earned it, but because of that little episode, I had all kinds of plans for Jackson Montgomery. I couldn't accept that this would be a "one time only" kind of thing. I wanted to wear this man out. If he could make it that much fun, I could easily do this again. I'd gladly fill his cap with feathers.

He sighed a heavy sigh and winked. "You gotta get off me. It's hot."

He started backing his cock out of me. That had never been my favorite part. The human body is so weird. As a woman, you open up and let a man shove his way in. Our bodies cling to him for dear life. Then, he just…leaves. All I know is it's a much better feeling when he goes in than when he comes out.

After Jackson withdrew himself, he flopped his parts and pieces back inside his pants and closed them up. He put his palm against my face and kissed my lips. His eyes met mine, and he winked.

"That was just what I needed, a bad girl with a tight pussy. Fuck! You're a lot of fun."

I felt bruised from his size, but also from the pounding my pussy had taken. Even with the ache, I'd do it again—even right now—if he wanted to. Jackson turned and picked my panties up off the floor. He dangled them from his finger as he sauntered toward me.

"I'm not a fan of these stupid things, but I actually like these. They're cute," he announced as he bent down, planting a kiss on my lips. "Mm! Get your clothes on, girl."

Chapter Three

"Now what?"

"What, what? What do you mean, *now what*?" he asked as his eyes shifted around the room.

"Do you think they'll know?" I asked as I pointed my thumb toward the closed door.

He shrugged. "Let's see. You've got that fresh fucked glow. I'm drowning in sweat. It smells like sex in here. Nah! Nobody will suspect a thing."

"Okay, so what do we do?"

He chuckled. "I'm not real sure. I probably should've thought about that before now, huh?"

"Let's rearrange your office. We'll move some stuff around. It'll look like we were just moving furniture."

He smirked and shook his head. "I'm not moving anything. I just busted a nut and moving furniture is the last thing I want to do, but that is creative. I admire your quick-thinking abilities."

"Okay, so what other options do we have?"

He shrugged. "Open the door. Walk out the door. Walk to your desk, just like normal. Sit down just like any other time you've come in here and walked out. If we act guilty, we're going to look guilty. Just act like you do any other time."

"Yeah, but you really are pretty sweaty." I smirked.

"Maybe I have a fever." He shrugged. "Don't make

it a big deal, and it won't be."

He appeared to be cool and smooth. He truly seemed like it was nothing to him. He looked like he didn't have a worry in the world when I started for the door. He sighed as he shuffled papers around on his desk.

About ten minutes later, Jackson came out of his office. His clothes had dried enough that it wasn't *as* obvious. In fact, had I not known, I *wouldn't* have known. He walked to the corner of my desk. He was suddenly so serious and professional.

"Miss Elizabeth," he said in a funny accent. "Do you have a fax number for Waynright, Cooper, and Bevins?"

I smacked my lips together as I turned in my chair and gazed up at him. "I don't think I do, but I can get it for you."

"I do, Mister Montgomery!" A woman's voice called from one of the cubicles in the middle of the room.

Jackson's eyes widened as he spun around to see where the voice had come from. It was Lisa Bertyn. Lisa was "limp." She was the frumpy girl who wanted men like Jackson but didn't quite get that she had to put a little effort into her appearance. She was delusional. If a man held a door open for her, Lisa thought he was hitting on her. If a man smiled at her, she thought he wanted her body. She just didn't get that she came off as annoying and bland. I couldn't stand her.

I watched as Jackson strolled over to her cubicle from my desk. Ugh! I had a feeling she would think that, because he walked over to her desk, he was flirting with her. What a troll! I had always hated her. Now, I hated her even more.

I stared at Jackson as he rested his arm on top of her cubicle wall, laughing, joking, and talking with her. I hated it. I didn't want him to give her the same looks he had given me. Maybe he screwed everyone in that office. Maybe *I* was delusional for thinking myself special in some way. "*Our* secret?" Yeah! Probably because he didn't want the others to know we all shared the same secret with him. I felt annoyed and irritable. I felt foolish, and I'll admit it, a slight bit jealous.

Okay! A lot jealous.

****

Though Jackson's size and his porn star skills left me feeling a little sore and bruised, I had never craved a man in all my life like I craved him. It had been two days since I had been his living sex doll. I watched him move through his day and every move he made only made me want him more. I wanted his body over mine. I wanted to feel him slamming in and out of me. Oh, the fantasies I had about him!

Working with him, for him, without giving away "our" secret was tough. How in the hell he could focus on anything work related was beyond me. All I could think of was how this diplomatic, proper, smart businessman became such a different man when his zipper came down. I *liked* it when his zipper came down. In fact, I wanted to make his zipper come down again.

Half of the office had gone for their lunch break. I went into Jackson's office. He had the sleeves on his button up shirt rolled up, just below his elbows. He stood, studying the papers on his desk in front of him. Even when he stayed focused and serious, he was still the sexiest man I knew. He seemed to be concentrating entirely too hard, making this the perfect time to distract him. I quietly cleared my throat to get his attention. He turned his head and looked at me.

"Hey, you! Do you need me?" His gaze returned to the papers in front of him. His voice was kind and warm. It felt like a hug.

I scoffed and softly whispered, "Um…yes!"

He sat down and turned in his chair, giving me his attention. "What's up?"

I smiled at him and bit my lip, saying nothing. He cocked his head, patiently waiting for my answer. His eyes scanned my face and then his serious face faded to a more playful expression. The edges of his mouth turned up into a smile.

"Oh really?" he asked incredulously.

"It's all your fault. You're the one that started this bonus program."

He rested his elbows on the arms of his chair and drummed his pen on his palm. He flipped his wrist, tossing the pen on his desk before he stood and walked toward me. His eyes narrowed, locked on mine as he approached. As we stood face to face, he gently put his hand on my hip and tilted his head as he kept watch of the door.

"Not here, okay?" he whispered.

"Okay. Where?"

"I know this will sound bad. I'm not blowing you off, but if you can give me an hour, maybe an hour and a half, we can go anywhere you want. I really do have to get this proposal out."

I sighed as I smiled. "Now I feel pathetic."

"I'll make you feel something entirely different

here in a little bit. I just have to—"

I cut him off. "I'll live! Geez! It's not *that* bad. Yet! Do that thing you do."

He kept his eyes on the door as he lowered his head and softly kissed my lips. "How the fuck am I supposed to concentrate now?"

"Don't know! I've had that problem for two days."

"It's just one stupid proposal. What's one stupid proposal?" He smiled. "No! I have to do this. I've gotta fire you. You're killing me."

"What was that you said? Something about bad girls with tight pussies? But, hey! Have fun with that proposal."

I turned and walked out of his office, flashing him a smile over my shoulder as I passed through the door. I really didn't want to cost him whatever job he prepared the proposal for, but I had a feeling he was disciplined enough to be able to work around me and my shenanigans.

After about an hour and forty-five minutes, he came out of his office with a stack of papers in his hands. He looked tired, or maybe frustrated. He held the stack of papers out to me.

"Can you please fax these over to Newton? After it sends, can you print the transmittal confirmation? I'm running late for a meeting with BGTP, so I *have* to get going. I won't be back this afternoon. Could you please just forward my phone to voicemail? Then, you're all welcome to leave early. Go home! Have a good night. I *have* to get going or this woman is going to kick my butt! If you can help me with that fax before you leave, I would appreciate it," he said as he pointed to the proposal in my hand.

"Uh, yeah! I can take care of this. Have a good meeting."

He raised his voice. "I want everyone out of this office within the next half hour. All of you people go home!"

Suddenly, the quiet office came alive with the sounds of shuffling and happiness. Jackson winked at me and turned to leave. I watched him rush out, and I felt confused. Maybe he had forgotten to mention this little meeting earlier. It felt funny. He had kind of made plans with me, so I had a feeling he was focused on work and my little problem would just have to wait. I felt foolish again. I felt like I had officially been blown off.

As I pushed my chair away from my desk to go send his fax, my phone rang. I knew that number. It was Mr. Montgomery, himself. This would be where he would tell me about how he had forgotten about this "BGTP" meeting. I picked up the receiver.

"Mister Montgomery, it's been such a long time," I teased.

His sultry, breathy voice came through the phone. "Do you know I've had a fucking hard-on for almost two hours?"

I gasped and feigned surprise. "That sounds horrible."

"Yeah? Well, you're the one that's going to have to pay for that, so we'll see how horrible it is. Did you send that fax?"

"No! Not yet. You just left."

"You better speed it up. You're late for the BGTP meeting."

"BGTP? What is BGTP?"

"Bad girl, tight pussy. BGTP! You had better hurry up. Call me when you're ready to leave."

I giggled. "Okay! Get off the phone so I can do what my boss told me to do."

His soft chuckle filtered through the phone. "Call me! Bye!"

The office cleared out within about ten minutes of Jackson leaving, with the exception of Ginger Fenley. That was no surprise. Ginger was the woman that came to work with a purple sweater, denim skirt, red knee-high socks and her brown, square-toed sneakers. She usually braided her oily hair into pigtails. She was just a little "off." She lived for praise, constantly pointing out the little things she did. She was like a mushroom—quiet and happy in her dark, depressing cubicle. Throw her some shit every now and again, and she was good to go. She tried to offer compliments, but they came out awkward and self-sacrificial. She was the brownnoser, and no one had anything in common with her, poor thing. We knew she just wanted to have friends, but she was just so strange. She would probably work well beyond the half hour, just because that was Ginger. Weird! Nerdy! She practically wet her pants anytime Jackson talked to her. I had the same problem, but in an entirely different way. I almost felt bad for her. She gave him one hundred and ten percent, desperate for his approval, and I was trying to hurry and leave so I could go fuck his brains out. It was sad. She tried so hard.

After I got the fax transmittal page, I clipped it to the fax and put it on Jackson's desk. I gathered my things and took out my cell phone. As I waited for the elevator, I dialed his number.

"It's about time!" he barked.

"Your fax machine is slow. Get a faster fax machine."

"I don't care about a fax machine right now. Where are you?"

"About to step off the elevator, then out to the parking lot."

"I'll come pick you up outside the door."

"Um, okay! Am I looking for you, or for a car?"

"I'm the only car sitting outside the doors, waiting like a drooling dork that's had a hard-on for two hours."

"Drooling dork? Oh, now I see you."

"Smartass. Get in the car and let's go!"

Sitting outside the doors sat a shiny charcoal and black race car-looking thing. It was sexy and sleek, hot, just like the driver. I opened the door and sat down in the seat. Before the door had even closed, Jackson started driving away.

"Where are we going?" he asked.

"I don't know. I'm having a cargasm right now."

"Oh-ho, no you don't! You don't have any kind of 'gasm until I get to be part of it." He gripped my hand and put it against his crotch. "You see what you did? For two fucking hours! That has got to be the worst proposal I've ever written, so no! No 'gasms for you."

"Poor baby! You sound incredibly whiney just now, just so you know."

He cut his eyes over at me and flashed his devious smile. "Woo, you're gonna get it."

"Oh, I want it," I taunted.

He chuckled as he jerked his head to the side. His hand covered his cock as his hips thrust up. He clenched his teeth and did a soft, low, throaty growl.

"Okay! Where the fuck are we going?"

I shrugged. “Do you want to go to my place?”

His eyes stared into mine, and he gave me that bad boy smirk. “No. I don’t want you to have to face your neighbors tomorrow. I wanna make you scream.”

All of a sudden, my panties felt damp. “Then you pick where we go. I just want your cock inside me again.”

He flipped on the blinker and made a left at the next street. He put his hand between my knees, rubbing his thumb against the inside of my leg. He pulled it away and upshifted before returning it between my legs. His thumb softly brushed over my skin, then he gripped my thigh, squeezing it as he pulled my leg toward him as though he were claiming it as his own. It was sudden and surprising. It took my breath away. It was just one of those animalistic gestures he did that drove me wild.

He turned into the driveway for one of the nicer hotels in town. As we pulled under the carport, my door flew open and there stood some guy in a white uniform, offering his hand to help me out of the car. He spoke with some accent, and he was very polite and gracious. He seemed confused when he asked if I needed help with my luggage and I answered with a negative reply.

After Jackson dealt with one of the other guys and received his claim check, he came toward me. He put his hand across the small of my back, leading me toward the hotel entrance. As we approached, two men opened the doors for us. I wrapped my arm around his waist, tucking myself under his arm.

“This seems a bit extreme. We’re just going to wreck their bed.”

“And, their sofa, and their shower, and their table,

and their counter, and their floor, and…" He stopped listing things and smiled at me. "I have to fire you. Seriously! This is a work night, and you're never going to be able to walk into the office in the morning. Your boss is going to be pissed off at the asshole that's about to pound your pussy all night long."

I felt all the blood in my body rush to my middle. My pussy ached. I wanted him so bad. He was good at the sudden, dirty, flashes of sexiness. With any other man, it would've just been perverse, but Jackson Montgomery was an entirely different animal. There was something so raw about the way the dirty talk just rolled off of his tongue. To look at him, one would never guess those words would fall out of his mouth.

As he got us registered for a room, I slid my hand over his butt, discreetly grabbing a handful and squeezing. He lifted his arm, hugging me to him as he scribbled whatever he needed to for the registration. He pushed the registration card across the counter to the girl behind the desk, and he wrapped both of his arms around my waist.

His voice harbored a sexy tone when he kissed the side of my head and breathily whispered, "All. Night. Long."

"Mm!" I smiled as his lips softly pressed to mine.

"Did you guys just get married?" the girl behind the counter asked.

"No," Jackson answered flatly.

"Oh! You just seem so in love. It's so sweet. You're really cute together."

"Wow! Really? I'm a prostitute. She just picked me up off the street corner about five minutes ago," he offered in a matter of fact tone.

Without missing a beat, she played right along. "You go, girl! That's smart. Make the prostitute pay for the room."

Jackson laughed and winked at me. "She's good! That was funny. I'm going to need to realign myself before I try that again. Maybe after I have a nap."

The girl pointed us down the hallway to a room on the left. I turned to start walking. Jackson tugged my arm, pulling me back toward him.

"If you can bump us up that tower, we'll stay for two nights."

"Oh, you want to be on one of the upper floors?"

He smirked. "Sure! That sounds great!"

"How high do you want to go? Like, which floor do you want?"

He smiled at me. "What floor?"

"I don't know. Remember? Five minutes ago, I was looking for a prostitute," I teased.

"Just put us at the top."

"Well, we have penthouses at the top, but I can put you on the next floor down, if you want."

"You don't have keys for the penthouses?"

"Well, yes. But… Oh! Do you want a penthouse?"

"No!" I scoffed and sang, "Ex-treme!"

Returning my song, he sang, "Two nights! Y-es!"

He turned and nodded at the girl behind the counter.

"My boss is going to be really pissed off if I don't go to work tomorrow," I said. "Really. This is a bit much."

He kissed the top of my head and softly said, "You're worth it. Shut up!"

In that moment, I wasn't sure how he meant that.

Maybe my "tight pussy" was just that good. Or, maybe he meant that in terms of me, as a person, but regardless, for just a little bit, I chose to believe he valued me as something other than just a way to get laid.

Chapter Four

When we got in the elevator, I turned to face him, interlacing my fingers in his. "You really didn't have to do any of this. I would've jumped your bones while you sat in your desk chair."

"I'm not a sappy, sweet kind of guy most of the time. I'm having a moment. It'll pass, so enjoy it while it lasts." He smiled.

Still holding my hands in his, he wrapped his arms around my waist and hugged me to him. When the doors opened, it really was beautiful. Ivory and metallic brown adorned everything in the room. A huge television was mounted on the wall with a fireplace under it. Ivory colored leather furnishings circled the gas fireplace, and floral arrangements were dotted around the room. It was beautiful. It felt formal, yet comfortable. The view was indescribable. There were windows all the way around, even in the bedroom. I tried to play it cool.

"It's beautiful," I casually said as I smiled at him.

I draped my arms around his neck and stared into his eyes. His hands drifted over my hips, to my ass. With one rapid jolt, he pulled me in closer to him. The smirk on his face split the difference between a little sly and a little ornery.

"All night long." He smiled and raised his eyebrows.

"I hope you mean that."

"Oh, I do. I promise!"

He sounded almost cocky about that promise. It was sexy when he showed that cocky side. Actually, Jackson was just sexy, no matter what he did. His confidence when it came to anything sexual made him so different from anyone I had known before. Before him, sex had been so boring! In, out! In, out! There were a few "Yeah, baby's" here, some "Oh yeahs!" there. It made sex so predictable, and the encounters ended long before I ever even got turned on.

With Jackson, the rich, sultry pitch of his voice set me on fire. His deep blue eyes were the color of a raging river racing around his pupils, and they pulled me into the undertow. His carefree, devil-may-care blond hair, always imperfectly perfect, summoned my fingers. His warm, yet wicked smile inspired all kinds of naughty ideas. His lean, toned body made me feel protected from the world when he wrapped his arms around me. Even the way he smelled turned me on. He wore just enough cologne to tease—a fresh, woodsy, spice scent. He was the whole package, and speaking of his package, his was definitely a pleasant bonus.

I knew better than to believe it was love. The temperature of our interaction was like a billion degrees sexual. It had to be lust. After all, it wasn't like I really knew that much about him outside of work. He had become a familiar stranger, if that made any sense. The erotic chemistry between us had changed me. I wasn't the kind of woman who gave myself so freely to a man, but Jackson made no apologies for anything he wanted from me. He made me feel like I didn't have to apologize for what I wanted from him, either. Maybe because I knew it wasn't "love," it took most of the pressure off to be "perfect." We were two people with wants and needs. He didn't seem to mind when I brought my wants and needs to his doorstep. I wanted to be the same for him.

I turned and walked toward the window to look down at the world around us. I'd be lying if I told you this sort of place was typical for me, or that I wasn't impressed. I grew up halfway across the country. My dad worked in real estate and my mother as a schoolteacher. My sister and I started out with a simple life. Places like this penthouse would've never been a thought in my parents' minds. In fact, due to my upbringing, places like this weren't really an option in my mind, either. We just didn't spend a lot of time living the posh, pampered life. I appreciated his effort, but it still seemed excessive just for us to have sex.

Jackson came up behind me and wrapped his arms around my waist. He rested his square, dimpled chin on my shoulder. I realized, as I peered out the window, that in the years that I had lived here, I had missed out on seeing a huge part of this beautiful city. I asked Jackson questions, and he answered if he knew. "What is that bluish building over there?" "What street is that?" The answer to almost every question started with, "Do you remember blah, blah job?" He used his job sites as landmarks, as though that meant anything to me. I wasn't familiar with all the streets he knew. I knew my typical course of travels. I rarely went to any of the job sites. I leaned my head back on his shoulder and listened to him talk. I loved the sound of his voice, especially when he talked about his passion—his jobs.

After he tired of the conversation, he reached down

and gripped the top of my thighs, sliding his hands up them as he pressed his hard cock against me. He raised my skirt and slid his fingers inside the thin band of lace at the top of my panties. His warm breath fell on my neck shortly before I felt his lips caress my skin. His fingertips delivered a feather soft touch to the fleshy part of my abdomen, just inside my hips. It was one of the most sensitive, excitable sensations I had ever felt. It felt relaxing but arousing as the same time. His hands slowly made their way toward the middle. I could already feel my body reacting to him. Then, his patient, but steady hands gently inched down inside my panties, to my throbbing, aching sex. He began stroking me, teasing me, making me eager to be filled. My chest rose and fell from the thrill of his touch. He drove me insane.

"I want you."

"I want you, too," he said in a velvety tone. "But, not yet."

His fingers kept tracing softly over my skin. Then with a gentle touch, his finger entered me. His soft lips danced along my neck and over to my shoulder as he slowly fingered me. It wasn't like before. It wasn't dirty. This was different. So different! My head dropped back to his shoulder as his hand pleasured me. There I stood, in a floor to ceiling window, while he finger-fucked me. I wasn't sure whether anyone could see us or not. I found something highly erotic about that.

I let my hands rove over all the parts of his body I could reach. His hand moved in slow, forceful bursts. I began to grind my clit against the heel of his hand. He made it easier for me, pressing it in against me. His other arm moved from my hip and wrapped around the front of me, holding my body up. He took his finger out of me and began massaging my clit. He made a few slow circling caresses. Then, without warning, he pressed harder and circled his hand faster.

"I want to feel you, but not yet."

He had me so close when he took his hand away. I dug my fingernails into the arm he had around my waist. He reached between us and unfastened his pants, freeing himself. He kicked my feet apart, pulling my panties to the side, out of his way. He guided his erection back and forth, through my wetness. He pressed the tip of his cock to my opening. I drew a deep breath in anticipation of what I knew I was about to feel. Smooth as silk, I felt him slide inside me. There was a faint hint of a moan as he entered me.

Holy shit! I was so in love with the way his cock felt as he sank it deeper inside me. The noises he made only added to the pleasure as he moved inside me. His hand began massaging my clit again. He bumped his hips a couple of times, and I felt my orgasm rolling over me like a backdraft in a fire. Heat raced through my body, and I owed the man another fucking feather for his cap.

My hand gripped the back of his neck as my pussy clenched his cock and released it again. His lips floated over my neck and my legs suddenly felt weak. He hummed approvingly. As I came, his hand rubbed my clit as hard and fast as I could take. He gently pumped his hips, making my orgasm even more intense.

As my body began to calm, Jackson's touch became softer and slower, until it stopped all together. He stopped rocking his hips, and I heard him sigh as he finally caught his breath. He hugged me to his chest.

"I want to play with you just like this, but, I'm too close."

"Isn't that the idea?"

"Um, not in my current state of 'undress.' I'm being really bad. I just wanted to feel you."

"I'm on the pill."

"So was my mom. I'm living proof of how well that worked out for her," he said. "I just need to settle down for a few minutes."

I smiled at him over my shoulder, and I began bouncing back against him, forcing his cock in deeper. He let go of me and threw his hands up. He looked down and watched me ride him. He made a throaty growl, grabbed my hips, and began thrusting into me, hard and fast.

"Is that what you want? Huh?"

I leaned forward, putting my hands on the window as he drilled his cock into me.

"I love it when you fuck me like this."

"Oh shit! I gotta stop," he said. "Fuck! Too late! Sorry!"

He ripped his cock out of me as fast as he could. That was by far, my least favorite dismount…ever. I turned toward him, just in time to see him bend over, resting his hands on his knees. His eyes clenched shut, and he dropped his head, then I heard him exhale. I hugged his head to my stomach, too late to help in any other way. I raked my fingers over his back until he slowly began to stand. He draped his arm around my shoulder, pulling me to him.

"I'm sorry. Are you okay?"

"That seemed sudden."

“Are you okay? Did I hurt you?’

“I think it surprised me more than anything.”

“I know. I’m sorry! You felt so fucking good. Watching you…I didn’t want to do that. Holy shit, you feel good to me. You made me come all over myself,” he said as he looked down at the wet cum streaks on his pant legs. “Oh, yeah! I’m going to be going by my house before work in the morning.”

“See what happens when you play on work nights?”

“I’m not sorry.” He smiled as his tongue pressed into my mouth, caressing my tongue.

After we kissed, I tucked my body under his arm, hugging my arms around him. He just stood there for a second, holding me, his body swaying with mine. As though he had a plan, he took my hand and led me toward the bedroom. He fought with the buttons on his shirt, trying to undo them with one hand. As we stood beside the bed, I helped him in his efforts. He draped his shirt over the arm of the chair in the sitting area at the foot of the bed. He raised his undershirt over his head.

My eyes widened as I gawked at his body. He had tone and definition, but not like a body builder. He had a “real” man’s body, and it was smoking hot. He smiled at me as I stared. He rolled his eyes and held his arms out, allowing me to stare before he tossed his undershirt at my face.

“Too many beers, not enough time spent working out,” he offered.

I held his shirt to my face, shamefully covering my gaping mouth. “Well, it looks good on you, whatever you’re doing…or not doing.”

He took foil packages out of his pocket and tossed them on the bed as he smirked at me. I picked one up and twirled it around my fingers. I watched as he unfastened his pants and let them fall to the floor.

"So, you had all of these in your pocket, and you…" I hesitated, waiting for him to fill in the blank as I pointed my thumb toward the living room.

"I told you, I wanted to feel you. You. Not the rubber. I wanted to feel you come without the rubber. You."

He picked up his pants and draped them over his shirt on the arm of the chair. He stood in front of me in nothing but his boxers. He chuckled and shook his head. He covered his mouth with his hand and dragged it down his face, as though he were wiping his smile away.

"I have to take a shower. Are you coming?"

"Naked? Um, no!"

"Do you wear your clothes in the shower? Is that some new way to wash your laundry?"

"Oh, hell no! I don't want you to… I'm shy. I don't…I'm not a centerfold."

"I hate to tell you this, but—"

"You've only seen me semi-naked."

He gave me a sarcastic smirk and rolled his eyes. "What if I promise not to look?"

"We're going to take a shower, and you're not going to look?"

"Yeah! If you don't want me to look, I won't look."

"Really?"

"Really!" he answered with that flat tone that he sometimes got, like when the girl at the desk asked if we had just gotten married.

"You won't look?"

"No! Let's go! Come on."

Chapter Five

I followed him into the bathroom. Jackson stepped into the shower stall and turned on the water. It was like an instant cascade in there. Water sprayed from the ceiling and from the corners of the shower walls. There were mood lighting and music options. Those seemed like odd features, considering the rest of the amenities were so posh and elegant.

I could see Jackson's silhouette through the fogged glass walls as he stepped into the spray. He put his head under the water. After a few moments, he called out to me.

"Okay, you can wash your laundry. It's ready now," he teased.

"You better not look."

"I won't," he growled.

I slid my skirt and my panties off. "Are you looking?"

"Is that an invitation?"

"No!"

"Then, no. I'm not looking."

I peeled my shirt over my head. Then, I took my bra off. I kept my eye on him, watching to make sure he didn't peek. The fact that we'd had sex prior to this moment meant little to me. He hadn't seen me completely naked. Right or wrong, I had always been self-conscious about my body.

"You're not looking, right?"

"I'm *still* not looking."

"How many fingers am I holding up?"

"I don't know. Bring them in here and hold them in front of my face so I can see them."

"No peeking, or I'll cry. I mean it, okay?"

"For the love! I'm not peeking. Just come on."

"What are you looking at?"

"The wall, but if you don't hurry up, I'm going to have to turn around before these sprayers start tearing into my flesh. These things have a lot of pressure."

"You promise?"

"Elizabeth! Get your ass in this shower."

I stepped into the foggy, misty stall. As he had said, he stood facing the wall. He had his palms against the wall, and he pivoted his head, letting the water run over his body. I slapped his bare butt.

"You sure you wanna start that spanking game?"

"You like getting spanked?" I flirted.

"No but slapping your ass would be a different story."

"You like spanking?"

"Yeah! Sometimes."

"I don't know why, but something about that kind of turns me on."

"Then, get over yourself," he said as he turned to face me.

I tried, in vain, to cover my nakedness. He wiped the water from his face and reached for my wrists. He fought against me to pull my arms away from my body. He stopped pulling and softly blinked as his voice softened.

"Just stop. It's like jumping in a pool. Just jump in

and get it over with. Then you can have fun." Again, he tugged at my wrists. "Trust me. Stop it."

I slowly relaxed my arms, allowing him to pull them away. His eyes stared into mine as he held my wrists out to the sides of my hips. He flashed me a sweet smile. His eyes began to drift down my body all the way to my feet. He sighed as he slowly blinked, and his eyes met mine again.

Almost whispering, he demanded, "Tell me what the hell is supposed to be so wrong with this?"

"I don't really exercise. I have a puffy gut. I hate my thighs. My boobs aren't big enough. I have freckles on my shoulders. And I have…"

"Shh!" he said, shaking his head. He smiled. "On a scale of one to ten, you're easily a…" His eyes scanned my body again, lingering between my hips and my feet. He pressed his lips together and shrugged. "One to ten, I'd give you a nine…teen, but I'm a tough one to impress, so others might rate you a full on twenty."

I giggled. "You said one to ten. Nineteen isn't on your little scale."

"I know!" His breath hitched as he arched his eyebrows and leaned down to kiss me. "Unbelievable," he said as he stared into my eyes and subtly nodded.

Then, he smiled as he drew a deep breath and pushed the air out of his lungs. He hugged me to him and pulled me into the stronger water stream. I loved the way our naked bodies felt together as the water rushed over us. We stood in a misty, foggy, warm shower and kissed as though we would die if our lips weren't attached to each other. Something about having his arms wrapped around me, and the way he made me feel like he thought I was beautiful melted me. He had quickly become my favorite bad boy, but this softer, sweeter side of him was definitely a pleasant surprise.

That shower was the best one of all my life. I enjoyed kissing him and not having to worry about getting caught. I enjoyed that there was no rush in this moment. Nothing felt hurried or dirty. His kiss was not about sex this time. We shared a completely different level of intimacy. We touched, petted, hugged, and kissed each other for the longest time. He pushed me to the wall, putting his arms out to keep me from slamming into the stone tiles. He pressed his body to mine as though I would be able to absorb him in some way—two becoming one. He had gone from being down and dirty to this tame, gentle, lover boy that drove me insane on so many levels.

If we had been seeing each other longer, it would've been the perfect, "I love you" moment. It seemed like it would've been all right to say, considering the current mood. For now, somehow, I decided I should contain that thought. I knew he felt it from me. I was pretty sure I felt something like that from him, too. I tried not to overthink it, since it wouldn't make sense. Love had to be built on so much more than the sexual bond we had shared. I was sure it wasn't "love," but it felt so intense, it could be love, right?

Jackson's arms were against the wall, creating a cage around my head as we kissed. He finally broke our kiss and stared down at me. He chuckled as he shook his head. He pushed off the wall and held on to my hips.

"I kind of think we should probably do something about dinner. What do you think?"

"Are you hungry?"

"Nah! Hunger happened, probably three hours ago. This has become so much more than hunger."

"Me too," I agreed.

"What do you want? Where would you go if you could go anywhere you wanted to go?"

"I'd go to Rome, and I would eat authentic Italian food, in Italy," I smirked.

He flashed me a sarcastic glare. "Good choice. The food over there *is* delicious. Maybe we'll plan that for another day, but I kind of meant for right now, smartass."

"And, you kissed me with that mouth?" I flirted.

"You have a problem with my mouth?"

I giggled, and before I could answer him, he dropped to his knees and started licking my pussy. His soft tongue licked against my clit. He dragged it over my engorged lips and tickled me with the tip of his tongue.

"What're you doing? I thought you were hungry?"

"I'm eating," he said.

He pushed my legs apart, gripping and squeezing my thighs as he sank his tongue inside me. The softer, gentler mood seemed to have passed. He was completely committed to being a bad boy now.

His tongue darted in and out as his thumb rubbed my clit. I tangled my fingers in his wet hair. When I looked down, he smiled and reached for my hand, interlacing his fingers in mine. He put my hand on my clit, wanting to watch me touch myself. I started rubbing, and he moaned his approval. My head fell back against the wall behind me. As I massaged myself, I felt him licking my fingers. He wrapped his tongue around them, taking them in his mouth, sucking on them. His hand came up, holding mine again. He covered my mound with his mouth. I felt his silky tongue brushing over me. His hand released mine, and he used his fingers to spread my lips apart. He pressed his mouth on me again, flicking his tongue as he sucked on me. I tried to resist the urge to thrust my hips. As though he could read my mind, he cupped my ass in his hands and forced my hips to move back and forth. He groaned and began sucking on me with even more intensity. His hands had a death grip on my ass as he forced me against his mouth. I could hear his heavy breath as my pussy ached to be filled again. The harder he sucked me, the more desperate I became to have him inside me.

His finger dipped inside me, and he hummed his approval, pleased by how wet he had made me. All of the blood in my body had rushed to my core. I felt nothing of my existence, other than what he currently had in his mouth. I bucked my hips, longing for my release. He buried three fingers inside me. I gripped his head as my pussy instantly began pulsing and throbbing.

"Oh, my God! Oh, yeah! Ooo! Oh, Jackson! Oh, baby!"

That was the fastest my body had ever reached orgasm. I had no warning it was coming. It just happened. It felt amazing. I have no idea what that man did with his fingers when he put them inside me, but it was like nothing I had ever felt. I never wanted that sensation to stop. It was the longest, one of the deepest orgasms of my life. When I began to twitch from being sensitive to his touch, he began to soften his oral assault on my anatomy. I didn't care if it was lust, love, or whatever. He could do that anytime he wanted.

When he finished with my womanhood, he stood and smiled his cocky smile at me. He dragged the heel of his hand across his mouth. He smirked as he shrugged his shoulder.

"So, what's wrong with my mouth?"

"I faked it," I teased as I flashed him a flirty smile.

He chuckled and sarcastically said, "Yeah you did!"

"Come to me," I urged as I pulled him toward me. I kissed him, wrapping my arms around his neck. I stared up into his eyes. "You're kind of getting to me."

"Getting to you?"

I hugged him and laid my head on his shoulder. "Never mind!"

"Hey." He patted my butt, prompting me to look at him. "We're just playing right? Is this supposed to become something? Because—"

"Nope! We're just playing," I sharply answered, feeling a stab in my heart that I couldn't explain.

I knew it. That was all it started out being, so why did it bother me so much when I heard him say it? I felt hurt. I didn't want to feel that. My body had just exploded in euphoria because of the same mouth that was now breaking my heart. Now, I felt like I'd just imploded.

It wasn't love. I knew that. Remember? I already told you that it wasn't love. It couldn't be, but maybe it bothered me that I was good enough to fuck and put up in a penthouse for a couple of days. Supposedly, I rated a "*nine...teen*," on a scale of one to ten, but no matter how flattering he could be, I wasn't good enough to be anything more than his plaything.

Fucking Jackson Montgomery!

After my short, snippy answer, I felt him pull away, emotionally, and physically. He stepped out of the shower and reached for one of the ivory robes hanging on the wall. He wrapped it around his body and looked over his shoulder at me.

“So, have you decided where you want to eat? Other than Rome, I mean?”

“No,” I snapped. Realizing how pouty I sounded, I followed it with a peppier, “What do you want?”

“I think we should order room service,” he offered.

Great! Now I'm not even good enough to be seen with out in public. Got it! Plaything! How dare I forget myself?

“Sure! Let's do that, then.” I faked a smile.

I turned the water off and stepped out of the shower. Jackson stood there, holding another robe open for me to slip into. I wrapped it around my body, and as I focused on tying the belt around my waist, he threaded his fingers through my wet hair. When I looked up at him, he smiled sweetly.

“Where's that smile?”

“I don't know. Do prostitutes smile?” I jabbed without thinking.

His forehead wrinkled, as the confused look flashed across his face. “What?”

“Sorry! I'm just relaxed now. My brain isn't working right. I was trying to make a joke, but it didn't work.”

I could see it in his face. He didn't believe me. “Sounds like you're trying to fake something,” he said with a smile. “But I can roll with it if you need me to.”

"So, do we have a menu for room service?" I asked as I pushed past him.

He grabbed my arm and pulled me to him, hugging me. This time, I folded my arms, balling my fists against my chest. He just held me for a few minutes, rubbing his hand up and down my back.

"You know you can talk to me, right?"

I faked a giggle. "I've been talking to you."

"Are you upset with me?"

"No!" I lied, or maybe not.

"I don't believe you, just so you know, but maybe you'll feel better after you eat, huh?"

"Mm! Eating sounds good."

Jackson and I scanned the menu. He felt torn between baked tilapia and grilled Mahi Mahi. I wanted an oriental chicken salad. Since the entrees came with a salad, I decided that I would order Mahi Mahi. That way, Jackson could get the baked tilapia and have the best of both worlds. I felt like it was the least I could do. He had put a lot of effort into making our little "sleepover" nice for me, so I wanted to do something for him, too.

I offered to call and place the order. He gave me a smug look and snatched the menu from my hand. He walked over to the phone, picked up the receiver, and pressed buttons. He squinted his eyes at me as he waited for an answer.

"What?" I questioned, flipping my hands palms up.

"You make calls for me all the time. I got this," he smiled.

Oh! Yeah! That! "Miss Executive Assistant." So, that was it. That was how I needed to see this. This had just become another one of my duties that had recently been added to my job description. I could file some job folders, run budget reports, and oh, bang the boss! I had just become the outlet for my boss' sexual frustration. There! Now, maybe I could make peace with those fluttery feelings inside.

I glanced across the room at him. Nope! There they were. Those feelings were right back on the surface with just a glance of his handsome face. I sighed and massaged my head.

I needed to put a stop to this before it got stupid. I needed to go home, call in sick for a few days, and let things die down. Maybe then I could come back and just be Elizabeth Roundtree, Executive Assistant to Mr. Montgomery. I had to tell him I wanted to go home.

I turned to see him straining to hear the person on the other end of the phone. He smiled and nodded as he answered, "That sounds right. Thank you!" He sounded so damn adorable! He looked hot! He was kind and sweet, no matter who he talked to.

He placed the receiver back in the cradle and turned to me, smiling. As he came toward me, he held his arms out as though he were spreading some kind of magic cape. He draped them around me, hugging me as though we hadn't seen each other in years.

Forget it, I thought.

I wasn't going home. I would have to get myself together some other time. I was right where I wanted to be. If it hurt like hell later, I'd deal with it then, but right now, I felt like I would wither and die if I weren't beside this man.

Something about that moment flipped a switch in me. I was able to smile at him, and not fake it. It might be temporary, but for the moment, I felt happy. Maybe

I'd be sorry when I ended up crying off my makeup because I knew he was a heartbreak waiting to happen, but for now, he belonged to me.

Chapter Six

After a beautiful dinner, in our hotel bathrobes, and after a couple of glasses of wine, Jackson Montgomery became a force to be reckoned with, practically swinging from the rafters. I, on the other hand, felt relaxed, happy and content.

"You know what we need?" he asked with a look of mischief plastered all over his face.

"Why am I afraid to even try to guess?"

He smiled and clicked his tongue against his teeth. "You're gonna love this. Just wait!"

He stood from the table and walked toward the living room. He scooped his phone off the coffee table. I went to stand with him, watching him as I slid my hands around his waist.

"Mm," he said, squeezing me tightly in his arms. "You're un-fucking-believable. Have I told you that lately?"

Still awash in adoration for this crazy, amazing man, I laughed at his flattery. He brushed his finger over my lips before leaning down and pressing his lips to mine. His phone crashed to the floor as he dropped it when he pulled me closer to him. He kissed me without worry or concern about his phone.

"I think you should go hang that robe back up," he said suggestively.

"Do you?"

"Or don't, but either way, I definitely think it needs to come off."

"What about *your* robe?"

"I'll let you wear mine with me," he offered as he untied the belt and tried to wrap me inside it with him.

I laughed at him and his playful mood. "Are you drunk?"

"Drunk? No, I'm not drunk, but if you told me you wanted me to make you come again, I would not have a problem with that."

"So, you're horny?"

His tongue flicked at my lips. "Uh, yep! You started it this time. I was minding my own business, trying to get a proposal out, and you came after me. I tried to be good, and you came wagging your tail in my face."

"My tail?"

"Take that fucking robe off," he sharply directed.

"Bossy!"

"Now! Take it off."

I playfully turned my back to him. I untied the belt and slid the robe off my shoulder and then back on again, teasing him. I glanced at him over my shoulder. To my surprise, he had closed the distance between us and stood right behind me.

He lowered his mouth to my ear. "Take…it…off."

His hands reached around me, rubbing up and down the tops of my thighs. I turned my head to kiss him, and he pulled away from me. My jaw dropped. I couldn't believe he pulled away.

"Who the hell do you think you are?" I demanded as I turned to face him.

I tried to kiss him again, and he smirked and turned

his head, pulling it away from me. I grabbed his hips and pulled him to me. Then I tried to catch his face and force him to kiss me. I laughed at the silly game he played.

He looked down at me, staring into my eyes. "Take it off," he repeated.

"No! You kiss me, and then we'll talk about me taking my robe off."

He chuckled and shook his head. "You're so cute. You know I could have you out of that in less than two seconds, right?"

"No, you can't," I teased and attempted to wrap it around me tighter so I could tie the belt.

Like it had never been there, the robe flew off my body and went sailing across the room to the sofa. I bit my lip as I shyly laughed. I looked up at him, and he arched his eyebrows and shrugged.

With a cocky tilt of his head, he said, "I told you."

"Okay, now you have to kiss me."

"Oh no! I sure do not! You didn't listen, so no kisses. I'm sorry! This hurts me more than it does you," he played.

"Okay, then," I said as I started toward the sofa to retrieve my robe.

He scooped his arm around my waist, stopping me in my tracks. "I wouldn't."

"You won't kiss me, so I get to wear my robe."

He stepped around me snatching the robe off the sofa. He smirked at me and went toward the bedroom. It was a childish game, but it was a fun one, for some reason, so I chased after him.

When I got to the bedroom, he stood beside the bed. My robe hung from the bedpost behind him. He looked at me with arrogant pride on his face.

I smiled and stepped toward him, sort of dancing my body as I moved. I planned to seduce him and steal my robe back. It wasn't because I wanted the robe. It was because he was so damned proud of himself. I wanted to wipe that arrogant smirk off his face. I pulled at the robe he wore, trying to tease his cock. He pushed my hand away and tilted his head as he rolled his eyes and faked a yawn.

"Ooo! You pushed me away?"

"You've gotta get up earlier if you're going to get one over on me."

"I want to get *all* over you," I said.

He pressed his lips together and shook his head. "Faker."

"Okay, so what do I have to do?"

"It's too late, babe. I gave you so many chances."

"Are you getting off on this?"

"I'm about to," he nodded.

"Oh, you think I'm that easy?"

"Maybe I just know how to get what I want."

"You almost sound too serious for that to be funny."

"Shh!" he quickly hissed at me.

I gasped and laughed as I stared into his eyes. "You are being so mean."

With a piercing gaze and a soft, low voice he said, "I'm being everything you want me to be."

Fuck! He had the most fuckable expression I had ever seen in my life. He raised his hands and slowly traced his fingers across my shoulders.

"Turn around," he ordered as he stared into my eyes.

"Why?"

"I'm not giving you anymore chances. Turn around."

I swallowed the lump in my throat, and my heart raced. I smiled at him and nervously turned around. He stood behind me and massaged my ass.

"See how nice I am when you listen? Now bend over."

"What are you going to do? I've never done…"

"Bend…over!" he ordered.

I leaned forward, putting my hands on the mattress. I looked behind me in time to see him untie the robe and drop it to the floor. I had never had anal sex. I got nervous about where he planned to stick his cock. For some reason, there was still something exciting about this game.

"Jackson, I'm serious. I'm too afraid to do that."

"I want your ass in the air. Get on your knees and put your ass in the air."

I stiffened and tried to face him. He stood too close for me to move. I pushed back against him.

"I'm not going to do anything to hurt you. That's not my thing," he said. His voice lowered to a whisper. "Trust me."

I sighed. "Ass in the air? On my knees?"

"Sounds fucking hot. Do it."

My pussy craved his cock like I had never craved a cock in my life. I was terrified, but excited at the same time. I could feel how wet I was, already. I climbed up on the bed, sitting with my back toward him. What if I didn't do what he wanted? What if I didn't understand what he asked me to do, and he busted out laughing? I covered my face with my hands.

"Come on! I'm running out of patience."

I slowly leaned forward and got on my hands and knees. I swallowed the lump in my throat and tried to catch my breath. By this point, I had moved toward the middle of the bed. He put his knee between my legs and one of his arms scooped around my waist, lifting me and dragging me back toward the edge of the bed. I giggled. I couldn't help it. It was so swift and unexpected. It was fun!

He put his hand between my shoulder blades and gently pressed down. I bent my arms, giving in to his direction. I lay face down, and he grabbed my hips and lifted up. I felt his breath on my calf, and then I felt his tongue trace up my leg to the soft place behind my knee. His tongue tickled me before he lowered his mouth to my skin and kissed the bend of my knee, his tongue traced the backside of my thigh all the way to my butt cheek. He kissed my ass as his hands gripped my cheeks and squeezed, massaging and pulling. I felt his teeth against my skin. He slowly dragged them, gently scraping them across my flesh. He repeated the same on the other cheek. I flinched when I felt his teeth on my skin. I heard him chuckle. His finger slid along my sex from my clit to my opening. Quick as anything, his finger plunged inside, and he fingered me for just a second. I felt his breath between my legs. His tongue flicked against my engorged sex a couple of times. Then, I felt the silky softness against me as he dragged it over my pussy, curling the tip, tasting me. He stood, and I saw him take a step back. He moaned as he admired the view.

"This is so fucking hot!"

He moved closer to me and reached for one of the

condoms he had thrown on the bed earlier. I heard the package tear, and he tossed the empty paper to the end of the bed. A few seconds later, he put his hand between my legs and massaged me. I rocked my hips, and his other hand gently raked over my back as he played with me for a few minutes. He placed his hand between my shoulder blades and dug his fingertips into my flesh, dragging his hand down my back. His hand stopped at my hip, gripping hold. Teasing me, he dragged his cock over my wet folds and guided it to my hole. He gripped my other hip and sank his erection inside me. I spread my knees a little in an attempt to force him in deeper. He stood at the edge of the bed and watched his cock move in and out of me.

"Okay, baby, tell me if I hurt you," he said breathily. He pulled his hips back, and then he slammed into me. "Oh, fuck!"

"I love it when you do that."

"Well, then you're about to be a very happy woman."

He started fucking me so deep and so hard, I could hear our bodies slapping together with every impact. It was so fucking wild. He slammed into me over and over again. Every thrust moved me forward on the bed. Then, he would grip my hips and rip me back toward him as he thrust into me again and again.

"Fuck yeah!" he said through his clenched teeth. He slapped my ass, gripping my cheek as he thrust into me again. "Mm, babe! This is so fucking good!"

I pushed my hips back toward him.

"What do you want?" he asked, breathily.

"Make me come."

"You trust me?" he asked.

"Um…yes."

He pumped his hips, driving his cock into me a few more times. His fingers traced over my dripping pussy, spreading my wetness to my asshole. Each time his finger moved around my asshole, I felt more and more pressure as he pushed in, threatening to penetrate me in a way no one ever had. Strangely enough, the more he primed me, the more I wanted it.

He withdrew his cock and moved my silkiness to my asshole. Satisfied that he had things as he needed them, he slowly slid his cock back inside me, fucking me like he had never stopped. I felt his fingers splayed on my lower back as his thumb began pressing against my asshole. I whimpered, filled with a desire—a craving I had never had before.

"Are you okay?"

"Mm! Yes!"

"Want me to stop?"

"No," I begged.

I felt the resistance just before his thumb penetrated me. I gasped as he pushed in deeper. Oh fuck! I had an entirely new "good" happening to me, and I wanted more. I moaned and his hips started thrusting wildly. He pumped his thumb in and out of me. Jackson's cock started getting thicker and harder. His body quaked. He started slamming into me harder and faster again. He pleasured my ass as he fucked my pussy so hard that his balls slapped my clit with his thrusts. I was on pleasure overload.

"Jackson! Ooo, fuck! Fuck! Fuck! Oh, yes! I love the way you fuck me!"

"You like getting fucked?" he asked, his tone breathy and demanding.

"Yes!" I moaned, feeling every sensation culminating and pushing me to my breaking point.

He pounded away, and I felt my orgasm building. Our bodies slammed together. I gripped the sheets in my fists as I rocked back into him. Finally, I couldn't stave it off any longer. My pussy clenched, gripping and squeezing Jackson's cock.

"Yeah, baby! Just like that!"

"Oh, my g… Ooo! Yes, yes, yes! Oh! Jackson!"

As I came, he pumped his thumb faster, but he drove his cock in deeper and held it inside me. I felt the thumping as he throbbed. He slapped my ass, a few times as his orgasm erupted inside me. He gripped my hip, ripping into me one last time.

As he finished, he let out a heavy grunt, and his head fell back as he fought for every breath. His grip on my hip slowly started loosening, and he eased his thumb out of me, softly patting my ass. He leaned forward and put a kiss on my lower back. He gently gripped my hips pushing me forward, lifting up as he pulled his cock out. I felt as though we had just been disassembled. I fell onto my stomach, lying across the bed, and my favorite playmate collapsed right beside me on the plush mattress.

"I need a minute, then a shower, but I've got a long way to go before sunrise."

"What?"

"It's only ten thirty. We've still got a lot of night left," he offered, with a hint of nervousness.

"Did you bite off more than you can chew?" I teased.

"I'll get my second wind. Then I'm going to tear you up." He smiled as he rolled over on his back and closed his eyes.

I wanted to touch him…constantly. I moved over beside him and threaded my fingers through his hair as I stared at his perfect face. He opened his eyes, smiling as he lifted his head to kiss me. I turned my head away, dodging his kiss, continuing his earlier game.

"No, you don't!"

He flipped my body, rolling with his. He put his leg over my hips, and he reached over my body, putting his hand on the mattress beside me, caging me. I had *almost* gotten beneath him. I looked up at him as he stared into my eyes, lowering his head to kiss me. I tried to pull him on top of me, but he seemed to resist my efforts, for some reason. I settled for the kiss for now.

After a few minutes, he dismissed himself to go to the bathroom. I stayed on the bed and stared at the ceiling. When he opened the bathroom door, the light cut through the darkness of our room.

"That light is bright."

"How do you know? You've got your hands over your face," he said as he sat on the side of the bed.

I glanced over at him, watching him as he dried his hands on a hand towel. He put his arm over my body and lowered his head, tickling my nipple with his tongue. It wasn't the wild tongue-flicking thing that he had mastered. This was more of a subtle, soft, sweet gesture.

"Are you done spanking my ass?"

He sighed. "Tell me you don't like it, and I will never do it again."

"It was hot. You're so much different than I thought you would be. You walk around giving this air of being some proper gentleman woven together with class and elegance."

"So, you think less of me, now?"

"Far from it. You're fun. You're just not at all as stuffy and fussy as I expected."

"Just because I slapped your ass?"

"No, because you're such a sexual person."

"If you're not going to enjoy it, why do it? The way I see it, if you sleep with someone, you're letting them be part of something you don't share with everyone else. So, the fact that I'm different than you expected is a good thing. I don't want everyone to look at me and know what I'm about."

I wiggled, attempting to sit up, and Jackson moved his arm from over my body. I sat up on the bed and traced my fingers over his arm and his shoulder. I smiled as my eyes locked on his.

"Why *are* you letting me know what you're about?"

Chapter Seven

I could see Jackson's wheels turning as he thought about my question for a few moments. I couldn't help but wonder how he would answer. I was hoping his answer would be filled with hope, with regards to what I meant to him.

"Remember the day you came in for that interview? Alice agreed to help me find her replacement because she was moving to Hawaii, and I just couldn't compete with Hawaii. She brought you into my office, and from the second your pretty face came through that door, I wanted to throw you on the desk and mess up your dress. You were shy, and you seemed so innocent that I wanted to corrupt you. Then you told Alice how she did that spreadsheet thing the hard way. Alice was untouchable, as far as I was concerned, but you were able to tell her things she did wrong. I wanted that. I liked the way you told her she did things wrong. You were tactful about it. I could see by the look on her face that you were right. She had never taken criticism very well, but you had her hanging on your every word, so I had to have you."

"So, you let me see you in this way because I can make a spreadsheet the easy way?"

"No. It's all about that lady in the street, freak in the sheets bullshit. Because I like this smartass, ornery side of you that likes to challenge me and argue with me. Then you turn around, and you're demure and sweet. I guess that makes you *proper* in some way, too. But you'll get dirty with me, and honestly, I couldn't stand the thought of you having to fake orgasms." He glanced at me, narrowing his eyes and shaking his head as though he were disgusted. "If you get nothing else from me, I will convince you that those fuckers owe it to you to take care of what you need."

"So, you see this whole thing as temporary?"

He sighed and dropped his chin to his chest. "I'm not trying to make it anything. We turned a corner with that email that you sent out. I saw the opportunity to do something I've wanted to do since I met you, and I went with it. I'm not regretting that. I hope you're not either, but I'm living for this moment. I'm not arrogant enough to think I'll be the best sex you'll ever have, but I'm determined to be the best you've had to this point. When you're done playing with me, I want you to be able to say what you want, how you want it, when and where. You don't have to lie back and take what they want to give you. Be bold. You're hot! If one doesn't want to play like you want, you will have no problem finding one that will."

"I don't think I want to think about what comes after you."

"Then, just live in this moment with me. To hell with all that future planning shit. The future may not even be there. What is the point in wasting what you know you've got for something you may not have?"

"How have you built anything without planning?"

"Oh, I assure you, business is a different situation. I do nothing but plan at work. Maybe that's why I don't want to do it when I'm out of the office."

"Maybe." I shrugged and faked a smile. "So, speaking of planning, we do have to work tomorrow. I don't think this is a good night to go all night long. We have to sleep."

"You're not working tomorrow," he snapped. "I'm giving you the day off."

"I don't need a day off. I have bills to pay. So, thanks, but no thanks. If you're working, I'm working."

"I'm going to be out a lot tomorrow. I have meetings all day. Bob Wardel is pissed off at the crew that's on his job. The guys are saying Bob is impossible, so I have to go regulate. I'm thinking I'll take him to lunch and try to get back on his good side. He has a lot of jobs coming up. It would be nice to have a foot in that door. Montgomery Construction would be set for the next year just off one of those jobs. No matter what, I want to make sure Bob is happy."

Naked as we were, just like that, Mr. Montgomery had made an appearance. I laughed to myself as I tried to imagine him at the office, working in his birthday suit. When he caught me laughing, naturally, he wanted to know what I found so amusing. I didn't want to discourage him from talking, even if it was about work. Since he seemed to be done with that topic anyway, I changed the subject.

"So, you were a birth control accident, huh?"

"I was, yes."

"I'm sure your parents were glad. I know I'm glad."

"My mom wasn't real happy, I don't think. My mother is one of those gypsy-type women who hitchhikes from one town to another. Her payment for their gas was not the kind that has a treasury stamp on it. She gets through life, I guess, but she's never worked an honest day in her life."

"So, how did you become the great Jackson Montgomery?"

"I don't know about *great*, but my aunt raised me. She never gave up on me, and I just wanted to make her proud. She's the main woman in my life. My mother looks me up when she passes through town. She stops by to borrow my shower and to tell me how much she hates everything I represent. We have a nice dinner, and then she's off, blowing on the breeze, again."

"That must be hard."

"I hate the calls that come when she overdoses. She's been tempting death for quite a while now. I can't change what she is. She doesn't try to live out of my pockets. I think she lives that life because it's truly what she wants to do. I don't know. I gave up trying to figure out why she does what she does."

"I'm glad you had your aunt. She did a good job with you."

He smiled a warm, loving smile, and his eyes sparkled. "She's the most amazing woman I've ever known in my life. Remember back when you first started? She's that one call that I told you I would take no matter what. My world stops for her."

"Oh! Winnie Fisher?"

"Yep." He nodded. "That's the one."

"I've worked for you for two years, and it took me sleeping with you to learn why she is so important. I've talked to her, what? Once? Twice? Now that I know her story, I hope I get to talk to her again."

"You want me to tell her to call and talk to you?"

"Sure." I giggled. "I'll talk to her. I'll thank her for

making you what you are."

I leaned over and kissed him. His arms scooped around me and hugged me to him. He reached up and raked his fingers through my hair. With all that family talk, he had gotten tangled in his emotions and needed to get away from talking about his aunt. I sensed a subject change coming, and I was right.

"You decorate this bed really well. Did you know that?"

"Oh yeah? I think we could both decorate it really well if I pull your body on top of me."

"Ah! The missionary thing?"

"Yeah." I smiled.

"Sorry! That won't happen. I'm not a missionary kind of guy." He smiled and winked.

"That's because you've never been with me. I'll change your mind."

"Nope! That's for husbands, wives, and forever type things. Maybe I'm just quirky, but that's not my place. However, I'll do anything else you want, but that missionary stuff is sacred. I just don't do it."

I stared at him in disbelief. "You're serious?"

"I want to be the man that drives you crazy and makes your pussy drip. I want to be the man that you can't ever get enough of—the dirtiest man you know. That's what I want to be. I don't want the sunset strolls through the park, or the cake tasting bullshit. Fuck that! I want to fuck you from across the room without ever having touched you—just by looking at you. I want you to want me. That's all I want. I want your legs to fall open when I walk in the room."

I dropped my legs to the side and smirked at him. "Like this?"

He slowly turned his head, looking over his shoulder as his eyes stared at my crotch. "Mm! Very nice."

He had so much sexual energy within his body that I could feel myself becoming addicted. I knew I would want it from him all the time. He just had something I had never experienced before. He was magnetic, and he drew my own sexual desires out of me. It felt like when you wake up in the morning and your body starts coming alive. Only this was a different kind of slumber. I felt like I had been starving for him—sexually starving—my entire life.

His eyes shifted to mine, and he smirked. "I'd love to watch you climax."

"You've seen that, quite a few times, actually."

"No!" he said in his velvety tone, dragging the word out as he tilted his head. "I want to watch you please yourself. I want to watch you come without me."

"Maybe one day when you're eye-fucking me from across the room," I said.

He put his nose to mine and flicked his tongue at my lips. "From across the room won't work. I want it in my face."

I kissed his lips and shyly smiled. "I've never been a sex slave before. It might take me a bit. I'm not ready for that yet."

He chuckled and pinched his lips between his thumb and his forefinger as he stared at the floor. He clicked his tongue and bobbed his head. His eyes shifted to mine, and he fought back a smile, attempting to be serious.

"Sex slave, huh? Yeah! I guess I'm okay with that."

"Well, what else would you call what I'm doing here?"

"*You're* not the slave. Don't get me wrong. I get plenty out of this little game, but remember? I said I want to be the best *you've* had this far. I never said I want you to be the best *I've* ever had. It's kind of a warped, roundabout way of doing things, but I'm doing this for *you.* It's all about *you.* Get it? Everything you've ever wanted to do, I want you to do it. I want you to believe that if you want it, I want to be the one to give it to you, whatever *it* may be. You! It's all about you. You deserve to feel good. If it feels good, and you want it, let's do it. I am your personal 'yes' man."

"Except missionary stuff," I challenged.

"You won't miss it. I'll see to that."

"You're a creepy, strange man."

"Faker. You don't believe that. You're just afraid to admit that you want this."

"Oh, I do want it!" I blurted out before I could stop myself. I covered my mouth, and he laughed at my emphatic declaration.

He pulled my hand away and kissed me. He brushed his thumb over my cheek as his eyes bored a hole into my soul. "I'll be whatever kind of sex toy you need."

"Aren't we both trying to be that for each other?"

He pressed his lips together and the edges of his mouth turned down as he shrugged. "Yeah! We are. Like I said, I get a lot out of this. It's not like I am suffering, but I do want to watch you one day."

"Okay! One day?"

"Yep!"

"Since this is all about me…?" I posed the question

as I smirked.

"What have I done?" He rolled his eyes, and a smile spread across his face. "Yes?"

"Can I sit in a nice hot bubble bath while you feed me bonbons?"

"Sweetheart, I'm not *that* kind of yes-man," he said. "Maybe if you had a bad day, I'd lower myself to that level of servitude. I'm like a union sex slave. I'm not kissing your shoes, crawling like a dog, and don't you ever hit me, but when it comes to your body, I'll make you feel anything you want. I'm *that* kind of yes-man. That kind of sex slave."

"This is fun right now, but I don't want a slave to be *all* that you are. You know?"

"It's an understanding. It's not a matter to address. Now you know where I'm coming from. That's all there is to that. I read you. You want to fight with me? I'll spank your ass. You want to get mouthy? I've got a way to quiet that. You want to tease me? I can play that game, too. You want to bring all of your broken pieces to me? I'll put you back together. Trust me! More than you will ever know, it's about you."

"You read me?"

"Oh yeah!" he said confidently.

"What do I need right now?"

He smirked. "You're not ready for what you need right now."

"Okay, what is that?"

"You need me to bend you over this bed, grab a handful of your hair, and fuck your pretty little ass. We'll get there." He nodded.

"I've never…"

"Because you've never been with someone that

makes it okay. You can trust me. You want it. You want to know what it's like. I'm not afraid of pushing your limits because I know what will happen for you just beyond that limit. There is nothing fun about a woman in pain. I'll never do anything that will hurt you in the bad ways. I won't say I won't hurt you in the good ways. You loved my cock tearing through your pussy that first time. You like it rough. That thought makes my cock hard. It makes me want to give it to you over and over again. Fuck! You make me so hard."

"That's okay. You make my pussy wet."

"I know." He smiled. "That's exactly how I want it."

"Well, you've got your wish. You know you're creating a monster, right?"

One amazing thing about Jackson Montgomery was that we didn't have the awkward conversations. He didn't need to ask my permission for anything. He said he could read me, and I don't know how, but I believed him. Every time I put a challenge in front of him, he licked it… Mm! He licked it.

Uh, where was I? Oh yeah! So, anyway, he had no issues just doing something, and I had no issues with it when he just did it. In fact, it was usually so much better than any idea I would've had.

When I told him I was wet and ready, again, he was done talking. He stood up off the bed and looped his arms behind my knees, ripping my body to the edge of the bed where he stood. He folded my legs around his right hip and pressed down on my knees, forcing my legs together. He caressed my silky pussy with his other hand. He put two fingers inside me, spreading them apart as I lay on my side. I felt tighter. His fingers felt different this way. When he took them out of me, he spread my lips apart, making me ready to receive him. He spread his legs so he could better reach me. I felt the head of his erection as he slid it in. He backed it out, not all the way, but almost. He stared at my face with a playful smirk as he slowly pushed into me again. He pulled his cock back, this time all the way out.

He reached for one of the foil packages at the foot of the bed. I watched him roll the rubber over his cock. Something about watching him handle himself made me burn. He put his thumb beside my opening, pulling it apart so he could access me again. This time, he only gave me a little, teasing me as he rocked his hips back and forth.

"You tease!"

"Did you want something?"

"You know what I want," I answered.

"You're right!" He clenched his jaw and rammed his cock inside me. "I do!"

I gasped. Holy shit! I loved it when he did that! His thick cock felt incredible. Especially when it slammed into me with the force he put behind it. Maybe he was right. Maybe I did like it rough, because for some reason, I seemed to enjoy it so much when he fucked me hard and fast.

He put one hand on my hip and grabbed my tit in his other hand. He pounded my pussy as he pinched my nipple between his fingers. It felt strangely exciting when he tugged my nipple, twisting it. His tongue slid across his lower lip as his eyes focused on my breast. He began driving himself in deeper, but slower. I felt his cock throbbing, I was sure of it. He lifted my leg and put it on his left shoulder. He slid his hands under me and jerked my body closer, using his pubic bone to grind against my clit. He circled his hips as he ground against me. Fuck! That was it!

"Oh, baby!" I shrieked.

He dropped my leg off his shoulder so my legs fell on both sides of him. If he weren't standing there, my ass would be off the bed and on the floor. He lifted my hips and pulled my body into him as he pumped his hips. His thrusts came in fast, short bursts. My back arched. It felt as though there was a fire racing up and down the inside of my thighs, like the burning fuse had struck dynamite, my orgasm exploded. He wasn't slamming and ramming. In fact, he was almost gentle. My fingers dug at his abdomen as the spasms raged. I desperately wanted his body on top of me. I wanted him to hold me and cradle me in his arms. My eyes fixated on his face as he swiped his thumb across his brow, wiping away a bead of sweat. His face looked so focused it became comical. He took this sex stuff far too seriously.

Then, something was different. There was a funny look on his face. It was a look of fear.

Chapter Eight

After my orgasm finished, Jackson watched nervously as he began backing his cock out of me. He clenched his eyes and pulled out. He put his hands on his hips and looked at me as though he was disgusted or terrified.

"What?" I demanded.

"Um…well…um…uh-oh…the uh…the fucking rubber broke," he cautiously offered as he pointed to my pussy.

"It's in me?"

"No, but something else is." He ran his hand over his head. "I should've pulled out. I thought I felt it snap right when I started to come."

I rose up onto my knees on the edge of the bed and slid my hand around his neck, pulling him toward me. I could see that he was annoyed. I pushed my lips to his and whispered, "It's going to be okay. Don't worry. There won't be a little you running around. I'm on the pill. Those condoms have spermicide, so relax."

He sighed, and his facial expression softened as he looked into my eyes. "I'm sorry!" He reached his arms around my waist and lowered his head to my shoulder. "I didn't mean to ruin your moment."

"You didn't ruin anything for me. I'm having the time of my life."

He backed away from me and looked down. "And,

then, there's my dick, looking rather proud of himself, I see."

I looked down and saw the head of his semi-hard cock poking through a tear in the prophylactic. I couldn't help it. I had to laugh. His dick did look rather happy to be free. I suddenly felt bad for penises everywhere.

"I'm going to go see my doctor," I said. It was a random thought that I, apparently, felt compelled to share.

"Your doctor? Like for a pregnancy test? But that takes a little time."

"No! I'm not worried about pregnancy. I'm going to do something different, so you won't have to worry about…this," I said as I motioned to his crotch.

"Don't do that. I would probably still do what I do, anyway, so don't worry about it. I don't want you to do something different because of me."

"I like it when I get to feel you."

He smiled and wrapped his arm around my neck, pulling my mouth to his. As our lips met, he muttered, "Mm! Me too!"

I hugged him, running my hands up and down his back. He tilted his head back and closed his eyes. I softly kissed his neck where I could see his pulse pounding beneath his skin. He brought his head forward and looked down at me.

"Is that bed comfortable?"

"It is. You should try it out."

"Let me run in the bathroom and take care of the prankster. Save me a spot."

I pulled the blankets back and wiggled my body to the middle of the king-sized bed. I closed my eyes and waited. When he came back, he fell into the bed on his back and folded his arms behind his head. I laid my head on his arm and cupped his balls in my hands.

"Mm!" He moaned with a chuckle as he flinched from the surprise of my touch.

He closed his eyes and let me play. His cock had softened, but even when it was soft, it was still nothing to sneer at. I massaged him for a few minutes. I felt like doing something devious to him. I threw my leg over him and slid my body on top of his. He pulled one of his arms from behind his head and put his hand on my hip. His eyes looked sleepy as he searched my face.

"What can I do for you?" He smiled.

"I want to do something for you," I offered as I lowered my mouth to kiss his neck and his chest.

He put both of his arms around me, trying to hug me. I pushed them away, pinning his arms to the bed beside him. He tried to lift them to touch me again. I pulled them over his head, and I licked his lower lip as I stared into his eyes.

"Leave them there, and I won't bite…as hard."

A challenging smile swept across his lips. "Yes, ma'am!"

I softly dragged my fingers down his arms and down his ribcage as I kissed his neck and his chest. I felt his breath rushing in and out of his lungs as his chest rose and fell under my fingers. It excited me when his breath hitched in response to what I did to him. I wanted to please him. I wanted to make him forget his name. I wanted to be the best he'd ever had, too.

I kissed his body all the way down to his hips, tasting his salty skin as I worked my way lower. When I got to his hip, I twirled my tongue, dancing it over his skin in the same place he loved to work on me. He flinched and drew a staggered breath. Then, I did the same thing on the other side. I dragged my tongue through the creased valley at the top of his leg that led to his crotch. I may, or may not, have added an extra sigh or two, just to make sure my warm breath teased his cock. I looked up his body and saw his chest rising and falling rapidly.

I loved every second of teasing him. I felt like I had him right where I wanted him…almost. I traced my tongue down the same path on the other side of his body. Knowing what he was anticipating, I lifted my body putting my hands on either side of his hips, hovering over him. I lowered my chest and pinned his cock between my tits as I pressed against him, sliding back down his body. When I could reach the tip with my tongue, I traced circles around the head. The noises he made only encouraged me. I wanted to tease him and make him want me in the same way he made me want him.

My tongue traced the fold beside his cock to the top of the inside of his thigh. I kissed down his thigh to his knee. I tickled behind his knee and moved to his other leg. As I moved up the inside of his thigh, I shoved his legs apart so I could lie between them. The force I used to push his legs apart excited him…and me. A moan followed his throaty chuckle. I was driving him crazy, and that felt sexy. I felt wild, daring, and dangerous.

His breath became rushed, and his body flinched when my tongue skimmed over a ticklish place. My tongue traced along where his legs and his crotch came together. I could hear his fingers tightening around the metal scrolls as he gripped the headboard. His breath grew shallow and rushed. He tried to be tough, but that only excited me even more, because this proved him right. Some things couldn't be faked.

I gripped his balls and gently pushed them up, tickling beneath them with the tip of my tongue. I heard a soft hum of approval as he flinched from my touch. I kissed him there, softly sucking and dragging my tongue over his skin, knowing from the way his body tensed that I was hitting my mark. I let go of his balls and licked them a few times before I took them into my mouth. I massaged them with my tongue as I sucked on them. He lifted his head and looked down at me. His eyes seemed pleading and desperate as he propped his body up on his elbows so he could watch me. It excited me to know that he wanted to watch what I did to him. I became content to accept that this man knew how to own my body, but this time, I wanted to be the one bringing him to his knees.

After I had my fun teasing and playing with his balls, I dragged my tongue up his shaft, purposely avoiding making it all the way to the tip. Under the peak of his head, I drew circles with my tongue, kissing him with a little extra suction. I kissed him again, only instead of breaking the suction, I moved down his shaft before I released him. I smiled at him, dragging my tongue back up, again. This time, I lowered my mouth over his cock until I felt the head in my throat. I closed my lips around him. Teasingly, I lifted my head off of him, then I traced circles around the head of his cock, tasting the salty, pearly drops of precum. I gently closed my fingers around his shaft, massaging the head with my thumb as my tongue flicked him. I moved my hand down, and I lowered my mouth on him again. I began sucking as I rippled my tongue against him. As my mouth slid up and down on him, I stroked the lower part of his shaft. He put his hand in my hair, and I looked up at him, gently pressing my teeth against him, a friendly reminder of my earlier warning. He softly blinked and nodded as though he consented to the punishment I had planned. I gently clicked my teeth against him a few times. As I lifted my head, my teeth lightly grazed his skin all the way toward the tip. He drew a deep breath through his teeth as he watched me. Before the head, I lowered my mouth on him again. I sucked him and teased his cock with my tongue as I moved up and down on him a few more times, stroking him. I opened my mouth and slapped his cock against my tongue. His eyes widened, his body tensed, and his mouth fell open. A gritty moan filtered out of his throat as his hips bucked a couple of times. I slapped his cock against my tongue harder and faster. His eyes had that wild, crazy look in them as he watched me, breathing through his clenched teeth.

"Oh, fuck yeah!"

He stroked my hair, encouraging me. The noises he made told me he was getting close. He started lifting his hips, desperately wanting to come, yet trying to hold back. A few seconds later, I had him! He put his fingers under my chin, trying to lift my mouth off of him.

"You better stop. Stop! Oh, shit! Fuck!"

He drew a deep breath through his teeth. His head dropped back, and he moaned as he thrust his hips, ramming his cock into my mouth. I closed my lips around him and sucked him as he thrust his hips up and down. He let out a throaty grunt as he lifted his head and looked down at me. His hand on my head suddenly felt heavy, pushing me down as he thrust his hips a few more times. He filled my mouth almost faster than I could swallow. As usual, he made no apologies for what he wanted—using my mouth exactly as he wanted. When his cock quit spilling cum into my throat, I brushed my tongue over the tip. When he flinched, I was confident I had given him what he wanted.

"Holy shit! You fuckin' swallow." He chuckled and fell back onto the bed.

I kissed him and softly ran my tongue up and down his shaft. It was more like a petting, soft stroking act than something I did to excite him. It made me feel good to do something for him. For the first time in my life, I had actually enjoyed blowing a man as much as he had enjoyed it.

After I felt Jackson had relaxed and was content, I crawled up beside him, resting my head on his arm. He folded it around me, and I cupped his balls, playing with them. I gently massaged them as I stared at his perfect face. He had his eyes closed, and he looked like he was about to fall asleep.

"You've only got about five minutes," his sleepy voice said.

"Five minutes?"

"I'm resting for a minute, then I'm coming for you."

I giggled. "You already came for me."

"Yes, I did, but you know what I mean."

I pulled my hand away from his crotch. "Jackson, it's almost three in the morning."

"So?" He opened one eye, peeking at me.

"So, it's late. We need sleep. This has been so much fun. But, really…"

"I'll change your mind," he insisted.

He pulled his arm out from under my head and propped himself up on his elbow. He pretended to bite at my lips before he pressed his lips to mine. His tongue swept into my mouth, brushing over mine. My fingers skimmed over his chest and his abdomen as we kissed. He slid his hand in mine, intertwining our fingers. He tugged my hand as he rolled onto his back, trying to pull me on top of him. I put my leg across his hips and mounted him. He stretched our joined hands up over his head, holding me flat against him as he kissed me. One of his hands released mine as he reached down between us, guiding his semi-hard cock inside me.

I tried to take it. I wanted to take it, but my body wasn't having it. My pussy was sore from the unusual amount of friction, slamming and pounding. I felt raw and bruised. I hadn't minded anything that put me in that position, but the thickness that had been so much fun earlier in the day suddenly stopped being as much fun. He pumped his hips a few times as our lips locked in one of the life and death type kisses.

"Ouch!" I muttered around the kiss.

He pumped his hips upward again. I broke the kiss and rested my forehead against his. His eyes locked on mine as he thrust into me, again.

"I can't do this. It hurts," I blurted, lifting my hips in an effort to avoid his effort to go deeper.

"Hurts how? What hurts?"

"I want you inside me, but my body wants you out. I'm so sorry," I shyly said.

"Don't be sorry. I can't do it anymore either," he

chuckled.

"Why were you doing it then?"

"I told you I was going to do this all night long. It's still nighttime. Plus, I don't feel right if I get mine and leave you wanting something more. I want you to be happy, too."

"Then, just let me be here with you…and sleep!"

"Okay." He smiled, with a hint of relief in his tone as he softly kissed my lips.

He reached down and lifted my leg, pulling it toward his hip as he quickly withdrew himself. He winced as his cock left me. He exhaled and clenched his eyes shut as he held my body on top of his. His fingers softly drew circles over my back.

"Get off me," he said. "You broke my pecker."

As we laughed, he hugged me, rolling us onto our sides. I turned away from him, backing against him. He draped his arm around me and buried his face in my hair. He mumbled something that I couldn't understand, but within seconds, he was sound asleep. Satisfied to the point of aching, I fell into my own slumber, my body pressed against him, happy and content.

The next morning, when I woke up and realized where I was, I panicked. I sat up, looking around the room. I stared at the clock. It was almost noon. Jackson wasn't in bed beside me, but he had left a note.

Good morning! Will you call me when you wake up, please?

Enjoy your day off.

—XO, ~J~

I got out of bed, and all too quickly, I was reminded of the "sexcapade" marathon from the day before. Flowers would've been a nice reminder. Maybe a box of chocolates, or even a bottle of wine would've been a nice refresher, but no! My lady business felt like it had taken a beating, and I felt tender.

I smiled to myself. *But I had a hell of a lot of fun!*

I went to find my cell phone. I dialed Jackson's number, and it went to straight to voicemail. I thought about hanging up but opted to leave a message instead.

"Good morning! I'm calling you. Now, will you call me back, please?"

Chapter Nine

I waited a little while for Jackson to call me back. I craved the sound of his voice. Sadly, the return call didn't come, so I decided I would go enjoy a nice warm shower. Naturally, as soon as I turned on the water, my phone rang.

"Good morning," I purred.

"Hi! It's Jackson Montgomery. I'm here with Betty Elwerth. She's with—"

"Martel and Wynder, yes?"

"Right! Okay, they don't want to let our guys get their supplies for the Haxley job. They're telling me something about a past due balance of eleven thousand, something dollars. Betty says she talked to you about this a couple of months ago. Do you happen to know anything about that?"

"Um…it sounds vaguely familiar. What happened with it?"

"Well, I hoped I wouldn't have to ask them that. I feel like that's something *we* should know. Why wouldn't she have talked to Dena? Why would she talk to you about that?"

"I don't know. I don't remember what the deal was with that. I vaguely remember something, but I don't remember specifics."

"Hmm! Well, I guess I'll pay it, but when you get back on Monday, can you run that down for me, please?"

"Of course."

"Thank you!"

The line went dead, and I felt a cold chill move through the once hot and spicy hotel room. I had butterflies. I felt like I was in trouble and try as I might, I couldn't remember what the deal had been with Betty. I knew I had talked to her, and I remembered that there was something funny with that account, which explained why I had to be the one to talk to her. I just couldn't remember why we had a problem.

I stood in the shower, nervous that I had done something wrong. My mind raced, trying to remember what the conversation with Betty had been. It just wouldn't come to me. I got out of the shower and wrapped a towel around me. I went to get a brush from my purse and suddenly I remembered. Oh, shit, did I remember! I called Jackson's phone again.

"Yes?" he said into the phone, with a hint of annoyance in his voice.

"Are you still there with Betty?"

"No. Now, I'm on my way to get my ass reamed by Bob. Why?"

"You're gonna kill me."

"Oh no! Come on! Please don't say that," he desperately pleaded. "Why?"

"Martel and Wynder won't take checks for payment on accounts. They will only bill a card."

"So?"

"So, Dena isn't an authorized name on the company card, so I had to pay it, but you had both of the cards for some reason. Then, by the time I had them back—"

"Are you fucking kidding me?"

"No. I was supposed to call her back, but I must've spaced it. I'm really sorry."

"I don't fuckin' believe this. I just defended my people and put all the blame on their people. I copped an attitude with that woman because I had confidence that my team had their shit together. That's a ding to our credit rating, by the way. Tell ya what! I don't care when it gets done. I'll do it myself if I have to, but I want Dena and Lisa added as authorized users for every single account we've got. Right now! I don't care if it's an account with the ice cream man. Dena and Lisa are to be added. We can't do this, Elizabeth. We can't just *forget* to pay people."

"Do you want me to take my name off the accounts?"

"Yeah! I honestly don't see the point. We've got the accounting girls. There's no reason they can't handle it. If you need something, go to them and get it."

"You're serious?"

"Oh, yes! I am!"

"That never happens. You never have both of the cards. It was a fluke. I never forget. This time, I just—"

"Elizabeth, that's a flimsy excuse. Please, just roll purchases and payments over to the accounting girls."

"Okay! I don't have my car to get to the office. I seem to be stuck in a hotel room at the moment."

He sighed. "Fine! Monday. It can wait until Monday."

"Are you okay, today?"

He sucked on his lips. "Sure doesn't seem like it."

"I'm really sorry."

"I heard you. Have a good a day."

My heart shattered. Even if I weren't sleeping with him, Jackson never talked to any of us like that. Anytime anyone made a mistake, he handled it with kindness and patience. He was pissed at me, and there was no mistaking that. It broke my heart, not only as an employee, but now we had the relationship aspect, also.

For the next few hours, each second passed with agonizing slowness. I kept hoping there would be a happy phone call coming, but that didn't happen. I felt stressed out, disappointed, and hurt. More than anything, I wondered what this meant for Jackson and me.

At a quarter to five, my phone rang. Instantly, my stomach tied itself in knots. I debated answering the call for a whole second, but I had to know how much trouble I was in.

"Hello?"

"Hey! I thought you might want your car. I'm going to be over there in a few minutes. Do you want me to bring you back over here?"

"Um, sure!"

"Okay, I'll be there in about fifteen, twenty minutes."

"Do you want to call me? Or do you want me to meet you downstairs?"

"You can just meet me downstairs."

"Is your day any better?"

"It's a day. I'll be there in a few minutes."

"Okay!" I scoffed.

About ten minutes later, I heard a heavy knock on the door. I walked over and looked through the peephole. Jackson stood on the other side of the barrier. Now, my heart was really breaking. Why would he knock, at this point? I opened the door.

"Why didn't you just come in? What're you doing?"

"Coming to get you so you can get your car. Let's roll."

"What's going on? Will you come talk to me, please?"

He glared at me as he heaved a heavy sigh. He stepped into the room, seeming formal and stuffy. It was unnerving. I wanted to remind him of the more relaxed, happier version of himself.

I put my arms around his neck and stretched up to kiss him. He pulled his head away from me. His voice sounded flat and course. "Don't!"

"What the hell?"

He arched his eyebrows as he stared into my eyes, driving his finger at me. "I'm fucking pissed off at you," he spouted before he pitched the key set in his hand across the floor, as though he were skipping a pebble on a lake. His head twitched to the side. "February happened seven fucking months ago. She gave us, what, five, six months to pay before she shut our account down? They had to shake me down for the money we owe them from seven, fucking months ago? Seven! That's a long damn time! The guys are late to the jobsite because they can't get their shit. The client is up in arms, wanting to know where they were. I made an ass out of myself, arguing with that woman because I believed in my people. I trusted you. I believed we had it together," he said as he splayed his hand across his chest.

"I made a mistake. I'm sorry. I feel bad, and I don't want to be in trouble with you. I just spaced it. I never would've done that on purpose."

"You had seven months to remember. Elizabeth! Shit!" His hands brushed up his face and into his hair and back down again. He wouldn't look at me. He just started rambling on some tangent.

"Spaced it? You spaced it? Be glad it's not *your* name on the front of that fucking building, because it *is* *my* name. And that name's not worth shit right now. *Delinquent* account, my ass! Not what I wanted! I pay you people to take care of this kind of shit."

I bit my lip, trying not to laugh. I couldn't figure out what I found so funny, but this all seemed a bit dramatic for one account out of all of them that we had. Yes, I messed up, and yes, it was pretty bad. However, it would hardly ruin his name. I covered my mouth with my hand, trying to hide my smile.

He glanced over at me, doing a double take before his eyes locked on mine. He looked *really* annoyed, now. "What's so fucking funny?"

I shook my head. He looked down at his blue jeans, which I had never seen him wear, by the way. He pitched his arms out to the side.

"Is my fly down? Do I have a booger? Is there an alien colony dancing on my head? What the hell is so fucking funny?" he demanded.

I shook my head, still trying not to laugh. He reminded me of a little kid, throwing a fit. I did feel bad, but he was so cute. I didn't want him to be angry, but no amount of pouting and bitching would change what had happened. I had to find a way to make him laugh.

He stared at me, watching me struggle, in vain, to wipe the smile off my face. As he stood there, with a blank face, the edges of his mouth started to turn up into a smile. He tried to fight it, too. However, the harder either of us tried, the harder it became.

"Are you just mad? Or really…*really* mad?"

He glared at me and sighed.

"I'm so glad you take me seriously." He pointed to his chest. "I'm pissed off. *Big* pissed off! And, my fucking cock hurts. I've had a bad day, and I can't do shit about it. I'm cranky. I'm tired, and I'm big, *big* pissed off," he said, fighting back a laugh. "You know what? You can laugh at me if you want to. I'm leaving! If you want to go get your car, you better come on. I have a meeting at five thirty. I can't play around."

"So, are we still friends?"

He glared at me, smirking as he stepped around me to retrieve the keys he had launched across the room.

"Is that a no, then?" I teased. "And, I'm sure it served a purpose, but throwing your keys across the room helped…how?"

He stood in front of me, and his eyes looked sad. He sighed. "I told you I had a bad day. Can you just do something nice instead of being the salt in the wounds?"

"I tried, but you pulled away from me."

"You want me to forgive and forget what you do, but you don't have to forgive and forget? Humph! Double standard, but okay!"

As I stared into his eyes, I stuck my lip out as though I were pouting. I reached up and pulled his head down to hug him. He laid his head on my shoulder, and I raked my fingers through his hair. His arms locked around my waist.

"I had a bad day, too. It hurts when you're mad at

me. It hurts even more when you're mad at me, and I can't fix it. I screwed up, and I'm sorry."

He sighed, and I felt him shrug. "We'll get it fixed."

"And my pussy hurts, and I can't do a damn thing about it."

He lifted his head with a smile on his face. He leaned down and forcefully pressed his lips to mine—obviously, a tension release. He stared into my face, smirking as he shook his head.

"I seriously have to go to this meeting. Are you coming with me, now? Or are we going later?"

"I'm ready, now. I need to run by my house, after I get my car."

He rolled his eyes and scoffed. "I should be back around seven thirty."

"A late meeting? On a Friday night?"

"Oh yes, sweetheart," he answered sarcastically. "I was rude to Betty, and I hurt her little feelings, so I offered to take her and Jim to dinner. Maybe Carlotta, too. I'm not sure if she's going to make it or not. I'm always going to back my team, but for the way I did it today, I've got a healthy serving of crow coming my way. Salt? Pepper? What goes good with crow?"

"A heaping cup of *I'm sorry*, a side of *Oh shit,* and for dessert, maybe you could have the *I'll never do it again*. That's just one suggestion."

His face softened as he squinted at me. "In two years, this has happened once. That's pretty damn close to flawless. I may have overreacted. Forget it. It's over," he said with a shrug. "But, if it matters, that really is a big deal to me. Please help make sure this doesn't become the norm."

“I wouldn’t dare let that happen. My heavens! The way you tossed those keys across the floor, I truly feared for the safety of the world. You have a serious temper, Mr. Montgomery.”

He rolled his eyes and shook his head. “You, sweetheart, are walking a very thin line.”

I bit my lip, giggling as he glared at me. I had no worries. I had a plan to help my Mr. Montgomery with his bad day. I had two hours! Well, once I had my car, I would have two hours!

I could make him forget. Bad day? Got you, baby!

****

We pulled into the office parking lot, where Jackson dropped me at my car. Then, he drove across the lot to meet up with Jim and Betty. My two hours had begun. *I’ll spare you all the boring details of what errands I had to run before I could get back to the penthouse, but I will tell you I’m one amazing woman!* That day, I did in two hours what would’ve, should’ve taken two *days* in any other situation. I even made it back with time to spare.

After two hours, still no Jackson. I started to worry that he had done something I had not planned for, like going home to sleep, rather than coming to play with me. Another fifteen minutes passed, so I sent him a text message.

—Are you coming back here?—

I waited for a few minutes. I started to feel silly. Finally, my phone pinged. I looked down at my screen.

—Took longer than expected. On my way up.—

I patiently waited. When the door opened, he did a double take, and his eyes met mine as he stepped into the room, closing the door behind him. The raspy voice in the background sang a soulful song with a sexy, sultry beat. He sauntered toward me with a suspicious smirk on his face as he tugged at the tie around his neck.

"What is this?" he asked as he motioned around us.

"This…is because you had a bad day," I answered.

I sat, naked as you please, on the breakfast bar, with my feet on the armrests of one of the stools. I had a cold beer between my thighs, waiting for him. There were candles burning at various places around the kitchen area. I sat with my elbows planted on my knees. I curled my fingers at him and took one of my feet off the armrest of the chair in front of me.

"Have a seat." I smiled.

His eyes stared into mine as he unbuttoned his shirtsleeves, rolling them up as he sat in front of me. I put my foot back on the armrest, and I handed him the beer. I leaned forward, slowly inching toward him so I could kiss his lips.

"I'm sorry you had a bad day," I offered as I reached for his shoulders, massaging them.

He still seemed skeptical as he stared into my eyes and took a drink from the bottle in his hand. I could see his mind racing, trying to figure out how I saw this whole thing going. He got that I had a plan. He just didn't know what. He slid his hand up the inside of my thigh, jerking his head back in confusion when I pushed it away.

I smiled. "You wanted to watch. You wanted me to do it without you."

He smiled as his eyes stared into mine. He poured more from the bottle into his mouth and swished it around before he swallowed, exhaling and offering a drink to me. As I took a sip, he pushed my legs apart, softly kissing all the way up the inside of my thigh. I could feel his warm breath on me. His tongue gently caressed my folds. It tickled, but in an exciting way. He kissed my clit and reached for my hand, putting it between my legs as he licked and sucked on my fingers.

"You're forgetting that whole, *without you* part," I said as I raked my fingers through his hair.

His tongue felt so good, I didn't want him to stop. His breath flowed over my skin, making me even wetter. I wanted him! But I wanted to do this for him. He looked up at me. His eyes looked so sleepy. His chin glistened with me all over him. As I kissed him, I could taste me on his lips. I never wanted him to ever have anyone else under his tongue. I had found something so good, and I wanted to keep it. I wanted my taste to be the only one he wanted. He pressed his hand against mine as he dipped his thumb inside me.

"You're so damn beautiful," he whispered as he kissed my shoulder.

His tongue trailed a little further up my shoulder and ended with another kiss. His hand closed around the beer bottle beside me. He stared into my eyes as he took his thumb out of me and caressed my hand.

"Show me something beautiful."

Chapter Ten

Jackson leaned back in the chair with his eyes locked on mine. He turned his beer up, again as his eyes shifted to my pussy. He licked his lips as he prepared for a show.

Something beautiful? Okay! What did that mean? What did he want to see? My fingers brushed over my engorged sex. It was erotic, having him watching me. I petted and stroked my pussy, soft and slow. I moved my body to the music in the background. I could feel my hardened clit begging for attention, too, but I knew that would be my "easy" orgasm. I didn't want it to be over before he got what he wanted, so I spread my wetness, making my pussy silky, smooth and ready.

As my fingers moved over my sex, Jackson adjusted himself in his jeans. He hummed his approval. His eyes locked on mine as he took another drink.

"Is this beautiful?" I nervously asked.

"This is very beautiful." He nodded as he arched his eyebrows.

"What would make it more beautiful?"

"If you would forget that I'm here and do whatever you want to do. I want to see real."

I sighed, trying to release my nervousness. I stroked my mound, being softer than I may have been, otherwise. He wanted to see real that was *beautiful*?

Finally, I made my mind up to give him one hell of

a show. I began rubbing my pussy a little harder. I gripped, squeezed, and pressed harder and faster. The smooth, silkiness as my fingers moved over my mound felt erotic. I felt naughty, racy, and wild. I sat here, in a penthouse, with my boss sitting between my legs, watching me masturbate, and he seemed to enjoy it. His responses encouraged me. With my other hand, I grabbed my tit, pinching my nipple, pulling it away from my body.

When I dipped one finger inside my dripping pussy, Jackson sat up in the chair, moving closer as he watched me. I popped my finger in and out, and he seemed to approve. A low rumble rolled out of his throat as he looked up at me with that wild, devious look in his eyes.

"Show me what *you* want," he said.

I put three fingers inside my pussy as I massaged my clit with the heel of my hand.

"That a girl!"

I drew a deep breath and stretched my back. His voice was so hot. The fact that he enjoyed watching me pleasure myself was a turn on. The fact that he knew "fake" when he saw it, and he wouldn't let me get away with it felt so sexy. Then, the fact he had been the instigator for this whole thing made me feel as though I had been unleashed and freed.

I rubbed my pussy as my fingers dipped in and out. I took my fingers out and began massaging my clit. Jackson moved closer and dragged the neck of his beer bottle down my folds as I rubbed my clit harder and faster. I was so close. Then, I felt the cold lip of his beer bottle enter me. I gasped as I looked at him. He had that bad-boy stare in his eyes—the one where he made no apologies and did whatever he damn well pleased. He pushed the bottle in further as he stood up in between my legs. As I massaged my clit, he fucked me with the neck of his empty beer bottle.

That was new and different! It was dirty. The lewdness of it seemed so naughty, and if I'm being honest, it felt pretty fucking good. My head fell forward, resting on his shoulder. I watched as he powered the beer bottle, rapidly sliding it in and out of me. Watching it made it feel even more real. I rubbed my clit harder, watching him fuck me with the bottle as I started to come.

Jackson's rapid breath raced past my ear as he moved the bottle in and out of me. He kicked the chair away, causing my legs to fall flat on the countertop. Apparently, he felt an urgent need to taste me. He dropped his head, licking me as I came. This man created one sensation overload after another.

When my orgasm began to fade, he slowly took the bottle out of me. He flicked his tongue across my engorged lips and up the center. He flicked his tongue inside me. He licked and sucked every part of my sex, staring up at me with a wild look in his eyes.

"You feel good?" he asked.

"That seemed a little naughty." I smiled as I bit my lip.

"That *was* naughty, but I don't like being replaced by a fucking bottle," he shook his head. "I'm not okay with that."

He gripped me around my waist and dragged me off the counter, standing me on my feet. His hand gripped mine, and he pulled me toward the bedroom. He pitched the beer bottle in the trashcan as he passed.

He brought his silk tie over his head and put it over mine as he winked at me. He looped his arm around my waist and threw me down, hard, onto the bed. It was so fucking hot and passionate. I giggled, loving every second of being his ragdoll. He ripped his fly open and grabbed my legs, jerking me back to the edge of the bed. He was right! I fucking loved it when he wanted to play rough.

He pushed my legs apart and rammed his cock into me. His abdominal muscles instantly flexed as he lifted his hips up, driving his erection against my G-spot. He swayed his hips from side to side.

"You missing that bottle yet?"

"Fuck no!" I answered, breathily.

He wound the tie around his fingers and tugged it, pulling me up off the bed. He stared into my eyes, eye fucking me as he moved his body in ways I had never experienced before. He gyrated his hips, and I couldn't hold back.

I gave him, yet another feather in his cap. Jackson Montgomery was the best I had ever had.

He pressed his tongue into my mouth and kissed me as though he owned me. I melted, in a good way. Everything he did was hot. It wasn't controlling in an abusive way, but a fun, sexy, *Master of Mayhem* kind of way. I wanted everything he did to me. It wasn't just the act itself, but the emotion and the point behind it. He was confident enough to run the show, but only because I wanted him to.

"You like it when I fuck you with a bottle?"

My chest heaved. The combination of the demand in his sultry voice, his eyes, the words that came out of his mouth, the tie he gripped in his hand, and the way he moved his cock in me were all part of one of the most erotic experiences I had ever experienced in my life.

"Answer me," he said, encouraging me, rather than demanding.

"I like everything you to do me," I answered.

He pursed his lips and tilted his head. He pulled the tie, pulling me closer to him as he lowered his mouth to mine.

As his lips met mine, he said, "You sure about that?"

"Mmmhmm," I confidently answered as he swept his tongue into my mouth and covered my mound with the palm of his hand. He kissed me as he rocked his hips side to side and pressed down on my clit with his palm. He massaged me for a few seconds. Then I felt a sting as his fingers slapped my clit. I flinched and drew a quick breath as he covered my mouth with his, again. I felt a stinging sensation, but it felt so good. I moaned, and he pulled his cock out of me. He pushed against my shoulder, shoving me back on the bed. He put his palm on me again and pressed harder as he massaged me. Then, he lifted it off me and slapped my clit again. My fingertips dug into my thighs, as the stinging sensation began to bring me to the brink of my next orgasm. He gently caressed me for a few seconds, and then he slapped me again. He was going to make me climax again, and he knew it. He grinned and began rapidly slapping his fingers against my clit.

"I'm gonna come. I want you! I want you inside me, now!"

I pulled at his hips as he complied with my needy demands and sank his erection inside me. As soon as he moved inside me again, it felt like lightning flashing. My pussy pulsed. As my body milked his cock, he stared at me with a smirk plastered on his face. He didn't move. He just watched me enjoy the pleasure of his hard cock pressing into me.

Once I relaxed, he hovered his body over me as he kissed me. I tried to pull him down on top of me, but he refused to give in. The harder I pulled at him, the stronger his resistance. He broke the kiss and pushed off the bed.

I felt like I melted into the mattress beneath me. My body had never felt more amazing than it did since Jackson Montgomery had brought me to life. I so desperately wanted to be beneath him. I wanted to feel the weight of his body pushing down on me.

He removed his cock and sat on the edge of the bed. I closed my legs and breathed a sigh, trying to catch my breath. He looked at me over his shoulder as his fingers skimmed over me, tracing circles on my thighs. He reached over my legs, lovingly hugging them to his body.

"This is all about me, right?" I asked as I sat up, removing the tie from around my neck.

"I've told you, I get a lot out of this, too, but most of this is about empowering you to stand up and say what you want and what you need. There's nothing wrong with getting what you want out of sex."

"You say you can read me?"

"Yes. Did I do something wrong?"

"Why don't you know that I need you and want you to lay your body on mine?"

"I do know that, but I also know why you need that and want that. I know I can't be that. Not for you, or anyone else. There is only one thing I won't do for you. Don't push me, okay? Let's just have fun."

"You told me I wouldn't miss it. You lied. I don't think you understand. Your body lying on mine would feel amazing. I don't know. I would feel…covered…protected…secure."

"Loved?" he interrupted. "I'm a lesson, not a lifer. I'm here to teach you things about yourself. I'm teaching you how to stand up and bust these men in the nuts. If they come at you, make them give you what you want. Don't just take what they offer you and smile like you enjoy it. Stop fucking faking it! When you're done with me, you'll be able to find your lifer, but don't confuse my intentions with your fantasies. I am not the guy that will *love* you. I'm the guy that cares, but I'm not the guy that loves."

"You're the guy that tells me I can have what I want, but then denies me when I ask for something."

"Okay, I lied. Two things! There are two things I won't give you. I won't give you false hope, and I'm not giving you my balls to carry around in your little purse."

"I like you better when you haven't had a bad day."

"Good day. Bad day. It won't matter. I want to rock your world, make your pussy wet, and get a little dirty with you, but that…is…it."

"I'm not asking you to love me. I'm not foolish enough to believe that's what this is, so just do it. I understand it doesn't mean anything to you, but I want it, so just give me what I want."

"You're fuckin' hot when you're sassy."

"I'm not trying to turn you on. I'm trying to get you to do this for me."

"It's not that you're not saying or doing the right things. It's that I'm not that man. Not your fault, okay? I'm not crawling on top of you. I'm not the type you're going to pussy whip. Save your energy for that lifer, but I want to make you feel good."

"What makes you think I want to just play along? What are you going to do when I decide I'm tired of being your personal whore?"

"You still don't get it. Just trust me. You're not a whore unless you want to be. That's not how I see you. It's quite the opposite, actually. But I'll fuck your brains out and throw money at you when it's over, if that's really what you want me to do."

"You throw money at me, and I'll rip your balls off your body. Got it?"

"Yes, ma'am." He smirked.

I tried to sound tough. It actually felt pretty good to be so assertive. I expected no return on my investment. However, I wasn't willing to just shut up and go away, like he may have liked for me to do. It couldn't have been sexual aggression. God knows, if that were it, I'd have no aggression whatsoever. I think I just wanted to push him, maybe just to test a boundary or two. I never liked boundaries, but I was content to let it go…for now.

I knew Jackson was tired, but I felt like being contrary. It would've been nice of me to let the poor man rest, but I wanted to play his game. He was the one who wanted to be my toy. Last I checked, toys don't complain. Ugh! What was my deal?

"You look tired," I said with a flat boredom in my tone.

"I had a long day. Last night was a short night, and

I've got this woman with an insatiable sexual need, and the only problem I have with any of it is that I don't have another one of those beers in my hand."

"They're in the fridge," I snapped.

He nodded. "Makes sense."

I sighed as though I were disgusted and was making it obvious that I was copping an attitude. I stood up from the bed and attempted to step around him to go to the kitchen. He stood up, wrapping his arm around my waist. He planted my ass back down on the bed before I could blink.

"I can get it myself. Relax. Shit," he grumbled, glaring at me.

In that moment, I figured it out. I didn't want him to be mad. I wanted him to throw me around again. I dared him to "teach me a lesson." I felt my pussy throb at the thought. I wanted him to be rough with me. Maybe if I "tricked" him into pinning me down, I could have what I wanted. Why? Because we were playing a game with a new goal to get him on top of me. That's why.

When Jackson came back from the kitchen, he held two beers in his hand. He twisted the top off one, handing it to me as he threw the cap in the trashcan by the door. I accepted the beer from his hand and took a drink. He twisted the top off his and turned it up, chugging.

He exhaled through his mouth. "Ah! That tastes pretty damn good."

He dragged the heel of his hand across his mouth and looked down at me. He smiled a knowing smile. He tilted the bottle in his hand, checking the level of the liquid contained within. He turned it up and drank the rest of it down before he turned to get another one.

"Are you thirsty?" I called at his back.

"Just trying to take the edge off your attitude."

I couldn't help it. That was funny. I giggled just as he rounded the door, leaving the bedroom.

"So, is it helping?"

"Not yet," he teased. "But I'm going to keep drinking until it does."

I heard the refrigerator door close. A few seconds later, he came back into the bedroom. I smiled and wrapped my arms around his waist. He draped his arm around my shoulder and rested his chin on my head. He put his bottle to my lips, offering me a drink.

"I have one," I said.

"Drink it! It just occurred to me that even if I'm drunk, you're still going to have an attitude. I need to get you drunk and see if *that* will fix the problem." He flashed an ornery, playful smile.

I smiled as I sighed and shook my head. "No! I'm bored with giving you attitude. You wouldn't play with me. That was no fun."

"Let's go take a bath. I want to feed you bonbons," he said as he led me to the bathroom.

I laughed. "No, you don't! We don't even have bonbons."

"Oh! Sorry for your luck. I wanted to do that for you," he said sarcastically. Then, with his flat tone, he stared at me and said, "I wanna fuck you."

"What?" I hiccupped.

He covered my mouth with his, sweeping his tongue past my lips. He scooped his arms around me, lifting me up as he hugged me. The bottle he held in his hand felt cold against my skin, causing me to draw a deep breath as I tried to move away from the chilled glass. When he felt me flinch, he pulled his head back to look at me, setting me back on my feet. He brushed his cold bottle over my nipple. It ached as it pebbled from the cold. He took my erect nipple in his mouth, sucking on it and tickling it with his tongue. He dropped to his knees, hugging me closer to his mouth. My fingers caressed his scalp, raking through his hair. He tapped my nipple between his teeth, threatening to bite it. He held the bottle to the other nipple, repeating everything he had just done as he massaged both of my tits. He tilted the bottle, pouring a splash of beer on my chest. The cold liquid running over me was titillating. The sensation of his warm tongue chasing the cold liquid off my body made me crave him again, especially when he breathed his warm breath on my chilled skin.

He smiled as he looked up at me. He stood and stepped around behind me. His head gently nudged my head to the side. His lips trailed down my neck and over to my shoulder. He splashed more beer over my shoulder. The cold liquid spilled down the front and back of me. He drank from my body, where the beer pooled around my collarbone.

My heart pounded against the wall of my chest. My breath quickened as he reached around me, slowly and gently dragging his fingertips over my abdomen. I leaned my head back, resting it on his shoulder. His touch felt soft and tender. I was sure that whiplash, switch flip would come any second. Any second, I imagined he'd be ramming some part of his anatomy in one of my orifices—maybe multiple orifices.

He turned me around and draped his arms around

my shoulders, pulling me to him. I wrapped my arms around him. He cradled my head in his hands and kissed me. No tongue flicking. No nipping at my lips. Just soft, sweet, tender kisses.

Holy…shit! I was probably about to pay for every second of this piece of heaven, but for this moment…holy…shit!

Chapter Eleven

As Jackson kissed me, he pushed me backward and set his beer on the bathroom counter. He cradled me in his arms, driving us as our lips locked, walking me backward toward the wall. He pressed his body against me, lowering himself enough for his cock to reach me. With a slow and gentle tilt of his hips, his erection moved against my pussy as his hands explored my body. His quickened breath rushed over my face. He broke our kiss and smiled at me, stacking his arms above my head on the wall. He bent his knees, and as he straightened them again, I felt the head of his cock as he slowly penetrated me. He softly blinked his eyes shut as he slid into me as though it meant everything in the world to him.

"You fucking son of a bitch!" I whispered as I pulled him closer to me and closed my eyes.

I knew he understood exactly what I meant. I had become his puppet, and he was pulling every heartstring I had. I was already too weak to resist him. In this moment, everything about every move he made seemed to be on an entirely different level. He was soft, and I swore I could feel his heart in everything he did. This time, he wasn't fucking, and I didn't want him to. Not now! My heart burned in my chest, aching to believe this was real. A playboy shouldn't be able to make love to a woman like he was to me. It felt as though he had forgotten that he only wanted to be the wild and fun guy. This fucking shit of grabbing my heart and acting as though he had a heart at all was bullshit! When he lowered his arms, placing his hands on the wall beside my shoulders, I wrapped my arms around his head, cradling his head in my hands. My soul longed for him to be more than some empty fuck.

He reached down and gripped my legs, wrapping them around his waist. I opened my eyes, and reflected in the mirror, I watched him thrust into me. I saw his back…his perfect ass…his lips kissing my neck. I looked at his face, and he had his eyes closed as though he was seeing with his heart. He put his elbow on the wall beside my head, and his fingers smoothed my hair. He lifted his head and kissed me as though he would die without me. I wanted it to be true. I had to quit watching us. I couldn't stand the lies the mirror showed me.

As his hips slowly, but rhythmically pressed into me, he lowered his mouth to my ear. "You're beautiful."

I blinked and tears dropped from my eyes. He nestled his forehead against my cheek. I dug my fingers into his flesh as my hands moved down his back. He lifted his head, as his hips maintained a slow, steady rhythm.

"Don't close your eyes," he softly said as he stared at me. "Do it with me, baby." He put his palm against my cheek, his eyes locked on mine.

His breath synched with the way he lifted his hips up, slow and deep. I loved it when he got rough, but the steady rhythm, his body pinning mine to the wall, and the sensation of his cock slowly moving in and out of me felt incredible.

The ripples of pleasure began surging through my body. He stared into my eyes, pressing into me and backing out again as my body appreciated his. My pussy tightened and released him again and again. I had never met anyone like Jackson. He was more than willing to be the source of my pleasure. He did it very well. He knew exactly what he was doing. When I finished, he smiled at me, tenderly pressing his soft lips to mine.

"Did you…" I asked as I brushed my fingers through the hair above his ears as I stared at him.

He looked right into my eyes. "Of course," he lied, with a soft blink and a nod.

I tilted my head, staring at him. I knew he could see that I knew better. He smiled and tucked his chin to his chest.

"It's not always about getting off. Besides, I didn't put a condom on." He winked at me and shrugged shyly.

He was killing me. He was stealing my heart. I just needed to get his, too. I was in a whole world of hurt. I couldn't figure out what I had experienced. We made love. It was that simple. Why he threw out the bad boy games, I didn't know. Unfortunately, the answer came, sooner than I wanted. That answer had a bitter sting to it.

"You're a lot to handle, Mr. Montgomery."

He leaned into me, kissing my cheek. He softly whispered in my ear, "See? I told you, you wouldn't miss it."

His words ripped me from my happy, delusional state. "You did this to prove a point?"

"It's all mind over matter."

"Jackson Montgomery! What is the difference in this and laying your body on mine? You're fucking impossible!"

"You want something from me. I'm trying to do the best I can."

"It was all a lie? This was a lie just so you could prove a point to me? But I felt like your heart was in this."

"No, you didn't! That's why you called me a fucking son of a bitch. Yeah! I heard you!"

"Get the fuck away from me. Just…move!"

He slid his cock out of me. I drove the heels of my hands into his chest, pushing him out of my way. I glared at him as I passed him and went to the bedroom. He was right behind me, realizing he had screwed up. Not interested in hearing his feeble attempt to excuse himself, I crawled under the blankets, pulling them up over my head. I felt his body fall on the bed beside me.

He chuckled. "What are you doing?"

"You can take your fucking job and shove it up your pecker with a bottle brush!" I fumed from under the blankets.

He laughed. "Ouch! No thanks! That was pretty vile."

"Please don't talk to me."

"Okay," he agreed.

He lay beside me on the bed. That fucking asshole started singing "Ninety-nine Bottles of Beer on the Wall." I think he sang to seventy-three before he started yawning. Anyway, the point is, he can be a real prick when he wants to be.

I don't know what irritated me more, him singing,

or the fact that he could actually go to sleep. I *was* pouting, after all! How dare he? I believe he made it to forty-something bottles when he started losing count. He jumped from forty-three to forty-seven, then I think he jumped back up to fifty-six. I pulled the blanket off my head to glare at him, only to discover that he had folded his elbow over his eyes. My movement woke him up enough for him to start singing louder. I kid you not. I wanted to belt him in the gut and knock the wind out of him, just to get him to shut up. Other than the annoying song choice, he sang pretty well, but still!

Eventually, the aspiring rock star gave up the ghost and went down for the count. I stared at him as he slept. He looked so sweet and innocent when he was asleep. It still pissed me off that he could sleep at all, no matter how cute he was.

I wondered about what his life must've been like when he grew up. I thought about how he wanted to steer away from emotional attachment. Maybe he did that as a result of his mother leaving him. Maybe in his mind, it served as a form of self-preservation, and maybe it was all an act. I saw the look in his eyes. He did pretty good at reading me, but maybe I had gotten better at reading him than he realized. Then again, maybe I wanted something so much I was willing to break myself trying to make it what I wanted. My mind wouldn't shut down. For whatever reason, I felt I needed to ponder everything in the universe.

As I lay there, staring at the ceiling, the silence echoed through the room. As I got lost in my thoughts, the creepiest thing happened. As though some force ripped up on his body, Jackson sat straight up and got out of bed. He walked from the bedroom to the living area.

"Now where are you going?" I asked.

He mumbled something that I couldn't understand. I decided to follow him so I could hear what he said. He tried to walk through the coffee table. Then he stood by the window, and he pointed toward the floor as he mumbled.

"What? What're you doing?"

"I put it in there," he plainly said.

"Uh, okay! Put what…in where?"

He swished his hand through the air and pointed again. My eyes shifted from his face to the floor where he pointed. His eyes were wide open, but his face had a blank, creepy stare. He clumsily dragged his hand across his mouth.

"Jackson, what are you doing? What are you talking about? You put what there?"

He blinked, and his eyes darted around the room. He seemed confused. That made two of us. Again, I tried to figure out the message he had tried to relay.

"What were you telling me? What did you put in the floor?"

"No! You're not blaming this on me too," he said, rubbing his eyes.

"Hello! Can you hear me?"

He turned and looked at me with his sleepy eyes. He held his hands out to his side, turning his palms up. As though there was nothing odd about this little episode, then he shrugged and said, "I was sleeping."

He walked back to the bedroom and fell back onto the bed as I stood, frozen, in the living area trying to figure out what had just happened. I just stood there with my mouth wide open. My eyes shifted around the room, trying to figure out if he was done roaming…or just…what? That was the freakiest thing I had ever seen in my life.

Deciding that he was done roaming, I went back and lay down beside him. I kept watching his face, trying to figure out if this was some kind of joke. He appeared to be sound asleep. I couldn't stop staring at his face, waiting to see if he peeked at me, or if he smirked, or started laughing. None of those things happened. Eventually, at some point, I finally fell asleep, myself.

When the sun came pouring through the window the next morning, my eyes popped open. Jackson slept beside me. I glanced at the alarm clock. We had twenty-five minutes before check-out time. I threw the blankets back and started pulling my clothes on. Jackson lay on his stomach and drew a deep breath, stretching. He didn't even lift his head off the pillow.

"What are you doing?" his sleepy voice asked.

"Getting ready to go. Check out time is eleven."

"No! Call them and tell them we're late."

"Jackson, wake up! We have to get ready to go," I urged.

He flipped over and glared at me. "Call down to the desk. Tell them we are going to be leaving later. Come back to bed."

"Okay! Don't bite my head off. I thought you were getting ready to do that zombie, walk-about thing again. I didn't know if you knew what you were saying."

"I can call them," he said as he looked at the clock, rubbing his eyes. "Come back to bed."

It surprised him when I sat beside him and cradled his face in my hands. "What the hell happened? Why did you do that? Are you okay?"

His eyes shifted around the room as he thought about my question. His eyes focused on mine. With an incredulous attitude, he arched one eyebrow.

"Uh, yeah. I think so."

"What were you telling me last night? In the living room?"

"In the living room?" he asked as he yawned. He shook his head. "I don't remember. What were we doing? What were we talking about?"

"I mean after we came to bed. You got up and went out to the living room and pointed to the floor, telling me you put it in there. You put what in where? You were pointing to the floor. There was nothing there."

"I have no idea what you're talking about." He shrugged.

"Your eyes were wide open, and you were talking to me, but it didn't make sense."

He shook his head. "Calm down. Just ignore me. I do that when I'm tired, sometimes. Sorry!" he said, nonchalantly. "So, are we staying later? I need to call them if so."

"Why do you do that? That's fucking creepy!"

"Because this crazy woman keeps me up all night, wanting me to screw her every ten minutes. You're wearing my ass out! I'm tired. You're…you're the one that's fucking *creepy*." He scrunched his forehead with an ornery grin.

"Jeebus, Jackson! That's a good way to get knocked the fuck out! What if I would've woken up to you roaming around and thought you were an intruder?"

He wrapped his arms around me, pulling me to

him. “Mm! Next time just spread your legs. Let’s see if I can make you come in my sleep.”

I giggled. “You’re so perverted. No! Stop it! I’m serious. You should’ve told me about that.”

“You figured it out.” He smiled. “I’m sorry for being a creep, but now I’m curious. I need to know if I can make you come when I’m like that. I want to see if you feel like you’re fucking some other guy.”

I slapped his arm. “Jackson, I swear!”

“You can swear at me. When I’m like that, I probably wouldn’t know anyway. Might make it even better for you.”

“So, next time you go for a walk, I’m supposed to have sex with you?”

He chuckled and raised his eyebrows. “Yeah! Sure. Should be fun. It will probably wake me up, but I won’t be mad at you.”

At first, I just stared at him. Wouldn’t that be like rape or something? Could I do that? Then, I imagined pulling him on top of me. I wondered if that would work. Maybe it would be worth a try.

Why? If you don’t understand by now, I’m not sure I’m going to make it make sense for you, but because I fucking wanted it, that’s why! I wanted his body on mine. I wanted that even more now, just because he refused to give it to me. It would probably be over before it ever got started, but if I’m being honest, part of it was the point that I wanted him to be on top of me. Sure, I wanted to feel his body over mine, but this had become a mission. Maybe that would be playing dirty. If he wouldn’t remember anyway, then why not?

At five after eleven, the phone in the room rang. Jackson answered it. I could tell from the part of the conversation that I could hear that the hotel staff wanted to see if we had left the room. Jackson checked us out over the phone, we gathered our things and left our two-day sex palace.

When we got to the valet desk, we both handed over the tickets for our cars. Jackson wrapped his arms around the small of my back and kissed my forehead. While we were waiting for them to bring our cars around, he insisted that I go eat lunch with him. He brushed my hair away from my eyes and kissed my lips. I saw his car coming up behind him.

"That car! That's sexy," I said. He immediately turned to see which car I referred to.

He smiled down at me and motioned with his head. "Go drive it."

My eyes widened as I gasped. "You're not serious?"

He shrugged. "If you wreck it, I'll snap your pretty little neck, but yeah! Go drive it."

"I'd be too scared. No!"

"It's just a car. It's just like any other car."

"Heh! Yeah! Right," I offered sarcastically.

Just then, another valet pulled up in my car. I had loved my car…until I saw it parked beside his. Somehow, it paled in comparison. He tipped the valet guys and pointed toward our cars.

"Is there someplace we can leave one of these?" he asked.

The valet pointed to a small lot to the right. "If you don't need to leave it for very long, you can put it over there. I wouldn't leave the Audi over there. We can keep an eye on it, but that's an R8! You can't leave that thing over there."

Jackson handed him more money and pointed to my car. "Tell ya what, hold on to this one for me."

"Yes, sir!" the valet said as he held his hand out to me, taking my keys.

Jackson turned to face me. He kissed my forehead as he put his keys in my hand, squeezing my hand in his. "Let's go."

"I can't do this! I can't drive your car. No! I'm too scared."

"Shut up," he said and opened the driver's side door for me, and he went to get in the passenger seat.

Chapter Twelve

He seriously expected me to drive his car—his beautiful car? I froze with fear. I wanted to drive it! Oh, how I wanted to drive it! I just didn't want to drive it if he intended to sit beside me and have a panic attack the entire time. Oh, no! I was going to have a heart attack. I needed him to be okay to cover for me when that happened. He leaned down and looked at me through the open door.

"Uh…we're clogging up their driveway. We should go."

I blinked, scared to breathe as slid myself into the driver's seat. I drew a deep, nervous breath. "Oh…my… I can't do it! Will you just drive, please?"

"Elizabeth, stop being silly. Fire it up and let's go. Hurry up! Go, go, go!" he coached as he pulled the seatbelt over his shoulder.

"I'm scared. I don't know this car."

"Huh. Okay! Elizabeth, this is Lucy. Lucy, baby, this is Elizabeth," he said as he stroked the dash. "Be nice to her."

I have no idea if that comment was aimed at the car or me. I had a feeling I knew, but a girl can dream.

When I started the engine, it had that low, smooth growl. I felt turned on for an entirely different reason this time. The leather felt velvety smooth and the shifter sat in the perfect place. The trim on the seats, the new car smell, everything was…unbelievable!

He looked over his shoulder behind us. "Uh, you're going to have to go, or they're going to start delivering mail to us here. We've been in this spot for forever."

I sighed and flashed him a sarcastic smile. The thrill of this whole situation was a completely different excitement. I moved the shifter into first gear and looked down at the red gauges.

"Oh, my God! I'm so scared," I confessed.

He leaned back in the seat and put his right ankle on his left knee. "Just don't wreck it," he said coolly.

We lunged a couple of times as I tried to figure out the sensitive clutch. Finally, smooth as a soft breeze, with a wicked smooth growl, the car rolled out from under the carport. My soul felt like it had been reborn. We rolled up to the stop sign before the street we had to pull onto. I looked over at him, and he casually chewed on his thumbnail.

"So far, so good," I said nervously.

"Yeah! You're doing great. At this rate, we might make it in time for lunch sometime next week. Good God! I'm gonna be mighty hungry."

I giggled. "I'm terrified right now. If you could just be patient."

He leaned up in the seat and clasped his hands together like an excited little kid. "Are you gonna do it? Huh? Huh? Are you gonna push the gas pedal?"

As I glared at him, I put the gas pedal to the floor as I let off the clutch. The tires screeched and the back end fishtailed. It was wild and excitingly terrifying. With a newfound respect for the power in my hands, I took my foot off the gas. That car had a lot more than I expected.

Jackson gripped his head as he sat back in the seat. “Oh, dear Lord! Just…do *not*…wreck it!”

“No, Jackson! You better drive. I didn’t know. I just wanted to play with you. I’m so terrified!”

“Drive before you get us killed. Holy shit!”

I wanted to shut him up, but honestly, that scared the hell out of me. I no longer felt the need to be ornery. I quickly found a way to be softer with my pedal foot. I drove that beautiful car as though my life depended on it. Actually, I believed it probably did.

When we got to the restaurant and got out of the car, I handed the keys back to him. He didn’t hesitate or argue a bit. He practically snatched them from my hand and shoved them into his pocket.

“I did pretty good, huh?”

“Yeah!” he scoffed. “I need four new tires, now, but you didn’t wreck it.”

He put his hand across the small of my back and led me into the building. We chatted, but it wasn’t about anything significant. I believe the conversation revolved around something about the flowers growing along the walkway. It wasn’t important, but we were creating a history just the same.

After we entered the establishment, the hostess led us to our table. The server immediately came right behind her and started introducing herself, without even looking at us. When she finally looked up, she saw Jackson and stopped talking. A devious smile spread across her face as she stared at him.

“Hey you!” she purred. “How are you, today?”

I felt the friendly smile fall off my face. Good grief, she undressed him with her eyes. I kept expecting her to jump in his lap and start grinding away. She tried to engage him in a conversation. I didn't care for her flirty demeanor, quite honestly.

"I'm sorry," I interrupted. "Can I please get some water with lemon? I am parched!"

"Uh, sure!" she agreed as she stared at Jackson. "And what about you, sweetie?"

This bitch grated on my last ass-nerve. He smiled at her and nodded. Apparently, she heard something I didn't. Like some chipper little schoolgirl, she spun on her heel and away she went. I watched her walk away and without turning my head, my eyes shifted to Jackson.

"A has been? Will be? Or currently is?" I asked.

He leaned forward, stretching his body across the table toward me. He had a smirk on his face as he wagged his finger at me.

"No, no, no! The only way I would play that game is if we were all going to play together. I'm not trying to play any games in that way with either of you. I didn't know she would be here."

"Play…*together*?"

"Yep," he answered matter-of-factly. "You would have to be okay with it, and she would have to be okay with it. I wouldn't pit women against each other like that."

"So, you fuck her, too?"

"Do you want me to?"

"No!"

"Then, don't give me any ideas." He winked.

"You would do that? The two at a time thing?"

"Don't ask questions you don't want answers to."

"Two at a time? Really?"

"Two is hot. Three is fun. Four? It's too difficult to

be everything to four."

"Oh, shit! I didn't want to know," I groaned.

He smiled, resting his elbow on the arm of the chair with his pointer finger along his cheekbone, as though he were thinking. "That would be hotter than you could handle."

"I'm going to take your word for it. That whole idea disgusts me, quite frankly. I don't want to be part of an orgy."

"Then, we won't play like that." He dismissively shrugged.

"Why do you like that? That's gross!"

He took a deep breath. "If you were to stop overthinking it and just let yourself go, you would love it. Imagine being bent over the bed. I spread your legs and ram my cock in your pussy. Our little playmate sits on the floor, between our legs, licking your clit while I fuck you. It's fucking hot. Now, I don't need to touch you to know that your pussy is dripping right now. That's why I love it! The mental image of your pretty face buried between some other woman's legs drives me out of my mind. You two finger each other, kiss, and suck on each other's tits, but after a little bit, I'm the one with the one thing you both crave. My cock can do things for you that none of you can do for each other. See? So, maybe you could be a little nicer to that girl that's about to quench your thirst. She'd do anything for you that I wanted her to."

"Why do you know that? Have you fucked her, too?"

"Never touched her, but I read people, remember? She's got ideas about what she wants from me. I know exactly what she wants. I won't lie to you. I want to give it to her. Now that you've brought it up, I would want to watch her please you while I fuck your pretty mouth."

I sat, oddly excited, but infuriated at the same time. I didn't want him to be this. I didn't want to share him. I didn't want him to want to be shared, but I didn't want him to want to share me either. It bothered me.

As my mind thought about what he had said, the girl came back with our drinks. He looked up at her and smiled his devious smile. He cocked his head, looking at me.

"Just say the word," he seductively said.

"Absolutely not!"

"What?" the girl asked with a curious smile on her face as she looked between the two of us.

Jackson stared into my eyes with his head tilted as he answered her. "We were just considering appetizers."

"We have a lot of good ones," she offered, opening his menu and holding it up for him.

She was such a helpful little thing. She pointed to the appetizer section as he looked over the top of the menu at me. With a seductive, beggarly look in his eyes, he asked, "You wanna try it?"

"No!" I snapped.

He dropped the seductive routine and became far more serious, and business like. "I guess we'll pass on that, so we'll probably need a few more minutes."

"Okay, I'll come back," she offered as she smiled her flirty smile.

There was no way! I was so straight there wasn't any deviation in my angle whatsoever. I was a solid one hundred and eighty degrees straight. Not one eighty-one. Not one seventy-nine. But a flat, perfectly straight, one-eighty!

"So, what looks good?" he asked as though nothing had ever happened.

I couldn't concentrate. I couldn't focus. Maybe I had lost my appetite altogether. The thought of burying my face in a pussy did not please me. The fact that my dream guy wanted that made me sick. Ugh! I wished I hadn't asked.

"I think I'm just going to try a salad," I said. "What are you going to eat?"

"I don't know. I'll figure it out. Let me finger you."

"What?"

"You're too far away. I want to see if I can make you come while you tell her what you want for lunch."

"You're freaking me out. This is too much."

He licked his lips, softly whispering. "Tell me you're not wet?" He stared into my eyes with that cocky grin. "Come closer. I'll take care of it."

"Are you insane? What the fuck is wrong with you?"

"I want to do it, just as bad as you want me to. Come on, dirty girl. Let me make you come, right here in front of everyone."

He was serious. He pissed me off! He was just being lewd and disgusting, so why were my nipples so hard that they ached? Why were my panties completely drenched? This wasn't what I wanted, but the hot look in his eye still turned me on.

"No," I said. "Not in here."

"Then, we'll go out, and I'll throw you on the hood of the car. We can let everyone out there watch."

"I'm not doing it. I'm not."

"Shut up," he smirked. "Come on! It'll be one of the best experiences of your life."

I stared at him in disbelief. My heart pounded. I felt nervous. I didn't want to be a buzz kill. However, I felt confident the rest of the diners would be okay without watching him ram his fingers in and out of me while they enjoyed their lunch. What could I do? You only live once, right? I slowly pushed my chair back as I heaved a sigh. I didn't want to be "boring." I studied his face for his reaction. Was he serious? The smile that spread across his face and the daring look in his eyes assured me he was quite serious.

Our server returned to take our order just as I got to my feet. He flashed me a disappointed look. I smiled at the woman.

"Could we have just a few more minutes? I'm sorry! I can't decide," I said and smirked at him as I moved the chair closer to him.

He arched his eyebrow. I could see the "game on" expression on his face. I was committed now. If I was going to do it, I wanted to make sure it happened just as he envisioned it. I sat down, and he put his arm around me, pulling me closer to him. I clenched my eyes shut and rested my forehead against his cheek. He drew a deep breath as though he were breathing me in. I couldn't calm my nervous, quickened breath. With his every touch, I felt jumpy and jittery as hell.

"Hi. You scared?"

I swallowed the lump in my throat and nodded my head.

"No one will know anything more than what you let them know. If you don't want them to know, they won't. Don't be weird, or you'll give us away. Relax. I want you to enjoy this."

He put his hand under the table, and his tongue slid over his lips. He gently traced his fingers up the inside of my thigh. My heart had perched itself in my throat, as he moved closer to the point of no return. I tucked my chin to my chest and took a deep breath as I anticipated his finger penetrating me.

"Open your legs a little," he whispered in my ear.

My heart banged and pounded as though it would jump out of my chest and run away. I thought I would die. I slowly slid my legs apart a tiny bit.

"More."

Chills raced all over my body. I whimpered a squeaky sound as I swallowed hard. I opened my legs a little wider. His fingertips brushed over the fabric of my dampened panties.

His breath rushed past my ear, and he softly growled. "So wet. Naughty girl!"

He slid his finger between the fabric and my body. His fingers traced over my silky skin. He squeezed me closer to him and smiled as he looked into my eyes.

He slowly blinked and softly said, "I can make you come right here, and no one will know. You gonna come for me in front of all these people?"

The look on his face became daring and challenging. My eyes shifted nervously at the people around us. No one seemed to notice us at all, let alone what we were doing under our table. I pulled at the tablecloth, attempting to insure I was covered.

He leaned his mouth over to my ear again. "They can't see. I promise." He kissed my cheek.

He looked over my shoulder, lifting his hand, curling his fingers at our server, indicating that we were ready, as he inserted two fingers inside me. I gasped. He slowly bobbed his fingers in and out of me as the server approached our table. I shifted a little, nervous that she would know what his hand was doing to me.

"Are you two ready?" she asked, seeming a little disappointed at our coziness.

He circled his fingers inside me as she stood right there. He kissed my cheek, nodding at me to order. I did my best to ignore what his fingers were doing to me. He did his best to make that impossible. As I talked, I felt them sliding in and out a little faster.

"I'm…uh. I'm going to have…I'm just going to have a salad."

"Okay! Dressing?"

I felt him spread his fingers apart inside me.

I gasped. "Um…vinaigrette…on the side, please."

"Okay, sweetie. What are *you* doing today?" she asked Jackson.

"Let's see," he said as he looked into my eyes. "I think I'll do the grilled salmon."

He rubbed my clit with his thumb.

"You want extra pepper, as usual?"

"Yes, please."

"Okay, I'll get those orders in for you. You need refills on your drinks?"

"Sure." He smiled giving a nod as his fingers toyed with me under the table.

He looked behind us, watching her walk away, but more so he could whisper to me again. A smile spread across his face as he fluttered his fingers inside me. "You're so fucking hot."

He circled his fingers inside me as he moved them in and out. His thumb thumped my clit, alternating with him pressing against it and rubbing in circles. He looked around as though nothing were happening. He appeared to be just some guy, cuddling his girlfriend for a cozy lunch. He nodded his head and smiled at anyone who passed by.

The way he handled me made me want to sit on his lap and ride the hell out of his cock. I felt like everyone around us knew what we were doing. It was unnerving, but he was getting me to the point of not giving a shit who knew what. I wanted to come. I swallowed hard and gently bucked my hips forward. I tried to force his fingers in deeper. I slightly moved my body a little lower in my chair. My pussy ached, wanting to be filled. He flashed me his devious grin.

"You're fucking spoiled," he said. "I can't do what you want me to do, unless you want everyone here to know."

He kissed the top of my head and took his fingers out of me. He pinched my clit between his fingers. I studied his face as he clenched his jaw. He started squeezing his fingers together, tighter with my clit between them. It felt incredible, then as he pinched me, he started rubbing his hand in a circle. I was about to lose my fucking mind. I was so close. He opened his fingers, firmly stroking as he massaged me. Then, he flicked my hardened clit. I wanted to come right then and there. My body twitched, as various sensations came over me. I panted as I breathed through my nose, staring into his eyes, hoping he could read my mind. His eyes scanned the other diners around us, and he took his hand out from under the table. He stole an ice cube from his glass. His hand went back under the tablecloth, and he rubbed the ice against me before he pressed it inside me. Then, he put his mouth to my ear.

"Come for me. Fuck yeah, baby! Come for me."

He rubbed his fingers in a circle, pressing as hard as he could, without being obvious. I pushed my mound toward his hand. A sound escaped my throat as the feeling I craved started building. I drew a deep breath, holding it as I clawed at the tablecloth. I tried so hard to look normal, while digging my fingertips into the tabletop to the point that they had turned white. Then, it happened. Gratification! My pussy finally began pulsating, and I exhaled through my mouth.

He had no mercy. He cradled me closer, holding my head up with his arm as he clenched his teeth, pressing his fingers against me as he rubbed me. As my orgasm surged through my body, the peppy server girl came to replace our drinks.

"I forgot to ask if you two wanted bread?"

Jackson chuckled. "Uh, sure! Why not?"

She looked at me, and I know in that moment, she knew exactly what we were doing. She quickly jerked her head away and walked off. I came crashing back down to earth by that point, but it was too late. I knew she knew.

"Better?" he asked, playfully slapping my sensitive spot before he pulled his hand away.

I flinched from the soft sting and sat up in my chair. I admit it. I had slumped down pretty far into that seat. It probably would have been far more obvious what had happened at our table, if anyone had paid any attention at all. However, thankfully, no one seemed to notice anything, other than our server.

When she came back with our breadbasket, she seemed preoccupied, straining her neck, looking anywhere but at us. She kind of ran by, practically throwing the basket at us, and she disappeared again. Jackson laughed.

"Yeah! I'm pretty sure we got caught."

"She looked right at me. I'm sure she knows. She has to."

"I should tell her I need to wash my hands and ask her where the restroom is." He laughed.

"I'm embarrassed. I tried, but you're the one that made me come."

"Mm! Say that again."

"What? That you made me come?"

"Mmmhmm! I'm fucking obsessed with being the one that makes you do that." He smiled.

"Me and three of my friends?" I asked with bitterness in my tone.

He smiled an ornery smile. "Come on, now! I can't keep up with one. What the fuck would I do with two or three more of you?"

"You're the one that said you wanted multiples."

"I lied. It's not that great."

"You lied to me? You made me think you're some orgy-crazed maniac."

"Shh! Please! Don't be loud."

I lowered my level. "Have you ever had sex with more than one woman at one time?"

"Um, yes!"

"When?"

"Probably four or five years ago. It's not my thing, but it sure seems to get you excited." He winked.

"I don't want that," I insisted.

"I know, and believe it or not, I'm happy about that. But, it wouldn't have been as risqué and fun for you if we had this conversation before, now would it? The threat of possibility has to be there. Taboo! Naughty! And, erotic even if you don't want it."

"You don't want the flirty little schoolgirl?" I asked, in hopes of confirmation.

"If I did, I would've had her a long time ago. She's easy. She's probably strictly missionary, though," he said as he rolled his eyes and shook his head. "I'd be so bored I'd have to turn the television to fucking golf or something. Golf would have to be more exciting and entertaining."

I giggled as I kissed him. Whether he meant it or not, he made me feel better. He said something I wanted him to say. Maybe he was just reading me, but I pretended he meant every word of it.

He hugged me to him. "I have to go take care of this mess," he said.

"That's sacred nectar, mister!" I said.

"You want it? I'll sit on the table, and you can lick it all off, if you want."

"Wait! What're we talking about?"

"I couldn't help myself. That was crazy sexy," he said. He stood, bending down to kiss me before he pulled his shirt over his crotch, winking at me as he made his move for the restroom.

I watched him as he moved out of my line of sight. I giggled to myself. I made Mr. Self-Control cream his jeans. We were ridiculous. I knew we were, but I didn't expect it to be a permanent situation. We fucked like rabbits. I had never wanted sex anywhere nearly as much as I did with this man. Even when he made me sore, it went away as soon as he turned me on again. He didn't have to do too much to make that happen.

Shortly after Jackson left our table, I heard a man's boisterous voice.

"Jackson! Hey buddy! I thought that was you. I kept looking, trying to figure out if you were who I thought you were. Now, I see that it really is you! How're you doing?"

I turned in my chair just in time to see the man extend his arm and shake Jackson's hand. *That* hand! I couldn't help but snicker to myself. I imagined Jackson was nervous as hell about now. It was only fair that he had to pay for his devious behaviors.

He talked to the man for a few minutes. Then he encouraged the man to call the office so they could schedule a lunch sometime in the upcoming week. He dismissed himself to go to the restroom, just as the server passed him with our lunch.

I feared our fun had come to a screeching halt since this man appeared to be a business relation of some sort. When he came back from the restroom, Jackson cuddled me to him, again, not seeming concerned about the man sitting behind us. I even reminded him that the man could see us.

"Who is that guy?" I asked, motioning with my head.

"Patrick Weller."

My jaw dropped. "That's Patrick Weller? He looks…older, now. A *lot* older. What if he sees us?"

"He's already seen us, baby. I'm not worried about it." He shrugged. "If his job suffers because of our sex life, then he's got a right to say something. This is *my* time. Considering that woman he's with is *not* his wife, it seems to me that he's got enough of his own business that needs tending to."

The remainder of our lunch turned out to be uneventful, considering. We snuggled, cuddled, and laughed. I don't think there was a single moment we weren't touching, kissing, or holding hands. Even when we left, our fingers were intertwined, and he looped his arm around my neck without letting go of my hand.

When we got out to the parking lot, I held my hand out. He kissed my lips and narrowed his eyes, squinting at me. He fished his key ring with the key fob out of his pocket and put it in my hand.

"Is this car expensive? Because I think you need to go buy one for yourself, now," I teased.

He scoffed. "Um, no! Not my Lucy. Sorry!"

He opened the driver's side door for me and waited for me to get inside. By the time he got in the passenger seat, I had already started the car. I loved the sound it made. The leather seats had a red leather piping trimming them, as well as the Audi logo stamped in red on the headrests. Everything about this car screamed "sex." Driving Lucy, I hoped, would become habitual for me.

Chapter Thirteen

After our lunch, we went back to the hotel to get my car from the valet. I didn't want to let him go, but I didn't want to be clingy. That's a lie! I really *wanted* to be clingy, but I wouldn't allow myself. How's that?

Jackson kissed me and asked me if he could call me later. He left me and went to his house or whatever he did. I went home to my apartment. There had been two hours since I had seen him when I got a text.

—Miss me yet?—

I replied with only one word.

—Excessively!—

So, I guess I deserved the one-word reply.

—Good!—

It only took a few more hours before we repeated, pretty much, the same exchange. I did miss him. Terribly, in fact. I wanted to be whiney and pathetic. Part of me wanted to be with him non-stop, but I knew that was a bit too ambitious for what he wanted us to be to each other. I decided I had to find a way to sneak in, grab his heart, and hold it for forever and always.

Maybe the fact I had known him for two years made it different. Maybe the amount of time we spent together at work, or maybe just the simple fact we had been naughty and naked together could be the reason, but I felt so relaxed with him. In all the time I had known him, I had never heard of him dating anyone or having a girlfriend or anything of the sort. Maybe he was good at keeping his personal life private. Then again, maybe it was because Jackson Montgomery found playmates to play his little “empowering” game with.

For just over two years, I would occasionally wonder what Jackson did when he wasn’t with us all at work. I wondered where he lived. I wondered what his hobbies were. I wondered what he did for fun outside of work. I had been afforded an opportunity to see for myself. He had taken me to a restaurant he visited enough that the server knew what he wanted. He let me drive his car. He put us in a penthouse for two days. I had learned about his mom and his aunt. I had seen him do that creepy zombie thing, for the love of God! Yet, here I was again, wondering what he was doing now that I wasn’t with him.

My brain started working. What if he spent time with someone else? What if he also entertained Lisa from the office? She seemed like she would love to spend time with him. She was pretty in an introverted, librarian kind of way. I had no doubt he’d have a lot of fun “corrupting” her. Maybe there were others…many others. I didn’t know, and I didn’t want to think about those things. I didn’t want to be jealous, but I couldn’t help myself. I had become addicted to this man’s cock. That’s a lie. Truthfully, I was addicted to more than that, which had become part of the problem.

I sent him a text.

—I miss you, again!—

It took him a while. Eventually, he replied with a picture of his car with the sun setting behind it. It looked awesome, of course, but not quite the reply I had hoped for. I played along, anyway.

—Hey! It's MY car!—

—Really? Then, why didn't YOU come wash it?—

—You gave Lucy a bath for me? You're so sweet.—

—The shit I do for you.—

—Are you calling me? Ever?—

—Never.—

But I didn't even have time to reply before my phone rang. We talked for a little bit before he started being dirty. He gave me the best sex I had ever had in my life. So, apparently, he wanted to make sure he was also the best phone sex I had ever had.

"You know I'm going to tear that pussy up, right?" he asked.

"Really? Can you do that over the phone? Because I'd let you."

"Wanna know what I want to do?"

"Do I want to know?"

His voice was sultry and smooth. "Yes. You need to know the things you make me think about."

"Okay, tell me."

"It's a candy game."

"A candy game?"

"Mmmhmm! I am going to find one of those colorful, big, thick, lollypops for you."

"A lollypop? Is this a blowjob fantasy?"

"Shhh! Listen," he softly said. "I am going to put my candy in your pretty mouth so you can have a little taste."

"Mmmhmm?"

"While you have a taste of that, I'll push your sexy legs open and I'm going to taste *you* because I love eating your pussy. I fucking *love* it! Then, when I feel like you've had enough, I'm taking my lollypop out of your mouth. I'm going to rub my candy all over your wet pussy, teasing you, until you beg me to put it inside you. I'll spread your lips wide open and watch as my pretty candy stretches your tight little pussy. I'm going to force you to take all of it. I'll watch your glistening, pink lips wrap around it as I pull it back out and put it in again. Then, I'm going to watch you drip as I fuck you with it. Every time you lift your hips, wanting more, I get to have a taste. Wanna play my candy game?"

"That sounds sticky,"

"I'll clean it up."

I giggled. "You're a pervert!"

"Did I make you wet?"

"Jackson, the sound of your voice makes me wet. If I even *think* I see you, I'm wet. You turn me on, just by breathing."

"I try," he said proudly. "Are you going to think of me?"

"Of course!"

"Do you know how much I want to be able to give you what you want? I want you to come crying to me when your pussy won't leave you alone. I want to be the one that gets to make her go to sleep and give you rest."

"You make it sound like some dragon that you're going to slay."

"Newsflash, Princess! There was never a sleeping dragon. It is just a way for men to talk about satisfying horny women. When your pussy sleeps, you're soft, subtle, sweet, harmless creatures. When your pussy is awake, you're a little more aggressive and demanding.

Your pussy becomes this raging, pissed off dragon. A needy pussy will take a man down if he's not prepared when he goes into that fight. A knight comes along, sticks his sword in, and slays the dragon. The soft, subtle, kind face that sits on top of the tower returns. He saves the princess. The knight becomes the hero and gets put in charge of slaying the next dragon. See?"

"Is that true?"

"Hell, if I know. I think I just made that up. It may be true. It feels like it should be true. As a knight, it feels like you've saved the world when a horny woman who has been clawing, tearing, and shredding her way to satisfaction, finally comes. That's a dangerous situation."

"I like your warped little fairy tale, until you talk about slaying the next dragon."

"A knight knows the prince is coming for the princess, but the knight has to be a warrior. He has to get the princess ready for when the prince comes, dragging his lazy ass and bellies up after the knight has tamed the dragon. Those sons of bitches piss us knights off. Why do they always get the princess? We do the hard part."

"I thought you didn't want to be stuck with just one dragon, or one princess."

"Well, some dragons are a little tricky. Some princesses are pretty tricky, too. If a knight's not careful, he ends up getting confused about what his job is."

"You're a bad-ass knight, Jackson! Fuck the prince up and steal his girl."

"Then, spend the rest of my life worrying about every other fucking prince in the land? No thanks. I'm just a knight. Women want Prince Charming. I'm only here to tame the dragon. I'm just a lowly knight."

"What if the princess prefers the knight? Personally, I'd rather have the knight. I already know he can save me and make my dragon his pet."

"A pet, huh?" he chuckled. "All right! This has gone too far. There are no dragons, knights, or princes. I made it up. You caught me. Next subject!"

We chatted on the phone for what seemed like forever. We both discussed getting off the phone tons of times before we actually did it. I was content to believe that for the moment, his sexual energy seemed to have been confined to a couple of naughty suggestions, a few dirty ideas and some perverted innuendos. I felt like maybe I had drained him and until he caught his second wind, he gave me all he had, which wasn't much.

The next few days were more like we were actually dating, rather than just fuck buddies. The energy that wafted through the office when we were both at work felt electric. The fact that I had been down and dirty with this man in numerous places, at various times, almost every day made it seem naughty when I referred to him as "Mr. Montgomery." I think he got off on that. I got off on the fact that he got off. I wanted to be the woman he gave it all to. He had become my addiction. I had a feeling he had his own addiction to me, too.

****

It had been a few weeks of our all-out sexual deviance and there was an ever-strengthening bond between us. He would drink from my cup if he were thirsty. I would steal a bite off his plate if I wanted a taste of what he was eating. It all became typical and comfortable. We had not spent the night at either of our homes. We just went to hotels or messed around in the office. Sometimes, we'd do things in the cars, or in public places, but we had insane amounts of fun no matter where we went.

Then, I learned something interesting. We were in the Jacuzzi at our favorite hotel. I rode him hard as my orgasm got closer. His phone rang, and he practically dumped me off him, tucking himself back inside his trunks as he scrambled to answer the call.

"Uh, what in the hell are you doing? Where are you going?"

"Sorry! That's Winnie. Hold on just a second."

I listened as he talked on the phone. We never went to his house. We never went to my apartment. As I listened, I figured out why. If we went to my apartment, then I might want to go to *his* house. That wasn't a good idea. Here's the thing…

"Remember? You asked me to put it in the rafters in the garage," he said into his phone in a soft, nurturing tone. "Don't try to climb up there. I'll get up there and look for it when I get home, tomorrow. I promise, I'll get it down for you. Will you be okay until then? Okay. I love you, too. Get some sleep. We'll get it tomorrow."

He hung up the phone, and I just stared at him. He had been so sweet and soft to her. He looked at me and realized what I had just learned. He stood on the top step of the hot tub and held his balled up fist to his mouth.

"I'm sorry about that. She, uh, wanted her quilt rack," he chuckled. "She wanted to try to get it herself. I don't want her to do that. Especially if I'm not home."

"She lives with you?"

"Yep!" he said defensively. "She gave up her life to take care of me. The least I can do is return the favor."

"That's sweet," I said. "Why didn't I know that?"

"Why would you?"

"Maybe because we've been fucking like lunatics for a while now. It seems like that would've come up at some point. You didn't have to hide that from me. I think it's sweet."

His response was a little defensive. "I wasn't *hiding* that from you, but I'm not taking you to my house. Winnie has a lot of old-fashioned ideas. I respect her and her views. She knows I'm up to no good," he smirked. "But I don't throw it in her face. That's her home, too. I asked her to come live with me. It wouldn't be right to ask her to come live with me and then do things I know she doesn't approve of. So as much as I like taming your dragon, it's not happening in my house. Sorry, princess!"

"She wouldn't approve of me?"

He chuckled and shook his head. "She wouldn't approve of what we do. If you were travelling and needed a place to stay, you could sleep in my room, in my bed. That would be okay with her. But it would upset her a great deal if I were anywhere near that room while you were in there. I would have to sleep on the couch or in the guest room for her to be okay with you being there. In Winnie's mind, some things you just don't do until you're married."

"That's kind of funny. You're such a bad boy, and you come from that kind of moral foundation?"

"You say that like you're disappointed," he said as he came down the steps, into the water, moving closer to me.

"And you seem concerned about what I think as though you care."

He kissed my lips and rolled his eyes. "Of course, I care."

"I can't imagine sleeping in your bed while you sleep on the couch."

"Heh! That would drive me out of my skull. Having you in my bed and not being able to do anything to you? Woo! Winnie knows I sleepwalk. We could blame it on that," he said. "No. I can't think like that. We'll be figuring out a way to pull that off."

He wrapped his arms around me, pulling me back onto his lap.

"Weren't you about to make me lose my mind?"

"I don't know. Was I?"

He let out a throaty chuckle. "Mm! Yeah, you were!"

I reached inside his swim trunks and gripped his cock. His breath caught in his chest as he laughed his seductive laugh. I covered his mouth with mine. I wanted to be in control and to make him "lose his mind." The steamy, bubbly water swirled around me as I stood and slid my bikini bottoms off. I climbed up on his lap, placing my swimsuit bottoms in his hand. I lowered myself on his cock, guiding it where I needed it to be. I sucked on his lips as I began rocking my hips back and forth. He untied the strings on my triangle top, slapping the wet fabric on the deck. His hands cupped my breasts as his mouth kissed and sucked on them.

I let my head fall back. I suddenly remembered where we were. We were in the courtyard of the hotel, surrounded, on all four sides, by guest room windows.

Knowing that little fact would turn him on, I cradled his head in my arms, putting my mouth to his ear.

"Anyone looking out their window is going to know what I'm doing to you."

He gripped my hips, pushing and pulling my body against him as he thrust his hips upward, into me. I hugged my arms around his neck, moving my body with his. I felt the muscles in my abdomen tighten, as though they were twisting. It was as though the butterflies were migrating from my stomach. Whatever he did, it made me feel amazing. My pussy began pulsing and tightening around him. He smiled at me, seemingly proud of himself. Hell, I was proud of him. He made me feel so good. He pressed into me a few more times, hard enough that the water spilled over the sides of the Jacuzzi onto the decking.

As my body started to calm, he got a devious smile on his face. "One more."

He started pumping his hips up and down as he pushed and pulled on my hips, driving my pussy down on him. The look of determination on his face as he fucked me with everything he had made me hot as hell. His pubic bone grinding against my clit made me want more. I pressed my clit against him and rocked my hips, grinding harder and faster. My pussy started pulsing again, just a couple of seconds before Jackson started to come.

He clenched his teeth and his body stiffened. "It's coming. Oh…yeah!"

He acted like a crazy man the way he ripped my body back and forth. He had a wild and unleashed look in his eyes. It fucking turned me on so much. I got to be the woman that satisfied Jackson Montgomery, but even better, I got to be the woman that he satisfied.

He breathed so hard I thought he would hyperventilate. Then, he stopped breathing at all. Eventually, he let out one heavy exhale and a growly grunt noise. He rammed his cock deeper into me as he came. He reached up my back and pulled down on my shoulders as he pushed his throbbing cock deeper, backing out a little, only to slam it in deeper again. When his stiffened body began to relax, I kissed him, sweeping my tongue into his mouth. I couldn't get close enough to him. He pulled his head back away from me, trying to catch his breath.

He laughed as his head fell back on the decking. "If I ever die while I'm fucking you, just know I died a happy man, okay?"

I giggled as I kissed his lips. "No! Don't die. I need you to keep doing this to me."

"You're going to be the death of me."

He lifted his head and smiled at me. Then, he dropped his head back again, laughing a cute laugh.

"I can't! I just can't move yet. I want to give your little panties…or whatever…back, but I just can't."

"I can get them," I said as I kissed his lips. "You just sit there."

I felt along the seat with my hand, gathering the bottoms of my swimsuit. If you've never put a swimsuit on in the water, you're not missing anything. It is not all that much fun. The damn bottoms kept rolling up as I tried to pull them up. Anyway, I got myself put back together and my swimsuit back on my body. Then, I trailed kisses along Jackson's jaw, to his chin and up to his lips.

He sighed a deep sigh and lifted his head, cracking

jokes. "Wanna do it again?"

"Come on, porn star." I giggled. "We should probably make ourselves scarce. Come with me."

I held my hand out to him. He sighed again and intertwined his fingers in mine. As I walked up the steps in front of him, he lifted our joined hands and brushed his finger back and forth on my butt cheek.

"Damn, you've got a nice ass," he said.

I stopped and turned to face him, hugging my arms around his neck, kissing him. He reached behind me to the towels draped over our chairs. He wrapped my towel around me and used it to pull me closer to him.

"Are you serious?" I asked as I stared into his eyes, feeling his hard cock pressing against me.

He chuckled. "What? You're fucking hot, okay?" His lips pressed to mine, "I can't help it."

We entered the elevator to go up to our room, passing a rather dignified, snooty-looking lady who already stood in the elevator car. She rolled her eyes and looked away as we stepped inside. Maybe she had seen us in the Jacuzzi. Then again, maybe she was just an ugly human being inside. Either way, I snuggled under Jackson's arm, and hugged his waist. He winked at me and flashed his ornery smirk.

"I'll never understand why people come to a place like this and go do perverse things in the Jacuzzi."

I shushed him, giving him an incredulous glare. He chuckled and glanced over at the woman. He shrugged.

"I guess some people just have no respect for others. If you ever want to do that sort of thing, you're on your own."

I smacked him in the gut and mouthed the words, "Would you stop?"

The lady exhaled heavily as she stepped off the elevator when the doors opened to her floor. After they closed, Jackson laughed, feeling proud of his ornery self. I'd be lying if I said I didn't love it when he got cocky like that. He was a fun challenge, but before I could say anything, he pulled me to him and flicked my lips before his tongue plunged into my mouth. Ah! When he kissed me like that, it set me on fire.

Chapter Fourteen

The next day we had a big day at work, getting ready for a special staff meeting. This special day came around twice a year when Jackson gave profit-sharing bonuses. One was a summer bonus that came in time for vacation, the other in time for Christmas. It was summer bonus time, and I had it on good authority…ahem…that the company had done quite well.

Jackson was kind enough to buy lunch for all of the office personnel. The catering company had called three times, trying to find us. Finally, we cancelled the caterers, which left me scrambling, an hour and a half before the meeting, to find something that everyone would eat. Pizza wasn't going to work. There were too many various preferences, and we would need twenty-seven pizzas for all twenty-seven office employees, so I opted for a six-foot sub sandwich and salad. That meant a trip to the sub shop down the street. I phoned in the order and since we paid extra for the rush, I only had an hour before I had to pick up the lunch.

"I have to stop for gas, but I'll be as quick as I can," I promised as I handed Jackson the stack of envelopes containing the bonus checks.

He seemed to be distracted, but he shoved his hand in his pocket and pulled his keys out. He dangled them, holding them out to me. As I reached for them, without ever looking at me, he closed his hand around them before I could take them.

"If you wreck it, I will cry."

"You want me to drive Lucy? Without you?"

He shot me a bone-chilling glare and sighed as he shook his head. "Lizzy, do *not* wreck that car!"

"I won't!"

He dropped the key set into my hand and went back to whatever he had his attention focused on at the moment. I swiped my hand across his chest, swishing his tie. His eyes shifted to me, and he puckered his lips. I put my finger across them, and he kissed it.

"Hurry up."

I raced to the car, drove very carefully, raced into the sandwich shop, and then drove very carefully back to the office. I think I even got up to thirty miles an hour at one point. I felt too nervous to have too much fun. Every little bug that flew at the windshield made me jump out of my skin, but I did it! I made it there and back without wrecking it.

I got back and went to return the keys to Lucy. Jackson proudly smiled and nodded his head. Then, he shoved the keys back in his pocket.

"Thank you," he smiled.

A short time later, everyone gathered in the conference room. As everyone filled their plate and found their seats, Jackson walked around handing the envelopes to the respective owners as he personally thanked each employee. When he got to Lisa, he offered her the envelope and teasingly pulled it back.

"Did you peek?" he asked.

Of course, she had peeked. She printed the checks. This had become a perfect example of a time when it sucked to be fucking the boss. He mingled with everyone in that room. Instead of getting to enjoy this little "party" at his side, I felt like the errand girl. I watched this charming man find something personal to chat with everyone in that room about. With John, he discussed baseball and which team did what. He talked to Dena about her son and his summer camp. He had something with every one of those people. When he got to me, he tried to downplay things so much that it looked like I was just some fungus that grew in the corner. At least that is how I felt.

He smiled at me and raised the cup in his hand as he nodded. "Thank you, Elizabeth. I appreciate your help in making all of this happen and for holding this place together."

I smiled an appeasing smile. "Sure. Anytime."

Jackson made his way around the room, chatting with everyone. I sat in the corner, staring at his ass, his package, and the way his body moved. I couldn't help it. He was hot, and I got the pleasure of getting to be the one that got to ride him like a bucking, wild horse.

After he had handed out the last bonus check, he got a turn to eat. He stood at the table, making his plate. I casually strolled over and stood beside him. We had our backs to the rest of the room.

"Did you eat?" he asked as he sweetly bumped his shoulder into mine.

"I want you," I said.

He smiled a devious smile as he picked up a piece of tomato and put it in my mouth. I wrapped my lips around his finger, gently dragging my teeth as he pulled his hand back. He put his plate down on the table and reached for one of the drinks we had in a bowl of ice.

"Keep it up." He smiled. "You're just making it harder on yourself, later."

"I want you in my mouth, right now."

He cut his eyes over at me. His eyebrow arched and a smile crept across his face. He turned to the rest of the group behind us and pointed to the plate on the table.

"I'm going to set this right here. Don't throw it away. I have to get a fax ready for Elizabeth really quick. We'll be right back." He held his arm out, encouraging me to lead the way. He ducked his head and politely said, "After you, Miss Elizabeth."

"No working, Elizabeth!" Lisa huffed, rolling her eyes. "Let the poor guy eat. Geez!"

I would've been annoyed, if I weren't so excited about the fact that I finally got to have him to myself. As we passed the supply closet, he looked over his shoulder toward the conference room. Content that no one was watching us, he wrapped his arm around my waist and pulled me into the closet. It was a small room, larger than a closet, but not big enough to be an office or any other room.

He pulled me into his embrace as he turned the light on and practically inhaled my lips. He put his hands under my shirt as our lips locked on each other. He brushed his fingers over my nipples, with a soft, throaty, devious chuckle. His body pinned me against the wall and his mouth skimmed over my neck. Fuck! He cranked the heat up so quickly.

"A fucking fax?" he scoffed. "That's not much time, Miss Elizabeth."

He gripped my thighs and ripped my feet off the ground. I wrapped my legs around his waist as he fumbled with his pants. He slid my panties to the side and rammed his cock inside me.

"Mr. Montgomery," I gasped, "I think you need to study some anatomy. That is not my mouth."

He thrust his hips hard. "When you're sulking and pouting in a corner, you don't get what you want. I'm not reinforcing your spoiled behavior."

I giggled. "You're damn sure not punishing me, if that is your intention."

"Oh, just wait," he smirked.

He bumped his hips, bouncing me like a ball on a court. It was fast and hot, but not as deep as I wanted to feel him. His mouth covered mine as his tongue rushed past my lips. Our quickened breath seemed loud in that little room. His sweaty body quickly dampened his shirt under my hands. He reclaimed his tongue and softly kissed my lips.

"What do you want?" He smiled.

"Mm! Harder and deeper."

He clenched his teeth and grabbed my hips, shoving me down on him, as he pressed deeper into me. My body practically melted, it felt so good. I let out a soft moan as he did it again…and again…and again. Each time, the force he used seemed harder than the time before. He pulled my legs off his hips, looping his arms around my thighs, holding me right where he wanted me. He quickly slammed his body into mine. He hit places I had never felt before. I closed my eyes and my head rolled back.

"Ooo, yeah! Oh, baby."

"You like that?" he asked.

"Oh yeah!"

He suddenly stopped bumping his hips. "Good to

know."

He withdrew his cock from me and released my legs, letting them fall as my feet reached for the floor. He turned away from me and put his anatomy back in his pants, zipping them up. I couldn't be sure if someone had opened the closet door or what had happened. It wasn't like him to end things so quickly.

"What happened? What are you doing?"

"Time's up," he boldly said as he turned back toward me.

"You had me so close. I…"

"I'll take care of it later. Like I said, I'm not reinforcing your spoiled behavior." He bit his lower lip and winked at me.

"No! Jackson, that's not funny. You can't leave me like this. You will have hell to pay."

He shrugged. "Maybe, but maybe I can handle that, too. Now, we should probably get back in there."

"You are not serious. Please don't be serious."

He chuckled as he stared into my eyes and with a smooth, lofty tone, he said, "I'm very serious."

He turned the knob, and before I could speak, he quickly peeked around the door and darted out of the closet. He left the door open and walked around the cubicles, distancing himself from me. Now, we were beyond playing. I was pissed!

I watched him walk up the middle of the office, his eyes locked on mine over the top of the workstations between us. He had that arrogant smile on his face. He knew what he had just done, and he was rather proud of himself. In loud whispers, we taunted each other.

"I can take care of it myself, and you won't get to watch," I teased as he strutted toward the conference room.

"It'll never be the same, and you know it."

"It might be better."

"Nope! You wouldn't be mad right now if you had a better option." He winked and went to eat his sandwich, the cocky son of a bitch! I stood there, giggling to myself.

Yeah? Well…well…so there, then!

I loved every second of those flirty conversations. He was so quick-witted that it was hard to get over on him. He wasn't going to take my word and just let it go. He was too smart and too cocky to let me get away with anything. I liked that feisty side of him so much. No matter how cute I found him, the fact is he had me close to my orgasm, and he stopped. I would find a way to get even.

For the rest of the meeting, everyone mingled, chatting and enjoying the opportunity to relax and socialize. I stepped into the office, going to the front to fill my water bottle from the cooler. I heard the door open and close. I turned to see a rather angry, larger man storming through the door. I looked behind me, toward the conference room. No one noticed that we had a visitor. To be fair, the cubicles, and one of the support pillars blocked the front of the office. When I looked at the man again, he pointed his finger in my face.

"Where the hell is that weasely, dumb shit?" he demanded.

What a shock! I started shaking my head and stuttering, unable to get any words to come out. He huffed a heavy breath.

"Is everyone in this fucking place just stupid?

Where do I find Jackson Montgomery?"

"H-h-he's in a meeting. Is there something I can help you with?"

"I don't want your help. I want to talk to your boss. Right now! Go get him." He swirled his finger through the air. "I'm sure he'd want to talk to me. Now! Go!"

Excuse me? I wasn't going to be ordered around by this hothead. Especially seeing as how I had no idea who he was, or more importantly, who he *thought* he was.

"Like I said, he's in a meeting," I retorted.

"Oh, forget it! Stupid bitch. Get out of my way. I'll find him myself."

"Hey, Bob!" Jackson sang out from the conference room door as he set his drink down and started walking toward us. He was oblivious to what he had just walked into.

"A *meeting*, my ass," Bob scoffed as his eyes narrowed, glaring at me.

As Jackson approached, he extended his arm to shake Bob's hand. Bob pushed Jackson's hand away and put his finger in Jackson's face. At that point, Bob began spouting even more of his verbal sewage.

"While you're in here playing arts and crafts all day, or whatever the hell you're doing in your little huddle in there, your degenerate crew is fucking up my job. Why? Because, again, you're in here, playing with yourself, instead of being a boss. You need to start firing these people, Jackson, and you need to start with this little dumbass bitch right here. She needs to be the first to go," he barked, pointing to me. "Having a centerfold greeting people is fine as long as she's got the intelligence of a stick of gum. This little dick magnet…"

"Bob," Jackson squinted, "you need to watch your mouth. Now, if you want to step into my office, we can discuss your issues, but you're not tearing into her like that."

"If she's so soft that she can't work in this field without crying over her feelings, maybe she needs to do you both a favor and go work in a teddy bear factory. This is a man's world," he said and spun to put his face in mine. "Deal with it, darlin'! You better get some thicker skin if you're going to play with us boys."

"Nope!" Jackson said as he pushed Bob away from me. "Get out of her face."

Bob scoffed. "Okay, hero. I'll let you look like a tough guy for the moment, but you better remember who butters your bread. I own you, boy. Have you forgotten?"

That pissed Jackson off. "You're not coming through that door, threatening my people. If you have an issue, you bring it to me. Leave the rest of them alone."

"Then, tell your little trick that when I come looking for you, she better start jumping instead of running her smart mouth."

"I'm pulling my guys off your job. We'll leave the materials for the next crew, and I'll check balances for your account. We'll take care of our end of things. You don't like us? We don't particularly care for you, either."

I gripped Jackson's arm. "No! Oh shit! What're you—?" I started before Bob interrupted me.

"Do you realize that you will never work in this city again if you do that? You better pull your dick out of her face and start thinking with your business brain."

Jackson drew a deep breath as he glared at him. "You owe her an apology," he bluntly noted.

"It's okay," I said as I reached for Jackson's arm.

Jackson scoffed. "No, it's not! He owes you an apology."

Bob broke the stare he and Jackson shared to look at me. He laughed sarcastically as he looked me up and down. Then, he turned his gaze to Jackson again.

"I'll let you take care of my apology, there, sport," he said with a knowing smirk. "You need to be out in the field, supervising your crews. Since you're such a sucker for a piece of ass, maybe you should start hiring beautiful women to work on your crews. Maybe then we'd actually see you on our job sites, rather than having to track you down here. Hell, if nothing else, maybe we'd all be a little happier about the fact our jobs aren't getting done. It trickles down, Jackson. Is some little gold-digging tramp really worth everything she's about to cost you?" Bob flashed his wicked glare at me. "I see right through you. I've seen scavengers like you shimmy into a successful business and rip the flesh from the bones. He doesn't know what you are, but I do. And so do you."

"Get the fuck out, Bob," Jackson snapped.

"Oh, give me a break! I'm your best friend, boy. You don't think people are talking about how you become a ghost as soon as you've got that contract? It's not just me. You need to be out there. You need to see what your boys are doing when you're not looking. You're giving them too much freedom. I'm trying to help you before you ruin yourself, and hell if I know why I care. All I know is you and your crew better be on that jobsite by nine sharp Monday morning or I'm coming back in here, and we're going to do things a little differently."

Jackson scoffed. "I don't think you heard me. I said—"

"Oh, I heard you, but before all of this, I also heard you when you said you and your boys were going to throw that building up for me. I want you to do what you said you'd do. Come nine o'clock Monday morning, *you* and your boys better be there, ready to work. You don't want me to have to come back here to continue this discussion, and I'm not talking about *just* your guys. I mean *you,* too! If I have to kick your ass every step of the way, we're getting that building up."

With that, Bob shook his head in disgust, turned and walked out the door. Without turning his head, Jackson's eyes shifted, locking on mine. I could see his mind racing as he clicked his tongue against his teeth.

"Are you okay?"

"Yes, but I don't care for that guy."

"We have to stop." He swallowed hard and sighed.

"Stop? Stop what?"

"This! Us! We can't have clients thinking I'm in the office because I'm chasing after you."

"You! You mean *you* can't have them thinking that. I don't give a shit what they think."

"That's because you don't have to figure out how to make payroll. I can't lose all of this because of…"

"Me?" I asked.

He didn't answer. He just pushed his tongue against his cheek and stared at the floor. I guess I had my answer.

"I need to take the rest of the day off."

I turned and stomped toward my desk, gathering my things to leave. Jackson sauntered toward me with some pathetic look of apology on his face. He plunged his hands in his pockets.

"Maybe we just need to slow it down a little. I'm sorry, but there's a lot of truth in what he just said."

"You think I'm a gold-digger?"

"Well, are you?"

I scoffed and rolled my eyes so hard they hurt. "Fuck you!"

"You already did that."

"Oh, you think you've been fucked? *You* haven't seen fucked," I spouted.

He pressed his lips together and nodded. "Do what you gotta do."

I pushed my way past him. I decided, in that moment, that I wanted to become the frumpiest looking, unattractive person I could be. I wanted to do my job, and I wasn't going to acknowledge him as anything more than my boss from now on. My heart hurt, and I was pissed. I didn't want to get even. I just wanted to make him un-say the things he couldn't. Forever, his words would stand. Forever, I would hear him questioning my intentions. I could be called numerous things, but a gold digger wasn't one of them. How dare he! I had never asked him for anything.

Chapter Fifteen

I left the office and went to a bar down the street. When the bartender asked what I wanted to drink, I told him I wanted something that would get me really drunk, really fast. He laughed and started mixing something, the mind boggler, or mind scrambler, or eraser…something. Anyway, it tasted like it should be some sort of vehicle fuel, and I was pretty sure it would do the trick.

I guzzled the first drink down pretty fast, then I looked at my phone and still nothing. I tried to figure out if this was a fight, or just another one of his games? The fact that I cared told me I hadn't drunk enough, yet. I ordered another drink.

As I sat there, drinking my drink, I noticed the song playing over the speakers. There were sad lyrics over the top of some sad, whining guitar. It wasn't what I needed. I flushed the bubbly beverage down my throat and nodded at the bartender for another. When he brought the third drink, I convinced him to change the music. He watched my face as he flipped through songs. Finally, he found a song I recognized.

As the raspy voice sang about preferring that old-time rock and roll, my heart nearly exploded. Of course, it would be a song Jackson frequently played. Of course, it would! I flashed the bartender a sarcastic smirk.

"Perfect! You better go ahead and mix up that next one."

I took my phone out of my purse. I had a text from earlier in the day that I had previously missed. It dug the knife deeper into my heart and twisted it.

—Do not wreck that car!—

I held my phone to my chest and fought back tears. I hated Bob! It felt like Bob and his big mouth were ruining my life. Fucking Bob! Fucking Jackson Montgomery!

After about an hour and a half, I felt no pain since my blood had stopped contaminating my alcohol level. I felt good. I kept telling the bartender that we were best friends. I told him, several times, that I loved him. I have no idea why, but I started telling him that we needed to be roommates. He graciously let me know that his wife would probably be a little weirded out if he brought home a customer from the bar.

Wife! There's a word! If I weren't drunk, I would've hated that word, too. I had a feeling I would never be a "wife." I would just be some wealthy man's "gold-digging tramp." But I didn't have time to think of such things. I felt happy and I was having fun.

When the bartender came to check on me, I convinced him to take a picture with me. I opened the camera on my phone and snapped the picture. I had a plan. It was devious, and maybe a bit catty, but I was drunk, and I didn't care about consequences.

I opened my text messages and clicked to reply to Jackson's message from earlier. I typed out a fake message to my sister, Ellery. I included all the pertinent details.

—Hey, Ellery! Should we take bets on how long it

takes me to bed this hottie? Tall, dark, and handsome! Just the way we like them.—

I sent the message, waited thirty seconds, and then sent the obligatory apology for "accidentally" texting the wrong person. Oops! Silly me! I even confessed to being drunk and apologized for disturbing him.

The reply didn't take long. When my phone pinged from the bar, I felt the wicked smirk spread across my face. I was proud of myself. I picked up my phone and read the message.

—Let me help you out. That guy that you're planning to fuck is happily married. His name is Jeff. Tell Jeff 'hi' for me.—

I felt my little plan falling around me. It wasn't supposed to go like that. I held my hand up, motioning for the bartender. He sauntered over, preparing to break it to me that he would not be serving me any more drinks.

"I can't serve you another drink. You have to wait about another half an hour."

"No, that's okay. I'm not ready, yet. Is your name Jeff?"

"Yes," he said with a questioning tone.

"Do you know Jackson Montgomery?"

His body seemed to relax. "I do. Good guy! Why do you ask?"

"He just told me he knows you."

"Yep!"

"How do you know him?" I noticed the despotic tone in my question.

"He's come in here for, probably, five years. I talked him into dressing up as Santa Claus a few years ago for a Christmas party that we booked in here." He smiled as though recalling an amusing memory. “That was a fun night. He started out doing *me* a favor and ended up owing me big for that night.”

Ah ha! This could explain how Jackson ended up being in a ménage situation.

“Oh really?” I questioned, hoping he would keep sharing.

“We laugh about that story quite a bit.”

“What story?”

“How do *you* know Jackson?” he asked with a surly tone, ignoring my question.

“He’s my boss,” I said, half slurred. “In *every* way.”

I tried to hint at the fact that I saw him as more than *just* my boss. I had a feeling I’d regret that when I sobered up, but for now, it felt good. I wanted to tell people about our relationship. I wanted to celebrate the way I felt about him. I couldn’t do that because of that whole “our little secret” thing. Ugh!

“Will he be joining us?” Jeff asked.

“Let me just ask him.” I smiled deviously.

It gave me an excuse text him. I’d gladly find out if he had plans to stop by to visit *Jeff*. Again, I took my phone out and typed out a text.

—Jeff wants to know if you’re going to come visit him. Maybe you could play Santa Claus, again.—

I camped there at the bar, staring at my screen. I hoped my message would inspire a flirty reply of some sort. I didn’t know what that meant, but I was drunk. If it would get him to play along with me, what the hell could it hurt?

Finally, my phone pinged.

—No. Not coming. Almost home. Next time.—

My heart sank. It would've been my preference for him to come skidding through the door, out of breath, and in a hurry to rush to my side, but instead, he had almost made it home. Annoying!

—Did you ever care about me?—

His reply:*—How are you getting home?—*

—Answer me, Jackson.—

—Yes! How are you getting home?—

—I'm going to call you for a ride, of course.—

—Should've talked to me first. I have plans for tonight. Do you need a cab?—

—No! I'll find someone to give me a ride.—

I looked up at Jeff and curled my fingers, motioning for another drink. Jeff flashed me a warning glance and nodded. As he made my drink, he asked, again, if Jackson would be stopping by. When I told him what Jackson had said, Jeff pointed to my drink.

"Then, you might want to slow down on those. They hit hard."

"Can I tell you something?" I asked.

Jeff pursed his lips and smiled as he considered my question. "Sure!"

"He's breaking my heart. I want to make him see what he means to me, but he doesn't want to. He just won't let me get close to him. I think I love him, and he just wants a dirty little secret. Tell me what to do? How do I make him love me?"

"First of all, I'm not making you anymore drinks, so don't even ask. Second, you can't make someone love you the way you want them to. All you can do is decide if you are willing to accept what he is willing to give you."

"But I think I love him!"

"A little while ago, you loved me, too. Remember? I think you might find a better solution to your problem when you're not drunk. For tonight, just enjoy your last drink. Then, we'll find you a cab to get you home. Tomorrow, it'll all look different."

"Will you play that song again? The one about rock and roll."

"You know, if you're trying to punish yourself, I've got one of his favorite playlists."

My vision was sufficiently distorted by now, but I tried to focus on his face through my blurry, tear flooded eyes. I nodded my head in agreement.

Jeff walked away, leaving me to my drink. A few moments later, the sound of a piano came sliding over the noisy background chatter. People started getting up from their chairs, dancing around the bar to the dance floor. I turned in my chair, watching them, gyrating my body to the beat. Jeff lowered the lights and turned on the strobe lights. We went from neighborhood bar, to dance club with the flip of two switches.

A guy that had been sitting at a neighboring table came and asked me to dance. I was looking to leave a scar, anyway. Why not? I smiled at the handsome stranger. He held his hand out, helping me off my chair. Jeff gave me a disapproving look, and his head twitched to the side. He studied the man that asked me to dance, glaring at him.

"Hey, thanks, man! I got her," I heard a voice from behind me say. The stranger seemed to vaporize. Like a ghostly vision appearing before my eyes, Jackson stood in front of me, bobbling his head side to side, with the beat of the music.

Jeff greeted him, confirming that he wasn't just an

alcohol induced illusion. My dream guy really had come to save the day. Jackson chatted with Jeff as he held his hand out to me. I put my hand in his, and he pulled me to him, wrapping his arms around me.

Jackson lowered his mouth to my ear. “You’re looking for the wrong kind of trouble,” he said as he passed me a disappointed look.

“I’m so drunk.” I giggled, poking my finger into his chest. “Like, really, really drunk. And so, if you’re thinking you can take advantage of me, you definitely can.”

“How much have you had?”

“I don’t know, but I feel good. I’m so happy you’re here.”

“You are a hot mess,” he said, shaking his head.

He leaned his head down and kissed my lips before he took my hand and spun me in a circle. Due to the fact that I was already inebriated, I had no balance for that. He held both of my hands and pulled me in and pushed me back, turning us in a circle, as he mouthed the words to the song. When the music took on a steady, pumping rhythm, he pumped his fist in the air as though he were at a rock concert. Granted, I was drunk, but holy shit, could he dance! Just like that, Jackson Montgomery had joined my party.

When the song ended, he smiled at me. “That is one of the best songs ever written.”

“I thought you had plans?”

“Yeah? Well, I thought we could have some fun and skip all the bullshit,” he countered, batting his eyes.

He pumped his shoulder to the beat of the music and folded his lips over his teeth as he raised his eyebrows. He took my hand and spun me again. He interlaced his fingers in mine and looped his other arm around my waist, pulling me closer to him. He snaked his body side to side as he held me against him.

"I think I'm too drunk to get the full benefit of this." I smiled as I stared at the bad boy looking down at me.

"Serves you right," he said, pushing me away and pulling me back again.

As we danced, Jackson put his thumb up in the air, pumping it upward, motioning to Jeff to turn the volume up. Everyone in the bar, with the exception of a few tables, had gotten up to show their moves on the dance floor. Jackson put his forehead to mine, mouthing the words of the song as he alternated rolling his shoulders toward me, like some looming monster. Only this monster was made out of sex appeal, making me lust for every fiber of his being. Jackson Montgomery was as dangerous as any other monster.

Then a velvety smooth voice blasted through the speakers, singing about some monarch of some tropical island. Between the breathy lyrics and the beat of the music, I couldn't help but move my body. Jackson lowered his mouth to my ear.

"I've seen you move like that before."

"No! What you've seen looked more like this." I smiled and turned around, moving my ass against his crotch.

He wrapped his arms around me, holding me to him and kissing my earlobe.

"You didn't have to do that. I'm there. Trust me."

"Where?" I played.

"Want me to show you?"

I slid my hand between us, over his crotch and

turned to face him. "Should we go do something about that?"

"I want you here." He smiled his devious smile.

"Um…here? Here, where here?"

He smirked and nodded his head as he moved his body to the beat of the music. He looked around the bar, before his eyes shifted to mine, and he raised his eyebrows.

"Yeah! Here!"

I giggled. As unpredictable as he could be, I had no idea if he meant it or just wanted to make me wet. I danced as my mind half attempted to figure out the riddle. He held his hands up, snapping his fingers as hips swayed, moving closer to me. He lowered his head and nipped at my lips. His tongue swept into my mouth, caressing my tongue. His lips moved along my cheek to my ear.

"Fuck me," he urged.

"Oh, my, God!"

My pussy had already been responding to him, but that was overload. My panties felt saturated all of a sudden. I couldn't believe that a man could have that effect on me.

He held me to him and slid his other hand between the top of my skirt and my skin, threatening to finger me right there. I drew a deep breath and put my palm on his cheek. He looked down at me and smiled.

"Should we go? We can go to my apartment," I suggested.

"Are you scared?"

I nervously bit my lip and nodded. "A little."

"They won't know more than you want them to," he promised. "I can make you come in front of all of them, and they'll never know."

He gently tapped my mound before he withdrew his hand from inside my skirt. He let go of me and started unbuttoning his shirt as well as any male stripper, smiling his ornery smile. Right here? Right in front of…everyone? Even drunk, this seemed a bit too "open." I covered my mouth, laughing nervously. The strobing circles of light danced over our bodies in an otherwise darkened room. He handed his shirt to me.

"Put that on."

Thankful to be gaining laundry, rather than him taking something away, I slid my arms in the sleeves. The shirt practically consumed me. I struggled to get my hands out of the cuffs. I lifted my hair out from the collar. When I looked up, Jackson tried not to smile as he stared at me.

"That's about the cutest thing I've ever seen," he said. "Never again will I see that shirt without reliving the way you look in it."

He drew a deep breath and shook his head, pulling me to him. His hands glided between his shirt and my body. He rested his hands on my hips as we moved to the music. His eyes locked on mine as he danced us to a darker part of the floor. I felt his hand slide under my shirt and tug at the waist of my skirt.

A cocky smile spread across his face as he walked his fingers down my stomach to my swollen sex. He brought his mouth to mine, kissing me as his fingers brushed over me, petting and stroking my pussy. I moved my body closer to him, afraid that the shirt wouldn't be enough to hide what he was doing to me.

His finger dipped inside me. He quickly flipped it back and forth. I gasped and nervously looked around the room to the others, to see if anyone seemed to notice anything. I could feel Jackson's eyes on me, waiting for a reaction as he finger-fucked me in front of a room full of people, again. When I looked at him, the look on his face turned me on so much. He had that animalistic, dominant expression he got when he wanted to do something he would have no regrets for. We were face to face as he gave me soft angel kisses, then his mouth covered mine. His tongue plunged past my lips, his breath rushing over my skin.

Our bodies moved with the music, and he walked me backward to a darker corner, just off the dance floor. Once he had me backed as far into the corner as I could get, his mouth moved down my jaw to my neck. He backed his head away, staring into my eyes as he started grinding against me.

As his mouth found mine again, he reached between us, unfastening his pants. I felt his hand between us as he rolled a condom over his shaft. He put his hand on the inside of my thigh, slowly dragging it up my leg, lifting my skirt as he moved. He tugged at my panties, moving them to the side.

"I want this," he said through his clenched teeth as he cupped my pussy in his hand.

My chest heaved. He made me so fucking hot. I spread my legs a little, and he forced himself between my thighs. He bent his knees. When he straightened them, he guided his cock inside me. There was no turning back. He really meant it. He fucked me right there in that club. He thrust into me, pinning my body against the corner. I looked over his shoulder at the moving bodies on the floor, under the twirling lights, none the wiser as to what we were doing in the corner.

Jackson gripped my hips and started slamming his body into mine. He put his hands on the wall beside my head, laying into me, pounding me with all his might. As my hands moved over his back, I could feel his body flexing as he pumped his cock in and out of me.

"Oh, Jackson!" I moaned. "Ooo, yes!"

"Come on, honey." He lowered his mouth to my ear. "You have no idea what you're doing to me right now."

"Come with me, Jackson."

"You want me to?"

"Yes! Oh, yes!"

He quickly popped his hips up and down, pressing his body against me. I pushed my hips toward him, trying to grind against him. One of his hands gripped my thigh, squeezing as he pulled it up to his hip.

"Oh, fuck!" He breathed and thrust into me harder, driving his cock deeper inside me.

The sounds he made told me he was about to climax. I reached between us and rubbed my aching clit. He pressed upward and to the side a couple of times. My body felt like my entire existence was wrapped around his cock. Like an explosion, my pussy began greedily squeezing his cock.

"Oh fuck yeah! Uhhh!" he growled as I felt him pounding like a heartbeat inside me.

He drove his hips up into me, pushing in deeper as his seed spilled. Drunk as I may have been, I realized that I wasn't just taken by the way he made my body feel, but how this strong, tough guy let himself be vulnerable to me. I had to admit, there was a rush that came from his crazy ideas. Since I had met him, sex had become something entirely different than anything

I had ever known it to be.

I cradled his head in my arms as the peak of our experience began to subside. He had quit thrusting and took a moment for his body to calm and for him to catch his breath. His hands gently rested on my hips, and he lifted his head enough to look at me. He smiled and drove his softening cock into me once more, just because he could, I guess.

As he began to pull out, he lowered the front of my skirt, covering me. He put his cock back in his pants and put his hand on my abdomen as he leaned down to kiss me again. This time, he did it soft and sweet, slow and tender.

He sighed and put his forehead to mine. "You really don't understand what just happened."

"What happened?"

"I don't know, but damn! Do you want some bonbons? I'll draw you a bath, and sit right beside you, feeding you all the bonbons you want. Did you want me to kiss your shoes?" He chuckled, shaking his head.

I giggled as I raked my fingers through his hair. "What do I do with you, Mr. Montgomery?"

He stared into my eyes for a few seconds. His hand smoothed my skirt over my hip as he leaned down and kissed my lips. He shook his head as he threw his hands out to the side.

"You seemed to have it all figured out, tonight."

I laughed and put my hands on his chest as I stared up at him. "Why is it that you seem so determined to force innocent people watch us have sex?"

"I *don't* want them to watch us. It's more the thrill of the game that gets me. I don't want anyone seeing us, but I get off on figuring out how to do it and make it good for you without them knowing what we're doing. It makes me feel like a fucking genius. There's this Italian place that has the wooden rafters overhead. They have a wooden platform up there. I want to find a way to take you up there right in the middle of the dinner rush. I want you to come way up above those people."

"You're insane!" I giggled.

He stared into my eyes. "Is that why half an hour ago, you were so willing to replace me?"

"You hurt me. I'm still pissed at you," I barked.

"I'm still pissed off at you, too, but dammit, I'm not out trying to fuck somebody else. That pisses me off."

"Why did you come here, Jackson?"

"I didn't want to, but what was I supposed to do?" He shrugged and hugged me closer to him. "I have no idea why I came here."

Chapter Sixteen

Something about the hot sex we had in the corner of the club sobered me to the point of a modest buzz. We danced to a few more songs before we decided to go back to my apartment. We closed the tab with Jeff and were on our way to the door when a muscular, attractive man with dark hair, a little scruff, and vivid blue eyes stepped in front of us.

"Hey! My name is Roman Ingrim," the guy said as he extended his arm and shook Jackson's hand.

"How're you doing?" Jackson asked rhetorically, trying to step around the man, protectively keeping me behind him.

"Listen, I don't mean to be too personal, but uh…that thing back in the corner…that was hot, bro. You just did what needed to be done. Damn, you're a bad ass!"

Roman raised his hand to give Jackson a high five. Jackson looked over his shoulder at me. He sort of slapped Roman's hand.

"Okay. Thanks, I guess."

"Do you two ever swing?"

Jackson chuckled a sarcastic laugh. "No!"

"You should. At least try a little ménage action. We could give that girl a dicking she would never forget. That would be hotter than hell, bro! We could tag team her. Fuckin' A, man. She's hot." Roman smiled as he looked me up and down.

"I think I've got her taken care of. I'll let you get back to your drinks," Jackson said, pivoting his body to walk away.

"You think maybe you should ask her? Talk it over. Every woman fantasizes about having two men fuck her. We could all go back to your little office back there, and we could fuck her good. Two cocks filling her up. We'd drive her crazy, bro. Let me jump in on it. We could make it a friendly competition. She'll love us for it."

Jackson shoved Roman's shoulder. "I said no, *bro*! We're not swinging, and we're sure the fuck not doing the ménage thing. You look at her like that again, and they'll be scrubbing your fucking eyeballs off this floor. I said no! Do you understand me, now?"

"Fuck," Roman said as he looked me over again and adjusted himself in his jeans. "I'm always in here, if you ever change your mind."

Jackson stared him in the eyes. "Don't push me, man. Go back to your drink."

Roman smirked at him and looked at me with a shrug. "Sorry, baby! I tried. We don't need him, though. You're a consenting adult."

Jackson looked over his shoulder at me. He was pissed off. Again, he laughed sarcastically and shook his head. I reached for him to pull him out of the bar, just as he lowered his shoulder and put it into Roman's ribcage, shoving him against the wall. He pushed up on Roman's chin, holding his head up and against the wall.

"I told you, don't fucking push me. Go back to your drink before you end up getting hurt."

"Jackson let's go. Don't! Just ignore him," I said as

I pulled at his arm. "Please? Don't fight with him. Let's just go."

Jackson glared as he shoved Roman's head against the wall. He backed away with his eyes locked on Roman's. I pulled his arm with more determination, this time, dragging Jackson out of the bar. I felt nervous and shaky as adrenaline surged through my body. Jackson turned and gave Roman one last glare as we walked out the door.

As soon as we were outside, Jackson stared into my eyes as we walked away from the building. He held up two fingers. "Twice! Twice in one day. First Bob and now this numb nuts," he griped.

"Why are you mad at me?"

"I'm pissed at myself. You wanna fuck that guy?"

"No!"

"You sure? Because…I don't fucking know. Get your ass in the car," he said as he swung his pointer finger through the air.

"What about my car?"

"Later!" he barked as he opened the passenger door on Lucy.

I slid my body into the leather seat and pulled my legs in. He scratched his forehead with his thumbnail as he closed the door for me. He walked around the car and dropped his body into the driver's seat. He started the car and tore away from the curb so fast the back end fishtailed. He had to slam on the brakes for a red light.

"Jackson, I'm sorry. I didn't mean to—"

"Hey!" he swallowed hard and shook his head. "Tell me something. Why do I care enough to fight twice in one day? What the fuck? You didn't ask me to speak on your behalf. Maybe you wanted everything he could've given you."

"I didn't!" I quickly returned.

"He would've had to step over my dead body, first, but guess what? I'm over the need to fuck you in public. He just fixed that urge. That's what I get! I don't need to be doing that. It is pretty fucking stupid to think that had ever been a good idea."

He spoke so fast it was almost comical. I reached for his hand, putting my fingers in his. He squeezed it and brought it to his mouth, kissing the back of it.

He looked at me and sighed. With a soft, sweet tone, he said, "I think I've got a problem."

"You're my problem." I smiled. "So, I'm okay if you have a problem, too."

"I'm not!" he scoffed, shaking his head. "I almost pissed my company away, today. That wasn't good enough, so then, I almost booked a stay with the county jail. All I can think about is how much I want to kiss your body. I want to taste you. I want to forget the rest of the bullshit. I want it to be just you and me. I want you all over me."

I leaned over toward him and muttered in his ear, "Then, let's go to my apartment."

I kissed his neck and gripped his cock through his jeans. I hummed my approval when I discovered he was hard. I lightly traced my finger over the bulge in his pants.

"Mm…" he hummed.

"I want to watch you."

His eyes shifted from the road to mine. I reached for the closure on his jeans, tugging to free his cock. He adjusted himself in his seat and helped me with the zipper. I put my hand inside his jeans, cupping his balls and pushing his boxers down so I could see his manhood. He drew a deep staggered breath as his eyes met mine. He exhaled and flicked his tongue at my lips.

"Let me watch you." I flirted.

"I'm trying to drive." He smirked as he merged into traffic on the freeway.

"This is turning me on. Show me how you do it."

He looked at me, trying to read my face. His hand moved from the shifter to his crotch. He scooped his balls in his hand and massaged them, pulling and tugging at them. It was erotic watching him touch himself.

"Is this fun for you?" he asked as he shifted gears and put his hand back on his balls.

"It's sexy when you do that."

My heart raced. My breath became fast and heavy. He stared into my eyes as he bit his lower lip, gripped the base of his shaft, and stroked his hand up his cock.

"You're so fucking hot! Show me."

"You want me to show you?

"Open your legs."

"I want to watch you, though."

"Open your legs," he said.

I spread my legs. He took his hand off his cock and walked his fingers between my panties and my flesh. He smiled his devious smile at me. He drew a deep breath and shook his head.

"Is this really that much fun for you?" he asked, my wetness giving me away.

"I can't fake that, right?"

"That's definitely not fake."

He stroked my pussy, dipping his fingers in and out of me. He removed his hand and spread my wetness over his cock. He closed his fingers around his thickness and pressed his hand down his shaft, gripping his balls as he reached the base. As though he were rucking a shotgun, he moved his hand up and down his erection. He reached over between my legs, again, winking at me as he rubbed his hand over my silky, smooth pussy.

I saw the precum beading on the head of his dick. He stole my wetness and spread it over his cock once more. This time, he closed his fingers around his shaft, and he shuffled his hand back and forth, squeezing and tugging as he handled himself. It looked sexy as hell to watch him stroke it. I wanted him, but I also wanted to watch him make himself come.

I leaned over the console between us and draped my arm behind his shoulders as I traced my tongue over his neck. "I want to watch you come, baby."

He leaned his head back and exhaled. He pumped his hand faster up and down his shaft, brushing his thumb over the swollen head. He draped his other hand over the top of the steering wheel, as he tried to focus on the road. He glanced over at me, and his body stiffened. I rubbed his stomach as I watched him jack off. His breath became rushed as he breathed through his teeth.

"Oh yeah, baby," I said. "Come for me."

"Fuck, fuck, fuck," he growled.

Then, his seed started spurting out. I gripped the inside of his thigh, digging my fingertips into him, sucking on his earlobe as he came. I watched his face as his orgasm rippled through his body. His heaving chest and the sounds he made excited me. I desperately wanted to fuck him. My pussy ached so badly.

The car raced down the freeway as Jackson finished. The speed we were travelling, the sounds and the erotic, primal events within the car made me want to come. I had never thought watching a man please himself would turn me on, but my Mr. Montgomery was fucking sexy, even when he masturbated for my enjoyment.

"Where in the hell are we?" he chuckled as he looked around.

"Heaven," I flirted.

"No, we're not there, yet," he said as he pressed his lips to mine. "We can't get there in this car."

He pulled his T-shirt over his head and mopped up the mess he had made. Holy shit! His half naked body, in that sexy car, after he had just jacked off had my heart racing.

"You know how you like my pussy wet?"

"Um… Yes?"

"You can't imagine what that did to my panties."

"We need a bed."

I took his hand in mine, and I started sucking on his fingers. The salty taste reminded me of what I had witnessed. He pulled his hand away from my mouth.

"You probably don't want to do that right now," he shyly said.

"I've had you in my mouth before."

"I know, and that felt amazing, but remember? I had my hand all over your naughty place before I jacked off."

"I've tasted me on your lips so many times."

He put his finger under my chin, bringing my mouth to his. He pressed his tongue into my mouth as his eyes watched the road. His hand went down and lifted my skirt. He put his hand inside my panties. I opened my legs for him. He put his fingers inside me and started popping them in and out. He took his fingers out of me and put them in his mouth.

"Wh…where are we?" he asked. "I'm trying to get laid and this shit of getting lost isn't working for me. Fuck it! We're here now, where ever here is."

He took the next exit and drove the streets, passing gas stations and restaurants. Then, we came to a row of various hotels. He turned into the parking lot for a major hotel chain. He glanced over at me.

"Want to have a sleepover?"

I giggled. "Yes! Whatever you want, the answer is yes!"

His eyes locked on mine, and he pulled my mouth to his. He kissed me like he meant it. It felt like "forever." It felt passionate, and sweet, soft and tender.

"I love it when you kiss me like that," I said.

"Really?" he asked, raising his eyebrows. "That's great. Now give me my shirt so I can go in here and find a place to show you something else you'll love."

"Oh! Yeah!"

I peeled his button up shirt off my body and handed it to him. My visual reality changed as he put his shirt on and buttoned a few of the buttons. He kissed my cheek.

"Ready?"

We got out of the car, and he waited for me at the front of the car. He held his hand out behind him, waiting for me to fit my hand in his. We strolled through the doors, like any other happy couple. In the lobby stood a rack that had various pamphlets and cards for the tourist attractions in this cute little neighboring town.

In his best attempt at a whiney voice, he said, "Why don't you ever take me to do anything fun? You never want to do anything fun."

I rolled my eyes. "I have tons of fun. I don't know what your problem is."

"Good answer. I like that, but if I don't take you to do something soon, I'm scared I'm going to find you in another bar, infested with another perverted, swinger freak."

We held hands as we studied the rack cards. Jackson reached for one and he studied it, reading the pitch on the card. He pursed his lips and handed the flier to me.

"Let's go do that, tomorrow."

"You want to go to a petting zoo?" I giggled.

He glared at me and shook his head. "It's not just a petting zoo. There's an old general store and some sort of gunfight. Look! Did you read the card? They have an antique car garage. They have an Amish village. What is wrong with you? That place sounds fun!"

I laughed. "Sorry! I apologize. If you want to go to 'Rustler's Village,' then I say let's go."

He hugged me to him and kissed the top of my head. He faked fanning his face. "You just made me the happiest man in the world."

"You're so weird!"

"I want to be Amish with you. It says we can live like the Amish. Will you do that with me?"

"You're serious?"

"Yeah! Actually, that sounds fun. I want to see what it's like to be Amish with you."

After we got in the hotel room, Jackson spent half

the night eating my pussy. He did that so well. Actually, he did *everything* very well, but he knew how to make my body do what he wanted it to do. He always seemed so eager to please me and make me feel good. His warm, soft tongue swept over my sex, flicking as he caressed me, teased me, and eventually pleased me. That man drove me crazy in so many ways. He was the most sexually giving man I had ever met. We had never had lazy sex, but for the first time, he fell asleep between my legs.

Poor baby! I thought to myself.

I brushed my hand over his hair as his head rested on my thigh. I startled him awake, and he climbed up the bed and fell beside me, holding me in his arms. Due to the fact that he lived an altogether different life in his sleep, I had no idea if he realized what he was doing or not. I snuggled against him, thinking that at least that way, if he went for a stroll, I would know it, and I could get him back to bed before he got too far. Then, it occurred to me that I could spend the rest of my life planning for his nighttime jaunts and keeping watch over him when he slept. I hoped for the opportunity, actually. I knew I loved him.

As he slept, I kissed the arm he had draped over me and I softly whispered, "I love you, Jackson Montgomery!"

****

When morning came, the sun poured through the light drapes that covered the window. Unfortunately, it came through the window, shining right on the bed. Jackson kicked the blankets off and grumbled.

"It's fucking hot in here!"

I went to the thermostat to see if I could get it to

kick on and cool the room. When the fan kicked on, it felt like instant relief. Jackson sighed and moaned as the air blew across his naked body. I couldn't help myself. I stood there, at the foot of the bed, and I just stared at him as he slept. He had to be the most perfect human being, ever. I snuggled beside him and softly placed kisses on his chest.

"Suck my nipple," his sleepy voice said as he chuckled.

"Are you awake?"

"It's too fucking hot in this room. I'm ready to take an ice bath. I'm dying. I can't sleep with third degree burns from the sun shining in that window. Fucking assholes! I know, now, how an ant feels, getting cooked by a magnifying glass."

"You should've faked it. I wanted to wake you up."

"Mm, sorry! I gotta piss."

"Oh, yeah! That's fucking hot, babe!" I said sarcastically.

"It's not hot, I know, but at least I told you, now."

He wiggled away from me and sat up. His hair was wild, and his eyes were sleepy. I felt so in love with everything about him. He wasn't "sexy" at that moment. However, it was the cutest I had ever seen him.

I reached around him and cupped his manhood in my hand. His sleepy eyes opened wide. He looked over his shoulder at me.

"I've been violated, and it felt awesome!"

He abruptly stood and started for the bathroom. "I'm sorry. I have to do something." He talked to me from the bathroom. "Hey, do you know I don't remember what happened with you last night? But I dreamed you let me fuck you up the ass. Did I dream that?"

"Yes! You know that wasn't real."

"I know. I didn't dream that. I'm setting the stage for what I want to happen."

"It's really hot when you talk to me like that while you're taking a piss. So disgusting." I laughed.

"I wouldn't still be taking a piss if someone didn't wake me up by giving me a fucking hard-on."

I laughed as I sat in the middle of the bed and clutched the sheets to my chest.

"That's not true. I always have a hard-on when I wake up. You can't be held responsible for that one, but I blame you for all the other hard-ons."

I heard the toilet flush, the water turn on and off again a few moments later. After he finished his business, he came around the corner and pointed to his erection. "He wants you to pretend that he's a trampoline park. He wants you to jump on him and bounce up and down for a few days."

He took my breath away. It didn't matter how crazy he wanted to be. I loved him. I curled my fingers at him.

"Come to me."

He crawled up the bed, putting his fists against the mattress on either side of my hips, and he kissed me. I tried to pull him down on top of me. He still wasn't having it. I so desperately wanted to feel the weight of his body on mine, but he slid off me to the side. I pulled away from his kiss in frustration.

"What? What happened?"

"Just forget it."

"No! What?" he demanded and propped his body

up on his elbow as he twirled a strand of my hair around his finger.

"You know what! You don't understand how much that means to me."

He fell backward onto the bed, and he sighed. "Elizabeth!" he growled and closed his eyes.

"If you don't want me to nag you, then just do it. Does it really take that much out of you?"

"Let me run this past you once again. I do know what it means. I understand. It would mean just as much to me, but I'm not ready to be that. I'm not trying to lie to you. I'm not putting on a fucking show. I'm being honest and telling you, that is a sacred thing in my eyes. I haven't earned the right to do that. I know you want that, but I'm not going to play with your fragile, beautiful heart, girl. Don't you understand that?"

"You don't think you're doing that very thing? Maybe you can fuck somebody and just walk away, but I'm already attached to you, you asshole! I want the fucking knight! I don't care about a prince."

He came up off the mattress as though he had suddenly been ejected. His legs straddled my hips and he kissed my lips. His nose brushed across mine. He drew a deep breath and released it as he clenched his eyes shut. He took my hands in his and held them to his chest then he moved them to his lips and kissed them. He swallowed hard and stared into my eyes as his head twitched to the side.

"I want to make you stop. I want to make you turn around and walk away from everything I am. You're going to end up hurting, and I know it's coming," he said.

"Don't you fucking do that to me. You don't get to make the choice of whether you hurt me or not."

"Listen to me. If I were watching you with some other guy like me, do you know what I would tell you? I'd tell you that you deserve so much more than this. I'd tell you he's only after what's between your legs. I'd tell you he's never going to be someone you can take home to your momma. I'd tell you that he has a long line of broken hearts behind him and there's no way he's going to change that now. I'd tell you to forget him. I'd tell you to play him the same way he's playing you. I'd tell you he doesn't want to be what he is, but he's *always* going to be what he is. He'll treat you like gold while you're in his bed, but the second you're not and you want something else from him, he's going turn tail and run.

"He's not a 'lifer,' honey. He's bad news. It's not because of you or anything you're doing wrong. He's just a fucking lost cause. He's good for a fun time, but joint checking accounts and doorknockers with a cute last name and wedding dates… It's just not my style. There were a lot of beautiful women before you. There will be a lot more after you.

"I love you blind in short spurts. I care about you, always, but I am never going to be in love with anyone. If you were smart, you'd bail out. This is a crash and burn kind of operation. It's imminent. It's just a matter of when," he said and put his palm against my cheek.

"If I could change what I am, I'd do it for you. It's not you. Run. Do you hear me? Start cutting ties. Because I'll take that pussy as long as you'll let me."

"You're breaking my heart."

He pursed his lips and nodded. "I know."

Chapter Seventeen

"Don't do it, Jackson. Just stop thinking this is okay. It's not. People fall for you. You can't just keep tearing through women."

"You deserve someone better." He exhaled. "And that's the purest truth I can give you. I love the way you taste. I get off on the sexual energy I get from you. You're the best sex I've ever had, if that helps, but I'm a young child on permanent recess, and I'm sorry about that, but it's the truth. Don't put anything into me. You won't get the same in return."

I sighed. It wasn't the kind of truth I wanted to hear, but I wasn't ready to give up. *If I'm the best he has ever had and he is the best I've ever had, there has to be something to that, right?* I decided I couldn't give up on him. I felt like he was capable of more than he realized, and I wanted to be the difference in his life. I wanted to be the one he couldn't live without. I told myself I would just have to be patient with him. I would corral his heart. I'd just have to do it without him knowing.

I sat up and kissed his lips. "So, what're we doing? Are we going to that village thing?"

"You don't listen," he said as he put his forehead to mine.

He sank his tongue into my mouth. His hand cradled the back of my head as he kissed me. Without words, I swore I heard his body and his soul pleading for me to ignore everything he had said. I swore I could hear him begging me not to cut and run. He lifted his head, and his eyes fixated on mine.

"You want to go do this village thing?" he asked with the sound of pacification in his voice.

"Yes."

****

As we drove to the tourist village, I stared at my Mr. Montgomery, completely enamored with everything about him. It started with his blond, wild, spikey hair, his beautiful blue eyes, and flowed past the knee he drummed his thumb on, all the way to his feet. I had never been this moved by another human being in my life. It took everything I had to sit beside him and not bust out crying just from my emotional investment and my overwhelming adoration of him.

As the soulful, sultry song spilled out of the speakers, he drummed his thumb to the beat. He mouthed the words as his head bobbed. Feeling my stare, he glanced over at me and smiled. He got a pair of sunglasses out of the console and put them on his face. He took my hand in his and the back of my hand became his drum for the moment.

He lip-synched the song as he stared out the windshield at the road, then a smirk moved across his face. He blinked his eyes and turned his head toward me, staring into my eyes behind the darkened lenses of his sunglasses.

"What?" he playfully asked.

"I don't understand."

"Oh, here we go," he said. "What don't you understand?"

"How can everything you do, no matter what that may be, be the sexiest thing I've ever seen in my life? I'm feeling consumed by all that is you." I giggled. "Everything! Even your name is sexy."

He chuckled. "Oh, yeah? I'm glad you think so. It doesn't take a lot of thought to name a kid after the hitchhiking route you were on at the time you got pregnant."

"What? What does that mean?"

"My mom hitchhiked from Jackson, Mississippi to Montgomery, Alabama. She thinks I came to be somewhere on that trip, so there ya go! Jackson Montgomery. Fuckin' beautiful story, huh?"

"But, how did she get to decide that Montgomery would be your last name? What's your middle name?"

"My birth certificate showed Jackson Montgomery Fisher. I legally changed my name, so now I just don't have a middle name. That whole process was a pain in the ass! But, at the time, I had an ax to grind, so I thought it would be worth it."

"An ax to grind?"

"I was a young punk, and I felt like I had a reason to be mad at my mom, so I thought I'd teach her a lesson and shed her last name. Boy, I showed her! Funny thing is it didn't change a damn thing that had happened. It didn't change her or what she does, so the joke was on me in the end. I'm one…big…joke."

I scoffed. "You are *not* a joke, Jackson. You're successful, smart, wild, funny, lovable, and you're a good man. The joke is on her. She's the one that missed out on getting to know you and seeing how amazing you are."

"So, there's no way any of this is making you wet.

Tell me something dirty."

"I don't want to talk about something dirty. I want to talk about you."

"Some other time, 'kay? What do you want to do when we get to this place?"

"Talk about you," I said, wishing I could wrap my heart around him.

He sighed and I quickly found myself on the business end of his tongue…only in a less pleasant way.

"Let me tell you all you need to know. I'm not talking about me, okay? If I wanted therapy, or whatever the hell it is that you're trying to do, I'd find someone that actually knows what the fuck they're doing. Thanks for your concern, but I don't want it. I get what you think you're doing and you're wrong. I am not giving you anything more than what I've promised you. You want a romp in the sheets? I'll make sure you get what you came for, but if you want sunshine, bluebirds, and pink music notes floating over our heads, you're talking to the wrong man."

"I'm sorry. I just like hearing your story. I like knowing about you."

"About me? Okay. I'm currently on my way to take this pretty little pain in my ass to do something fun. I don't like feeling like an asshole. I don't like snapping at people and being short fused, so let's just not dig at my scars, today. Let's just have fun, please?"

"Okay." I smiled. "But, just so you know, I just discovered that not *everything* you do is sexy. When you bite my head off, it's not sexy."

He chuckled. "No. Probably not." He glanced over at me, pressing his lips together, and he humbly nodded. "I'm sorry about that. I am. I just don't see the point in wallowing in that mud puddle. I'm trying to advance myself and make something with this life given to me, regardless of how that story started. I don't like pity and I don't want to hear how blah, blah, blah. I just don't need to relive that shit. It wasn't a happy time. That's why I'm trying to move forward. Okay?"

****

When we arrived at the tourist attraction, the car slowed, and Jackson waited for oncoming traffic to pass so he could turn left into the parking lot of this village thing. He parked Lucy at the end of the parking lot, away from the other cars. I couldn't resist the urge to be a smart ass.

"So, is there a shuttle bus that comes by these parts? This is quite a hike. We'll be exhausted by the time we get up there."

He scoffed with a smirk. He stared into my eyes as he put the car in reverse and started backing out of the stall. Instantly, I felt guilty.

"I'm teasing." I giggled. "Stay here. I'm just picking on you."

"No. You don't want to walk with me? I'll drop you off. I'll walk by myself." He pretended to pout. He drove to the entrance to the village to drop me off so he could go reclaim his parking spot. "Get your smart ass out of my car!" he said. "Remember stranger danger. I'll be back."

I got out of the car and waited for him to park and come across the parking lot to join me. That would be the last time I would need to make fun of him for parking so far away. I missed him every second that I wasn't right beside him. Watching him walk across the parking lot made me want to run to him, jump up, and cling to him for dear life.

He stopped in his tracks across the driveway from me and tilted his head. He rotated his finger, motioning for me to turn around. I smiled and danced myself in a circle, watching him over my shoulder. He shook his head and crossed the traffic lanes to join me. He put his hand across the small of my back, kissing my head as we walked toward the entrance.

"I missed you," he said.

"I think I've got a problem." I smiled as I tucked my body under his arm.

He clicked his tongue against his teeth and ducked his head as his eyes drifted to mine. "Yeah, I know."

When we got inside the park, we wandered, stopping by various handmade craft booths. I picked up a wooden gun that shot rubber bands, and I pointed it at him. Since those things are difficult to aim, of course it hit him in the face. He instantly froze. He closed his eyes as he cocked his head to pass a glare at me. He reached up and scratched his face as his eyes stared into mine.

I laughed, fearing what the devious look on his face equated to.

He lifted his eyebrows as he moved closer to me, pulling my body to his. "You think you're cute? Hmm? You think that's funny? I'll pull your skirt up and fuck you right here, and we'll see how funny it is then."

"Mm! You're sexy as hell."

"So are you." He smiled as he kissed me. "We should get out of here before I figure out how to make that happen."

We meandered through the village. Eventually, we got to "The Land of the Amish." Jackson plunged his hands in his pockets, standing in the shade. He watched what he could see from where we stood.

"Are we going in there? I thought you wanted to be Amish?"

He chuckled. "I was kidding about that. I just thought this place would be fun…different."

"We're going to be Amish. That's what I thought we were doing. We're doing it," I insisted, gently jabbing him in the stomach.

He pulled me to him and interlaced his fingers behind my back. He watched over my shoulder as some guy dragged an old plow through a dirt field. He shook his head.

"They go all out for that little theatrical production."

"Come on, Jackson. Come be Amish with me," I begged as I looped my arms around his waist and took a few steps backward, pulling him with me.

He finally gave in. He rolled his eyes but the smile on his face told me he wasn't as annoyed as he wanted me to believe. I decided he wanted me to make him do this.

As we walked around the little staged community, we saw women sewing clothing, men farming, and building buildings for the little fake community. We walked hand in hand, discussing how difficult it would be to live without modern conveniences. Then, we met Abraham Yoder.

"Hello," he said as he approached. "I'm Abraham Yoder. We are looking for people that might be willing to help us with one of our demos. Would I be able to convince the two of you to come help me out?"

Jackson chuckled and scratched his chin. "I don't

know. We're kind of just looking around."

"It'll be fun," Abraham said, enthusiastically. "It's just a small play."

"A play? Jackson, let's do it."

He glared at me. This time, I did not get the feeling he wanted me to make him do this. There wasn't a smile like before. Abraham stared at his face.

"Yeah, come on, Jackson. It'll be fun," he said as he clasped his hands.

Jackson sighed and shook his head. "Yeah! Okay!"

"Okay, what we're doing is a mock Amish wedding. First of all, you'll both need nice Amish names." He pointed to Jackson. "You are now Jacob Fisher."

"Fisher? Now, there's some irony," he said as he looked at me.

"You," Abraham said as he pointed to me, "will be uh, Mary Yoder. You will be my daughter. Sound good?"

"Jacob Fisher and Mary Yoder." Jackson smirked. "Got it! So, what do we do?"

"You are going to be the bride and groom," Abraham said.

"Oh shit!" Jackson chuckled, rolling his eyes. "Maybe we should just watch."

"It's just for pretend. She won't get half your house or anything," Abraham joked. "Come on. As the men, we have to lead. If you're afraid, she will be afraid. Come on, Jacob."

Jackson glared at me with a sarcastic smirk as he licked his lips, making a smacking sound. "Okay! What do I have to do to get to the wedding night? Are we demonstrating that, too?"

Abraham laughed forgivingly as I slapped Jackson's arm.

"What?" Jackson laughed. "It seems like a fair question, and don't hit me. I can't be part of an abusive marriage."

Abraham led us to a home in the center of the makeshift town, where the wedding was to take place. We learned what it meant to be "published" and how we weren't to attend church service on that day. Instead, I had to make dinner for "Jacob." We were to enjoy dinner alone, then, I had to introduce him to my parents. He had to go around and invite people to attend our wedding. The entire thing was fascinating. Jackson played along, taking his part to the extreme, especially when he got favorable feedback from the audience.

The clothes I had to wear were entirely different from a regular wedding dress. Jackson looked cinched up and uncomfortable in the outfit and bowtie they gave him to wear. My wedding dress had a navy-blue hue, and I had to wear a black bonnet type thing. We fit a week or so into one day, including milking cows on our "wedding day." Then we had this little reception type thing. I had the arduous task of pairing up other potential couples. Jackson didn't care for the fact that if it were a real Amish wedding, we would have had to stay with Abraham on our wedding night. Then, the next day, we would get up and clean house before our honeymoon had to be spent visiting family.

"So, Abraham." Jackson chuckled. "We have to spend the night in your house tonight, right?"

Abraham nodded. "Yes, Jacob."

Jackson chuckled. "I'd just like to apologize, in advance, for the things I'm about to do to your daughter."

The audience laughed and clapped. Abraham blushed and ducked his head. He patted Jackson's shoulder.

"My boy, the Amish don't prevent nature by means of birth control, and you will need little helpers to help you maintain your own home. I respect your eagerness to start a family."

I think Jackson almost choked. He looked at me and turned white as a ghost. He held his finger in the air, shaking his head.

"Oh! Uh-oh on second thought, we'll all be sleeping peacefully this evening," he said.

He looked at me and winked with a confident nod. Abraham raised his hands and began his closing speech for the mock wedding. We all stood after his speech concluded. He addressed Jackson and I as our Amish names one last time before we went to change our clothes again.

"Thank you, Mr. and Mrs. Fisher, for your willingness to play along with us."

When we shed the Amish life, Jackson chuckled and shook his head. He took my hand, and we left the little pretend community. As we walked past the gates, he smiled as he looked down at my face.

"Did you have fun?" I asked.

"I've seen that all before. Did *you* have fun?"

"You've done this before?" I asked, disappointed.

"No. Not here. Not like this. Before my mom went sideways, she had been a nice Amish girl. My grandmother is out in the real Amish land somewhere. I'm the evil creature born to an Amish escapee," he laughed. "When we could sneak in, I got to see all of this in reality. It's pretty crazy, huh? From horse drawn buggies to this," he said as he pointed to himself.

"Do you miss it?"

"Miss what? Hiding? Lying? I never really got to live that life. We weren't supposed to be there, so when we'd sneak in, we couldn't do much more than hide so no one would know we were there."

"Is your aunt Amish?"

"Once upon a time, yes, but she left them to pick up my mother's slack," he said, motioning to himself again.

"So, you were raised Amish?"

"No," he countered. "That life and this one don't mesh so well. Winnie tried to pull the good into my life and put it in my heart. She's got her old-fashioned views and ways. She left because I wasn't welcome in that community. My mother…" He paused and shook his head. "Well, never mind. We all made it through it, though, huh?"

He leaned against a tree, smiling at me. I could see that he was reliving old memories in his head by the distant look in his eyes. He pressed his lips together and shook his head.

"Fisher? What are the odds?"

"About as likely as the odds of you ever getting married for real."

"That wedding seemed sweet and easy. A whole week done in one day. There was no cake tasting stuff. Just quick, easy, done, over, and I don't feel any different."

"So, if you could do like a Justice of the Peace type thing, you'd get married some day?"

"Absolutely not! This sucked! What happened to

'you may kiss the bride?' I only did that whole thing because I thought I would get to kiss you."

I put my fingers inside his pockets, gripping the top, more as a place to rest my hands than anything sexual. I leaned into him, standing on my tiptoes. I pressed my lips to his.

"Better?" I asked.

"Not really," he flatly answered.

He stared into my eyes and cradled my face in his hands as he lowered his mouth to mine. I looped my arms around him, hooking my fingers on his belt loops. He smiled a sweet smile as his lips pressed to mine. Then, as though we were the only two people in the world, his soft tongue gently swept over my lips. His tongue caressed mine, soft and slow, as though he had nothing else to do with his life other than to kiss me.

When our lips parted, he sighed a heavy sigh and pulled me into his embrace. It may have only been temporary, but for that moment, Jackson Montgomery had surrendered. I knew it because I felt it. His touch, his voice…his heart all reflected sweetness.

"Can I take you to bed?" he asked as though it would be the first time.

I felt chills race all over my body. I looked up at his face. He stared down at me, patiently waiting for my answer. The look in his eyes meant everything to me.

He shrugged as though I had asked him to explain. "I just want to hold you for a little bit."

"If it doesn't mean something, don't do this."

He brushed the tendrils of hair away from my eyes, and he softly blinked and looked away. He folded his lower lip over his bottom teeth, and sucked on it, making a squeaky noise. He nodded his head as his eyes returned to mine.

"You're right. That's not fair, is it?"

"I wanted you to say something different just now."

"Considering I've never said anything like that before you, it feels like something kind of big just happened."

"Why can't you just throw out this silly idea that you have to be temporary? Why can't you just let it be what it's going to be?"

"Probably for the same reason you can't let go of the silly idea that I need to be permanent. I know what it's going to be."

"I don't think we need to discuss this anymore. Every time we do, I just end up hating you."

He scoffed. "Yeah? Well, you married me!"

"That's not funny, Jackson."

He smiled and pulled me to him. "I'm sorry. I just wanted to see you smile. Bad timing, maybe?"

"I love you!" I blurted out as I looked up into his eyes.

When I realized what I had said, I swallowed the lump in my throat. I wished I could take the words out of the air and put them back in my mouth. Too late! I had already said it. Even worse, he had already heard it. I had to own it.

He stood, stoic. After a few minutes, he lifted his eyebrows and nodded his head. He nervously brushed my hair away from my eyes, again. It seemed he studied every individual strand. For the first time, he kissed my lips without closing his eyes. A smile crept across his face.

"You are a problem."

I threw my arms around his neck. I feared that I had just scared the shit out of him. I clung to his neck like a silent plea to his heart for him to stay. I couldn't think of any way to take it back. I meant it. I did love him. It just came out of my mouth faster than my brain could think.

He hugged me, burying his face in my hair that had fallen over my shoulder. I heard him draw a deep breath. I couldn't look at his face. I just wanted to hold him to me. If this would scare him away, I wanted to hold him while I could.

His hand gently patted my ass. "You ready to go?"

"I didn't mean to say it out loud." I kept clinging to him, fighting back tears.

He slid his hands under my shirt and put them flat against my back. "You want me to pretend I didn't hear it?" he asked sympathetically.

"I don't know."

"I wanted you to say something different just now," he teased, mocking my previous statement. "I need you to be patient with me. This defining moment doesn't count. I fucked it up. Okay?"

"Okay," I said as a few nervous tears fell. I sniffled.

"Are you getting my shirt wet?" he asked, as he rested his cheek against my head.

"I have no idea what you're talking about."

"Mmmhmm!" he said sarcastically. "Let's go. I've got a song for you."

"A song?"

He gave me a pitiful glance as he dragged his thumb over my cheek, wiping the tears from under my eyes. "Don't do that. I'm just not good at this. Doesn't mean anything. I just suck." He put his hands in his pockets as he looked down at me. "It's a good song. It makes me think of you. You want to hear it?"

"It's good?"

"Come on. Listen to it. You tell me." He held his hand out to hold mine. "There's no shuttle, limo, helicopter, or cab coming for you. Are you okay to walk to the car with me?"

"Be nice to me," I whined.

"Okay!" he said, hugging me to his side as we walked toward the car.

When we got back to Lucy, he dropped my hand and played with the keys in his hands. He pressed the button to unlock the doors. He opened the passenger side door and sat in the seat. He played with the stereo for a few minutes. Then, a smooth song with a jazzy, sultry rhythm started playing.

Jackson stepped out of the car and wrapped his arms around my waist. He moved our bodies to the beat of the music. The sexy song that filtered through the speakers had a jazzy grit to it with gravelly lyrics, but the words touched my heart. The singer sang about how long he had wanted to make love to his love interest. He sang about how much he loved her. Then, he sang about his plans to rock the house off the foundation when he finally did get to make love to her. It fit Jackson's style. It wasn't a poetic and frilly song. It had a sultry rhythm that was great for dancing to, absolute perfection. It gave me hope that maybe I had made it past his cast iron rib cage and somehow snuck into his heart.

As we swayed in the parking lot, he mouthed the words to the song.

"I'm in love with this song," I confessed.

"You like it?"

"It's sexy and beautiful. I love it!"

"Good. Because I think of you every single time I hear it."

"But he sings about that 'L' word," I said.

He nodded his head. "I know exactly what he's singing about."

"You're seriously working on getting laid." I smiled shyly.

"Okay. Just as long as you understand, I'm not just trying to get laid. I'll take that, too, of course, but this song makes me think I've got a problem. I kind of like that problem."

****

When we got back to the hotel, as soon as the door closed, I turned to face Jackson. He could read me. As soon as our eyes met, he nodded and curled his finger at me. I stared into his eyes as I stepped to him. As though magnetically drawn to it, I ran my fingers through his hair. I folded his shirt collar away from his neck and planted soft kisses.

He lifted me off my feet as he hugged me, spinning me, pushing me against the wall. His kiss had more passion in it than it had ever before. He slipped his fingers in between mine and he held our hands over my head. His kiss deepened as he sucked on my lips. He pulled his head back, brushing his tongue over my lips, my mouth desperate to catch it. Then, he plunged it past my lips, sucking every ounce of love I felt for him from my mouth. He released my hands and slid his fingers over my shirt, down to my hips.

I unbuttoned the buttons on his shirt, kissing every part of him that I could reach. His fingers pushed their way under my shirt, the fabric resting on top of his hands and he slid them up my body. He lifted the shirt over my head and tossed it onto a chair in our room. I pulled his shirt off his shoulders and threw it on the chair with mine. He easily unfastened my bra and slipped the straps off my shoulders. When there was no fabric between our upper bodies, he pressed his chest to me as he kissed me again.

I lightly caressed his sides between his ribs and his hips with my fingertips, as I tasted his lips. I pulled at the closure for his jeans opening them and folding them back. He rested his arms on the wall beside my head, caging me in with his body as he stepped out of his shoes. I slid my arms inside his, holding his hands to the wall beside my head as my lips skimmed over his neck and along his collarbone. I softly bit his shoulder. He exhaled a heavy sigh, and I felt him submitting to me. I pushed my palms against his chest and pushed him toward the bed. I pushed his jeans over his hips and down his legs before I pushed him to sit on the edge of the bed. Then, I slid my skirt and my panties off my body and mounted him. I tangled my fingers in his hair while grinding my pussy against his cock. Our eyes were locked as I moved my body against his.

I reached between us and cupped his balls in my hands, lowering my mouth to cover his as I massaged him. I stroked his shaft for a few moments before I slid my hand up his cock and guided the tip inside my pussy. I hovered my body over him, teasing him before I lowered myself to take him deeper inside me. I slowly bobbed my hips up and down. Then, I quickly lowered myself on his shaft. He drew a deep breath and held it for a few seconds before he released it. I lifted off of him and slowly slid my body down his shaft, again. I reached behind me and massaged his balls as I moved up and down on him. His hands played with my tits while he took them in his mouth, sucking and flicking my erect nipples with his tongue before gently pinching them between his teeth.

He started sliding his hips back and forth under me, as I slid up and down on him. As if someone had pulled his chain, he gripped my hips and pushed my body down on him as he lifted up. He exhaled and clenched his eyes shut. He pushed my hips away as he pushed upward into me. He fell back on the bed.

"Hold on," he said as he lifted his hips and moved our bodies closer to the center of the bed.

"Show off." I giggled.

"I don't want to buck you off," he said sweetly.

"You're not bucking me. I'm doing this to you this time."

He laid back and let me bounce up and down on him for a little bit. His fingers gripped my thighs as I rode him. He moved one of his hands to my clit and massaged it as my body moved. Then, in a sudden sweep, he sat up, hooked his arm behind my back, pulling me down on top of him. He hugged me to his chest as his hips thrust up and into me, driving his cock deeper, harder and faster.

"It feels so good when you do that."

"Harder and faster?"

"Mm! Sounds fun." I smiled.

It surprised me when he slapped his hands on my ass and pulled my body down on him as he pumped his hips upward. He clenched his teeth and breathed through his mouth as he pumped his hips as fast as he could. Then, he drove his cock to the side, and I about lost my mind.

"Ohh, yeah! Oh, whatever you're doing…" I didn't have to finish my statement. He already knew. He always knew! Something about how he moved his cock made me feel the need to move my body up and down on him.

"There ya go." He smiled, encouraging me.

I bounced up and down on him as fast as I could as he moved his cock into me at a slight angle.

"Oh, yeah! Mm, baby."

He held my hands to his chest, as we both got ready to come. I rocked my hips as I moved up and down. We were both out of breath, our bodies soaked in sweat, giving each other everything we had.

"Ooo, baby!" I moaned.

I quit moving my body, trying to hold him in the position as my pussy started pounding against his cock. My head dropped back, and I rocked my hips as my orgasm exploded. Jackson held my hips, driving his cock deeper inside me.

"Mm," he moaned, approvingly.

I felt his cock erupting inside me, more intense than ever before. Every time he came, it felt almost as good as my own orgasm. I sat on him, dancing my hips side to side as he drove his erection deeper into me as his orgasm finished. He gripped my thighs, again, as though he wanted me to stop moving. He exhaled and his body began relaxing.

I relaxed and let my body settled down on top of his. As he exhaled, I gently sucked on his lower lip before I pressed my lips to his.

"Hey, baby."

"Hey, yourself."

There was a look in his eyes. He looked as though he had been satisfied in an entirely different way. I felt overrun with emotion and hope that I had finally made it to his heart. His eyes seemed to be giving him away. I kissed his lips a bunch of times, really fast. He laughed at my playfulness. Then, I sat up, lifting my body off of him so we wouldn't die from heat exhaustion. I fanned him, swishing my hands through the air. He took my hands in his, stretching our arms to the side, against the mattress, pulling my body back down on top of him.

"I love you," he said as he stared into my eyes and kissed my lips.

I gasped as my eyes went blurry from the tears flooding in. I blinked them out of my eyes and stared into his face. "I love *you*!"

He softly kissed me again. "I really do."

I tried to flip our bodies over and pull him on top of me. It still wasn't something he would give me. He turned to his side, but that man would not lie on top of me for anything. I found myself wondering if it meant that much, or if it had become the point, but I wanted that one thing from him, now, more than ever.

We spent the rest of the weekend getting tangled in sheets and each other. I believed with every beat of my heart that we had turned that corner. Finally, I felt like I had him. Everything about the sex felt completely different. It felt like two souls dancing outside of our physical bodies, while our physical bodies made love to each other. It was bliss!

Then, Monday came in like a lion, and we got back to business again. Jackson raced around the office, trying to get word to all of the guys to meet him at

Bob's jobsite by nine. He gathered drawings and various permit papers. He had Lisa pull reports for the financial side of Bob's job. The more paper she put in front of Jackson, the more he decided he would just take anything Bob threw out at him. It was funny how seeing the numbers in black and white changed what he could tolerate from the crankpot.

As he prepared to leave the office, Jackson stood in front of my desk. "Okay, I'll most likely be out the rest of the day. If you need me, call my phone. If I don't answer just text, or whatever."

I nodded as I smiled up at him. I softly whispered, "I love you."

"Don't," he barked, scrunching his nose. "I can't get into having to say that all the time. I have to go. Call me if you need me."

Like a tornado, he blew through and off he went. The emptiness he left when the door closed behind him amplified with each passing second. I hoped we had not just taken a step back. I hoped that his thoughts were so preoccupied with appeasing Bob that he didn't realize how cold he had been. I didn't want to be a distraction for him. I didn't want to hurt him or his business in any way, so I'd be content to take the backseat for the moment.

A few hours later when he called to check in, he said he was going to his house to change his clothes. He had started to see part of the problem Bob had with the guys, and it irritated him that Bob was right. He planned to help his guys with the physical labor side of things. He was hyper about dovetails, trench something or the other, and a bunch of other things. He seemed excited, talking too fast for me to keep up. The point is he seemed happy, and he chose to see the whole thing as something fun, rather than the battle that it truly was. He actually looked forward to getting out of the office.

"Bob's right. I do need to be out, checking on these projects a lot more frequently. I trust my guys. I don't want to be the dickface boss that hovers. Though, I think I'm just going to have to tighten my belt and stop worrying about friends. I have to get my head in this game."

"Is there a point you're trying to make for my benefit?"

"Elizabeth, I know this is going to be the last thing you want to hear. But I really do think about things other than just you all the time. I have a business to run. I'm talking in terms of the whole, rather than just how it relates to *you*."

"I'm sorry. You just kinda bit my head off when you left. It made me a little insecure," I softly spoke into the phone.

"You have to separate the two worlds."

"Right! Until you come through the office and need a place to stuff your cock. Then, we blend the two worlds."

"Fuck this! I didn't call to fight with you. I'm not in the mood today. I'm trying to save our ass because I almost handed it over. Why? Because I got my priorities confused. We have to separate the two worlds for now."

"I can't promise that I can do that. I can't turn it off and on like you do. It's too hard for me to see you and know how I feel about you."

"Is it harder than writing a resignation letter?"

"Are you threatening me?"

"Nope! I'm saying if you can't do it, then there are other ways to separate the two worlds."

"Okay! Don't worry about it. I'll figure it out. Thanks." I slammed the receiver down in the cradle as I growled in frustration.

Half of the office peeked around their partitions to peek at me. I rolled my eyes and stormed to the women's room. I slipped into one of the stalls and closed the door. I leaned back against the wall, crossed my arms across my chest and put my hands on my shoulders, trying to comfort myself.

Was I wrong to get excited about our relationship taking that next step? I let myself believe it would be different this time, but now, I had become a selection in a list of entertainment options. I just wanted to know he would still say it. Right or wrong, my feelings were hurt, and he wasn't the only one that wasn't in the mood. I wasn't in the mood to do anything other than cry, pout, and snivel. Maybe it seemed needy, but my grip on his heart seemed to be very slippery. I felt that if I couldn't keep a constant grip on it, I'd lose it, forever. Now, my options were really thin, if he wasn't even going to be in the office with me.

I went back in the office and gathered my things. I just wanted to go home. He could fire me or do whatever else made him feel like a man. A man? Right! That "man" could go fuck himself, for all I cared.

Have you ever been fed up, burned out, pissed off, and a slight bit emotional? It's not always the most rational bag of emotions.

I decided I would teach him a lesson. I made up my mind that I wasn't taking any more of his calls. In fact, I would just ignore him altogether.

Chapter Eighteen

When I got back to my apartment, I took my iPod out and found the song Jackson had played for me. After it downloaded, I let it play, and I cried, wallowing in a giant vat of self-pity. I sat on the floor, because for some reason, that always makes a good tantrum seem even more pathetic.

As my pity party got going, my phone rang. Naturally, it had to be the source of my pain. It also happened to be the only person who could make my troubles any better. It was the person who most likely *wouldn't* make it better. Even though I had said I wasn't going to answer his calls, trust me when I say I scrambled to get to hear his voice.

"Yes?" I answered.

"Miss Elizabeth, I need a favor. Can you go to the file room and pull that Daily Wilgood file?"

"I'm not in the office."

"Oh! Late lunch?"

"I'm taking the rest of the day off," I boldly announced.

"Okay, then never mind. I'll call Lisa instead."

I sighed. "Yeah! Let Lisa take care of you."

"Guess I have no choice this time, huh?"

"Why is this hurting me so much? Why does this feel like every step we took this last weekend never happened?"

"I'm at work, Elizabeth. I do not have time for the bullshit today."

"Oh! Okay! Bullshit? Got it!"

"Do you have any idea how much I want this to stop?"

"Want what to stop?"

"I want the petty, childish, immature bullshit to stop."

"I just wanted you to tell me you love me."

"Now, you're going to dictate what I say?"

"Just be honest, Jackson. Tell me. Did you mean it?"

"I've told you before. Sometimes I mean it. Sometimes, I remember this kind of shit, and I get myself straight. Then, I'm the knight with no desire to be the prince anymore."

"So, what does that mean? You're taking it back?"

"Would I say it today? Oh, honey, no! Not today. Today, I feel like throwing you all around the bed. I want to tie you down and make you take whatever I want to do to you. Today, I want to see my red handprint all over your ass. Today, I want to hurt you in the best ways. I want down and dirty, hard and heavy. Today, I don't feel like I love anything but fucking you. The more you fight with me, the more I feel it. You wanna piss me off? Go right ahead."

I sighed. "So, we're back to this?"

"I've told you…"

"I know! You've already pushed me as far away as you can. You've done your part. Now I'm crying and that's my own fault, but stop telling me it's all about me when, in truth, this has nothing to do with me. *You* want to fuck. *You* want to talk about fucking. *You* want to finger me or fuck me in front of everyone. *You* want a whore."

"So fucking what?" he growled. "Don't act like it puts you out. Does it not work out for you? I don't ask you for anything."

"You ask me to do a whole hell of a lot more than you realize."

"I told you how I see things from the word go. I never misled you. I can't help the fantasies that you build up in your head. You know what? I don't give a shit. I don't care enough to fight this out with you."

"Tell me why you want to rip my heart out?"

"Because your heart was never supposed to be in this in the first place, Elizabeth."

I heard him take a deep breath. "Just stop, okay? Get it through your head that I want to fuck you. You're hotter than hell, but that's where it ends."

"Okay! Got it!"

"Oh, don't do that mind trick, psychotic shit on me."

"No! I mean it."

"Okay, then," he said, sounding completely confused.

"Am I going to see you this evening?"

"I told you the mood I'm in today. Do you want to deal with that?"

"Sure! How can I help you? Would you like me to spread my legs wide enough for a beer bottle, your cock, or a fucking whale's dick? What do you want to see this time, Mr. Montgomery? What lewd thing can I do for you, today?" I asked sarcastically. "Maybe you could nail me right out in the middle of Main Street and Downtown Avenue? Would that be enough witnesses to make you blow your load?"

"Yep! I think I'm probably done with the phone for now. Let me know if you want to try again later."

"Jackson, this has to stop. I can't do this, anymore. This is over."

He chuckled. "Now, now, honey. You don't want to play that card until it's all you've got left. I'll cut you loose and never look back."

"I'll cut *you* loose. Apparently, I'm the one that's been holding this together all this time, anyway."

"I've spent my entire life getting cut loose. This is nothing new to me. You'll miss me first. I guaran-damn-tee you that."

"Guess we'll find out."

"That's what you want to do?"

"Yes. I can't do this." I swallowed hard. "But I need time to find another job."

"Do whatever you need to do. Let me know when I need to bring someone else in to fill your position."

"This isn't hurting you at all?"

"No. I told you a long time ago that this is where we've been headed all along."

"You told me you loved me."

"You said it first."

"How can you tell me you love me and then a day later just let this go?"

"Hey! You told me you loved me, too. Now, you're pulling the plug. I can't do anything about that."

"Yes, you could. If you wanted to save this, you could."

"Save what, Elizabeth? Save myself from having to start looking for the next skirt on my floor? I don't mind that game. That's easy! I tried to tell you. You're hot, but you're just another pussy to play with."

"You're breaking my heart."

"It would've happened sooner or later. Sorry! So, you're coming to the office tomorrow, right? No offense, but I either need you to be there, or I need you to just resign so I can do what I need to do. I've got a business to run."

"Oh, I'll be there," I sighed.

It killed my pride to have to need him for anything, but the thought of someone else taking my place hurt. I had already had time to process what it would mean if I left my job. What else could I do? I felt myself dying inside. Maybe more than fear of not being able to pay my bills, I wanted to believe he wouldn't let me go. I hoped he would come after me, chasing me down, and begging me to love him. What if I had said something I couldn't take back? What if he didn't care? What if our relationship never truly mattered to him? Maybe I needed to be there to see it for myself.

My heart hurt. I felt it burning in my chest. I knew what he had said all along, but we had been building a life together. He wasn't making it *just* about sex. I wanted it to be something that he never intended it to be. Nothing that matters comes easy. We all know that, but what if it meant nothing to him?

I sat on my couch and kept staring at my phone. Nothing! Were we fighting? Were we really over? Why did I feel like I was the only one giving this an ounce of thought?

Chapter Nineteen

After a night of crying my eyes out, and my heart heaving itself up in my throat about thirty thousand times, I gave up the ghost of getting sleep. I got up and got in the shower, determined to be heart-stopping gorgeous for work. I'd strut right past Mr. Montgomery, make him wish, and I'd rip his heart right out of his chest.

Once I had put the finishing touches on my look, I went out the door on my way to act the biggest part of my life—a frigid bitch that wanted nothing more than a paycheck from the sexiest man I had ever met in my life. I felt good. I could do this. I tossed my bouncy, curled hair over my shoulder and set out to own his world.

When I got to the office, my heart stopped. The sight of him crippled me. My plan was already failing, but something seemed funny. He and Dena were both racing around the office as though the IRS wanted to audit us.

Jackson looked like he had been there all night. He had his sleeves rolled up, his two top buttons on his shirt were undone, and he had his tie loosened around his neck. His hair looked a mess. If it weren't for the fact that Dena looked so "fresh," I would've questioned what the two of them had been doing. In the back of my mind, I knew Dena's marriage meant more to her than that. I was on such unstable ground, I felt suspicious of the silliest things. I watched Jackson race around for a few more minutes.

"Good morning," I said, trying to get his attention.

He didn't even look at me. "Good morning," he returned as he kept himself busy.

"What are you doing?"

"I should have worked on this proposal this last weekend. I spaced it. Now, they're coming here at nine, and I've got half of the shit to show them," he grumbled and sighed. "Fuck!"

"How can I help you?" I asked sincerely, skipping my own issues for the moment.

He looked at me with a desperate, pleading look in his eyes. "Can you please make the conference room look like we're ready for this? Folders, notepads, uh…pens. We need some sort of donuts, bagels, coffee…shit!"

"Okay! This is okay. Calm down. We can do this. I'll take care of the conference room. You go lock yourself in your office and make that the best proposal you've ever written."

He breathed a sigh of relief and hugged me to him. "Thank you!"

I pushed away from him. "It'll be okay. Go! Do that thing you do."

He took his keys out of his pocket and handed them and the company credit card from his wallet to me.

"We've only got two and a half hours. This time, I really screwed us."

"Stop bitching about it. Go make it happen, Mr. Montgomery."

When his eyes locked on mine, I could see apology and regret in them. I looked away, feeling the tears coming. I looked at the keys in my hand and extended my arm.

"What is this? I have my own car."

"You wreck it, and I'll snap your pretty, little neck." He faked a smile. "I don't want to worry about mileage. Just take Lucy, and then it won't matter."

I left the office and started racing to get things done. If I didn't beat the morning rush to the bagel shop, we wouldn't get much in terms of selection. I did want to help Jackson. I don't know why, but my heart was in it. Maybe it gave me a much-needed distraction.

As I made my way down the street, I kept having visions of Jackson stroking his cock as he drove down the freeway the Friday before. I thought about him holding my hand as I sat in the seat beside him. I recalled how he put his fingers inside me as he navigated this beautiful car. The way he danced with me when he played that song replayed in my mind. Then, out of nowhere, I felt the car jolt, and the back end spun around. It took me a second. Then, the reality hit me like a freight train.

"Oh, my God! Oh, no! Oh, no!" I wailed.

I got out of the car and saw a car to my right with a demolished front end and steam rising from the hood. A blonde lady who looked as stunned as I felt, peered out her windshield at me. As the world started flowing in slow motion, I covered my mouth and fought for my breath. I slowly made my way to the back end of Jackson's car. The passenger side was smashed to oblivion. My knees fell out from under me. I hit the ground and started crying.

The woman got out of her car, apologizing and babbling about what happened from her side. I couldn't care less. No matter what she said, it wouldn't change the fact that she had smashed into Jackson's car. I could've used a break and couldn't understand why fate hated me so much.

After a little time had passed, the cops showed up and ushered the woman and I to the shoulder of the road. As we stood there, telling our versions of the story, the cop asked for all the important information for Lucy. I went to the car, and I couldn't find the insurance card, only the registration.

"This isn't my car," I explained to the officer. "It's my boss's car, and he's going to kill me."

"It is a nice car, but you weren't at fault, and if he had any worries about it, he shouldn't be letting his employees drive it," he said, attempting to comfort me. "I hate to be the bearer of bad news, but you're going have to call him and ask him for the insurance information."

"He's going to kill me. He's trying to get a proposal done before nine. This is going to completely destroy his concentration. He's going to kill me," I cried.

Without missing a beat, the cop said, "Well, then I'll arrest him for murder. Go ahead and give him a call while I go talk to this lady. I'll be right back with you."

Realizing there was no other way around it, I got my phone, and I called Jackson. As soon as I heard his voice, I believed I had flatlined right there in the street. I couldn't feel any part of my existence. I had an out of body, out of reality, experience.

"Hey!" he answered.

I tried to respond but no sound would come out.

"Hello?" he pressed.

I swallowed hard and faintly muttered. "You're going to kill me."

"No bagels?"

"I'm so sorry, Jackson." I cried.

"Uh, what? What's…what? What's wrong?"

"There has been an accident. The cop needs your insurance card."

"Not funny! What's up?"

"I'm serious. I'm so, so sorry." I sobbed.

His nurturing tone came through the phone. "Okay. Are you okay?"

"I'm so sorry! I feel so bad. It wasn't my fault. This lady slammed into me. I'm so, so sorry. Please don't be mad. I didn't do it on purpose."

"Elizabeth! Are you okay?"

"No! You're going to be so pissed. It's pretty bad."

"Where are you?"

"Uh, Main Street and Downtown Avenue," I answered as I looked around.

"Are you fucking with me?"

"No. This cop needs your insurance information. I can't find it."

"Main Street and Downtown Avenue?" he asked for confirmation.

"Yes!"

"All right," he said. "Let me see if Dena can drive me over there."

"I need to give the cop your insurance information. Where do I find that?"

"In my wallet," he scoffed. "I'll be there in just a few minutes."

When Dena's car pulled up, Jackson got out, and she kept going, making a U-turn to go back toward the office. His jaw dropped and his fingers arched over his lips, covering his mouth. His eyes darted around, taking in everything to do with the accident scene. The cop saw him standing there and approached him.

"Are you Mr. Montgomery?" the cop asked.

"Uh, yeah!" Jackson answered as he fished his wallet out of his pocket.

He handed the laminated insurance card to the officer. The cop thanked him and started scribbling on his clipboard. Jackson sauntered toward the car. He bent his knees, squatting down to look at the damage as he covered his mouth with his hand, dragging his fingers down his face.

I walked over toward him. "I'm so sorry."

He stood up and plunged his hands into his pockets, refusing to look at me. He sighed and shrugged his shoulders. Finally, he glanced at me. I'll never forget how the expression on his face made me feel. I busted into tears.

"It's not going to fix a damn thing to stand here, crying. You can quit that."

I covered my face with my hands, crying into them. He reached for my arm, pulling me toward him. He hugged his arms around me.

"Hey! It's just a fucking car," he said. "It's repairable. Are *you* okay?"

"I don't blame you if you hate me. You really can snap my neck," I bawled.

He chuckled and rolled his eyes. "No. No, I can't. There are too many witnesses in this intersection… Remember?" He tilted his head and arched his eyebrows.

All of a sudden, I remembered the conversation from the day before. We had been so mean and nasty to each other. Ironically, this intersection happened to be the one I had sarcastically mentioned in my jab at him. I gasped as it all flooded back in.

"I'm so sorry." I exhaled, clenching my eyes shut.

He shook his head. "Just take it back. Take it all back."

I stared into his eyes. "I can't."

He wiped tears from under my eyes as he sighed. He pressed his lips together and slowly blinked as he bobbed his head. "Okay." He hugged me tighter, kissing the top of my head before he let me go. "I have to go see what I need to do to clear all this up. I'll be back."

I watched him as he strolled over toward the other driver. As he talked to her and the cop, I fought back tears. I wanted him to tell me he wasn't giving me the option of ending our relationship. I wanted him to want it bad enough to fight for it. Instead, he stared at me as though I were naked. I have no idea what the cop told him, but Jackson wasn't listening. He fucked me, just by looking at me. He had to be a mental patient. I had just wrecked his car, and he wanted to start some seductive game. Honestly, it drove me crazy. I wanted to fuck him and for things to be okay for us, again. However, I knew giving in now would be the equivalent of taking three steps backward.

During the crash, the back-passenger side wheel was folded up under the car, leaving it immobile. Jackson's insurance covered him for a rental car in these cases. The cop offered to take him to the rental car company. Instead, Jackson wanted to hurry to get back to the office to meet with the people he wasn't prepared to meet with at nine o'clock. Thankfully, the officer gave us a lift back.

As we rode in the back of the cop car, Jackson stared into my eyes with that devious smirk plastered all over his face. Apparently, thoughts of sex fit every circumstance as far as he saw things. His fingers brushed over mine as his tongue slid over his lower lip.

"I just had a fun thought," he said. "How much do you think it would take to get this cop to look the other way for about twenty minutes? I'd throw in extra if he'd turn the lights on for us."

I giggled. "You're such a sick pervert!"

"Psht! Tell me you weren't thinking the same thing." He playfully winked.

"What are we going to do about that proposal?"

"I'm not getting married. That's just the way it is," he snapped.

"Uh, what? I meant your nine o'clock."

"Oh! Well, I guess I'm going to get my dick knocked in the dirt. Shit happens! But the day I started this, I had one client. I've gotten this far, starting with that one. If I end up with one, I know what I did to get here, so I'll just do it again." He shrugged.

"I never meant for any of this to happen. I'm sorry."

He sighed. "I'll get through this meeting. It's not like it should take that long, considering." He chuckled as he flipped his hands palm side up. "Then, I'll go cry like a little bitch about all the things going incredibly fucking wrong in my life. After that, I'll be right back at it, so don't worry about it."

"I'm sorry for being part of all of those things that are going wrong."

"If you mean that, I know what would help the situation." He smiled a flirty smile. "Seriously, you need to quit apologizing. I'm a grown man. Everything that's happening is happening because I steered that ship. I don't blame you. It all started with me," he said as he pointed to his chest.

"What would it take to make you like this all the time? When you decide to be a dick, you're cruel and evil. You break my heart. Then, you're like this, and it makes me feel like I'm a bitch."

He drew a deep breath and leaned his head back. He lifted his hips off the seat and adjusted his jeans. He pinched his lips between his thumb and forefinger as he stared out the window. Instead of pushing him for an answer, I let a soft giggle escape my throat.

"So, you thought I wanted to con you out of a marriage proposal?"

"I'm an easy target today. I think I had just fallen asleep when it occurred to me that I had this meeting at nine o'clock. I raced to the office, before *someone* wrecked my car, and I started working."

"I'm so sorry. You know how much I love that car. I'm dying inside. Poor Lucy!"

"I'm so pissed off at you right now." He chuckled as he shook his head.

"Well, thankfully, you don't seem that pissed off."

"Oh, I am. You have no idea what's happening behind the scenes. A few weeks ago, it might've been worth fighting about, but I found something else that kind of gets my goat."

"Do I even want to know?"

He abruptly changed the subject. "How much do you think I'd have to pay that cop? I'm serious. Twenty minutes, and we'll have a lifetime of getting to brag about having sex in the back of a cop car," he muttered. "That would be hot!"

"I'm not having sex with you in the back of this car," I protested.

"Okay, then where? Where do you want me?"

"Stop!" I said. "I don't just want your cock. I want your heart, too."

He leaned closer to me as he winked and whispered, "I'm too tired to fight you. You can have anything you want right now."

"That was so fucking sexy…until you added the 'right now' part."

"Lizzy, you can't do this freeze out thing. I'm not going to make it if you do. I'm going to die from a multi-sperm pile up. It's going to be bad. You can't just cut a man off like that. I'm used to unloading a few times a day. That's your fault, so the least you can do is not cut me off. I need you. I need you to cooperate."

I wasn't giving in. In this moment, I had the upper hand. If I gave in now, I'd give that up forever.

The cop car pulled up in front of the building. The officer got out and opened the back door for us. Jackson shook the cop's hand and thanked him for his help. The officer gave him a card with phone numbers and the relevant address. He offered to help if Jackson had any further questions. Then, the officer smiled at me and wished me a better day.

When we got back upstairs, Jackson raced back to his office. There were no bagels, no donuts, no coffee, nothing. He didn't have a proposal. He had half of a brainstorming session that occurred at some point during the night, through the early morning hours.

Just before nine o'clock, Dena came through the door with breakfast sandwiches and breakfast burritos. She had an urn with coffee in it, along with various creamers and sweeteners. We both raced trying to beat the arrival of our guests. Jackson came out of his office and saw us fluttering around the room. He stepped to the door, leaning against the doorjamb.

"I have no idea how or why, but thank you both."

"Dena made it happen, Mr. Montgomery," I smiled.

"She helped," Dena said, pointing to me.

"If I can pull this off, we're celebrating, ladies." He nodded.

****

At nine o'clock, Jackson Montgomery walked into the conference room and tossed the half-written proposal on the table in front of the group. He scoffed incredulously as he looked at the client.

"I thought it over," he said with a cool, carefree shrug. "I'll write a formal proposal all day long, if that's what you want, but the bottom line is you know what you need to have done. You know what your budget is. I know it's people like you that keep a roof over my head, so we're here to do whatever it is that you need. I can write you a proposal. I could do that in my sleep, but that's me telling you what you need. I'd rather sit here with you and listen to you tell me what you want me to do. You're the client. I'm going to do whatever you need done. If you want the job done right, then, obviously it all needs to be done. I don't like writing addendums. It's a waste of my time, but more importantly, it's a waste of *your* time. Just tell me, right off the bat, what you want me to do. Do you want me to do it all? Or, am I stepping on toes? Because if it's just Montgomery Construction, we'll get it done, regardless of what this paper says," he said, knocking a knuckle on the half-written proposal.

It had to be the biggest bunch of bullshit he'd ever spouted in his life, but he sold it. He basically wrote the proposal as he sat in the meeting with that group. They found his method to be innovative and considerate of their needs and their views, as the client. When the meeting drew to a close and the door opened, he walked out, laughing and shaking hands with every person that had just witnessed his quick thinking.

After the men left, Jackson walked over and handed the stack of papers to me.

"I have to go get a car. Then, I need to go stomp around in the field and visit some job sites. Can I leave this with you? John needs to write up the contract for this…whatever *this is*," he smirked as he shook his head. He looked so tired.

"Are you okay?"

He leaned down, resting his elbows on my desk. "My cock wants to talk to you."

"No! It doesn't want to *talk*. It wants to use me."

"Same thing." He shrugged and rolled his eyes. "Last chance. I'm going, and I'm probably not coming back today."

I smiled at him. "Has anything changed for you?"

"You're so mean!" He grumbled as he turned away from me. "I've got my phone if anybody needs me. Freeze outs suck, by the way."

The phone rang just a few moments after he

walked out of the office. I went through the greeting. "Montgomery Construction, this is Elizabeth."

"Did I tell you how beautiful you look today?"

"No. I'm a mess now, thanks to all the tears."

"Look up, toward the elevators."

I looked up and out the glass lobby doors. He stood there by the elevators with the phone to his head. His eyes were all about the seduction as he stared back at me. When he did that, it weakened all the strength I had. Even when he had me pissed off and fighting mad, he still got to me. Compared to past relationships, that was a new experience.

"I want to make you come. Don't tell me you don't want it."

"I want quite a bit," I said sarcastically.

"You're fucking gorgeous. Come with me. Let's go rattle some walls."

"You're killing me."

"I'll make up for it. Stand up, get your things, and come rock this elevator with me."

"You're being so unfair," I said as I stared out at him, propping my chin on my palm.

"I know," he agreed. "I'm a real bastard, but I want you."

"I want you, too, but I can't. Not if I can't have you like I want you."

"Okay. What? Tell me what that means? What would I have to do?" he asked as he leaned against the wall beside the elevator doors.

"I've already told you."

"Tell me again."

"I don't just want to be an easy fuck. I don't want to be a shameful, dark secret. I don't want to be your whore."

"Is it wrong that I get off on the thought of *you* being *my* whore? That's a sexy thought to me. I get off on the thought of you being my dinner date, too. Oh, and my travel companion, my best friend, my dance partner, my Amish mock bride, my slumber buddy, my lunch friend… Where have you been, girl? You're getting what you want, but what? I'm not delivering it all the only way you're willing to accept it? If I'm doing something wrong, then I deserve whatever punishment comes for it, but just make sure I'm actually guilty of what you want to put on me. You don't want to be my whore? Okay! Who would you rather I look to for that?"

"I want to feel your body on mine."

"It's *that* important to you?"

"Yes! As silly as it may seem to you, yes, it is."

"Okay!" He nodded. Then, he sighed a heavy sigh, pushed off the wall and pressed the elevator call button. "I have to get out in the field. I told the crews I would be there to help them today."

"Do you want to take my car?"

"I would, but I have no idea when I'll be back, or if I'm even coming back today. I'm tired. That's only going to get worse after I jack off in the elevator, thanks to you."

"You're a big boy, and I've seen how well you *handle* that."

"Take it back. Please, just take it back. Let's pretend none of this ever happened."

"Not this time. I'm really sorry."

"C'mon, Elizabeth. You're starting to worry me." He flirted.

"You're only worried because you don't have time to line up your next lay. You've got a busy day. What will you do with that hard-on if I don't cave in? Right? I just can't."

"No. I'm not worried about getting laid. I'm worried about self-fulfilling prophecies. I'm not ready for you to run out on me."

"That's sweet," I said as tears welled in my eyes.

"Good. I need to win some points somewhere along the way." He disappeared behind the elevator doors. "Lizzy," he sighed, "I think I've got a problem."

"Uh-huh, and what would that be?"

"The same problem I've had for what? Four, maybe five months now."

"Oh! That *problem* seems to pass pretty quickly for you. Just hang in there."

"No. It doesn't *pass*. It just gets to be a bigger and bigger problem."

"Get to your job sites." I sniffled. "If you need anything, let us know."

"Did I let it go too far this time?"

"I can't talk about this right now. I need to separate the two worlds, remember? I need to do my job."

He clicked his tongue against his teeth. "Oh, yeah! I asked for that one, didn't I?"

"Have a good day, Mr. Montgomery."

"Yep! You too."

Somehow, after that phone call, I felt strong and powerful. I had resisted the most tempting human being I had ever known. I felt strong for almost three whole hours. It was nothing more than a passing victory, however. Shortly after that victory passed, I crouched in the bathroom stall, bawling my eyes out. I wanted to call him. My stomach tied in knots, afraid he would make good on his word and have me replaced quick as a blink. It would be tough to find out he had started fucking someone else. The mental images that my cruel mind served were killing me. It would be hard to see him with someone else, lunching, or her random stops by the office to visit him. Ugh! I couldn't win! This situation seemed impossible.

After I washed my face and dried my eyes, I freshened up my makeup and went back to work. I decided, as pathetic as it seemed, to go sit in his office so I could feel close to him. I had a mission. I bolted through the office, practically dashing for his door.

When I rounded the corner, I instantly felt furious. Lisa sat in his chair with her dirty feet up on his desk, using his phone. She sat, leaned back and cozy, in his chair as she listened to the person on the other end of the line. When she realized I stood there, staring with my mouth gaping open, she smiled and flailed her fingers in a greeting. She covered the receiver.

"I just needed to make a quick personal call. I didn't want everyone to hear." She hinted, wanting me to remove myself.

"Ugh!" I fumed as I turned and stormed out of Jackson's office.

I immediately called Jackson. I have no idea why, but apparently, this had become something I felt passionate about. I listened to the phone ring a couple of times before I heard his breathy voice come through the phone.

"Hello?"

"Hey! Can you tell me why Lisa thinks it's okay to use your office?"

"What? I don't know," he grunted, again, breathily. "But I don't care as long as she's not moving anything on the left side of the desk."

"What are you doing?"

"Working. Constructing shit," he announced with a hint of pride.

"I just don't think she should be in your office just because you're not here."

"Then, tell her to get out. I don't care either way."

"Well, it pisses me off."

"I can't be everywhere. Is this something the two of you can work out?"

"I just wanted you to know. If you don't care, then I don't guess I should either."

"That's the spirit."

"Okay! Fine. Just wanted you to know."

"Thank you. It's not a problem. Don't worry about it."

I couldn't help it. To me, it was as though Lisa would change the one way I had to feel close to him. I didn't want her to change anything. I didn't want her using his phone. I didn't want her mouth anywhere near where Jackson's mouth had been. I didn't want her body wiggling around in the same chair his body had wiggled around in. It felt like a personal violation, to me. I was livid. Realizing he couldn't be more indifferent if he tried, I would just have to accept that Lisa was using his office, regardless of how I felt about it.

That would be the last time I talked to Jackson for the rest of the day. I hated that. I missed him. I hated being a cry baby, but I wanted the opportunity to spar with him. I wanted to keep this alive. I was afraid that if

I didn't keep it in his face, he would get strong enough to be without me and just give up on us.

The next morning, I went through every effort to be pretty, again. I didn't know if I would see Jackson or not, but just in case, I wanted to be the kind of beautiful he couldn't resist.

The day passed with no Mr. Montgomery. It drove me the bad kind of crazy. He didn't call or come into the office. I got to the point I felt like I had died inside.

Finally, the next day, around three o'clock in the afternoon, he finally came through the office. He looked a mess. He was dirty and sweaty. He carried a hardhat in one hand and some sort of architectural drawings in the other. He stopped and talked to John for a brief little bit, asking about one of the contracts. Then, he started for his office, and Lisa called him over to her desk. He stepped inside her cubicle, sitting in the chair at her desk.

After about ten minutes, he stood up, and I could hear the two of them laughing over something as he left her workstation. I felt so jealous. I sat in my own boiling pot of envy and bitterness. I tried to look busy as he approached my desk.

"Good afternoon," he tossed out. "When you get a minute, can I get you to help me with something?"

"Right now?"

"Do you have a minute right now?" he asked with his cocky smirk.

"Of course, Mr. Montgomery."

I stood and followed him into his office. I had butterflies. Internally, I reminded to myself to stand my ground. I wasn't going to give in, no matter how thick he piled on the seduction.

I followed him through his door. I reached for the doorknob. I didn't want to seem eager.

"Do you want me to close this?" I asked.

He flashed me his devious smile and bit his lower lip. "If you close that door, you know what's coming."

"I'll just leave it open, then."

He rolled his eyes as he stared off to the side. "Do you have any idea what's happening to me right now?"

"What did you need me to help you with?"

"You're still mad at me, I take it?" he asked as his eyes locked on mine.

"I'm not mad. I'm hurt. There's a difference. Now, what did you need me to do?"

"If I call you tonight, will you talk to me? We could go to dinner. I'll take you anywhere you want to go."

He strolled toward me with that stupid, sexy smile. He reached his hand out, tangling his fingers in my shirt, trying to pull me closer to him. I looked up into his eyes, and I was sunk. Then, I remembered what my goal had become.

"It's not going to work this time." I swallowed hard. "I'm serious. I can't be your plaything."

He turned away and sat on the edge of his desk, folding his arms across his chest. He crossed his legs in front of him and sighed. He pursed his lips and shrugged.

"Why not?"

"What…did you need my help with?"

He held his hand out toward the door. "I haven't seen you for a couple of days. I don't know. I kind of thought maybe you would be as happy to see me as I am to see you. I want to make you wet. I want to make you come. Mm! I want to taste you."

"I am happy to see you."

"E-liz-a-beth," he softly sang with a smirk. "I've missed you like you can't believe." He reached his hand out and curled his fingers. "I want to kiss you. Just a kiss."

I couldn't look at him or I would give in. He looked so damn cute with his hair a mess like that. Actually, everything about him had my heart pounding.

Be strong, Elizabeth!

"What do you need me to help you with?" I asked, again.

"I'm not having fun," he admitted. "I'm here. I'm trying. What do you want?"

"You're trying to get laid. You're not trying to get me. You're trying to get a piece of ass."

"If that were all I wanted, why would I bother with you? I could go find a piece of ass anywhere. I'm here. I'm chasing after you."

"Because I'm convenient. You've already had me. You don't have to apply yourself if I give in. You think I'll roll over. I'm sorry. I just don't see where you trying to get in my pants is of any significance, but hey! A man's gotta do what a man's gotta do, right?"

"Am I wasting my time? Are you done with this, completely? As in you have no interest in seeing what we could be?"

"I don't want it like it's been. I want something deeper, with meaning."

"So, you're done?"

I scoffed. "If you can't see me as anything other than a fuck, yeah. I'm done."

"Really?" he asked, shaking his head. He pursed

his lips and shrugged, again. "That's all I needed."

My internal body dried up, shriveled, and crumbled into a hollow shell. I turned and walked out of his office, terrified that maybe this really had been all he needed. Maybe I would be fired. Maybe he was about to make my life hell. But, even worse, maybe I would have to accept that he would never be what I wanted him to be or what I needed him to be.

For the next few days, with every passing second, I missed him more and more. I wouldn't see him, but I would see stacks of papers with sticky notes attached, piled on my desk every morning. *"Pls. fax to* blah, blah, blah,*" "For file," "Review for John,"* or any other task he needed me to complete.

Then, the phone rang, and I answered.

"Montgomery Construction, this is Elizabeth."

"Hey!"

"Hello?" I sang, happy to hear his voice.

"I just wanted to let you know that I'm not going out in the field today. If anyone calls looking for me, can you forward the call to my cell, please?"

"Sure! Is everything okay?"

"I had a death in my family. I need to take care of some personal business today, so if you could just forward any calls…"

"What happened? Are you okay?"

"We do what we have to do, right?"

"Your mom?"

"Winnie," he bluntly answered. "I gotta go."

As though I knew her personally, I felt like a knife had sliced through my soul. Tears flooded my eyes. I had a lump in my throat, and I couldn't breathe. I knew how much he loved her.

"I'm so sorry. Can I do anything?"

"Just forward calls, please."

"I meant for you. Can I do anything for you?"

"No," he said. "Thanks anyway."

"I miss you," I muttered. "I want to help you."

"Okay, I'll keep that in mind. I appreciate it, Elizabeth. I have to go."

Just like that, the line went dead. There were a couple of calls that came in, and I forwarded them to Jackson's cell phone, just as he had asked. After a couple of hours passed, I took my phone from my purse. I called to make sure the calls were going through, and to see if he needed anything from me. My call went to voicemail. I left a sympathetic, concerned, supportive message, and asked him to call me when he got a chance. After another hour or so, I sent him a text.

—How are you doing?—

His reply:*—Can you put the Ireland and the Crendale files on my desk, please? Thanks!—*

—Sure. Are you okay?—

—Just need to work. I'll be in tonight for those files. If you can, leave them on my desk.—

—Okay. Will you call me when you get a minute?—

—Is everything okay?—

—I just want to talk to you. I'd give you a hug if you were here.—

—Thanks, Elizabeth. Have a good day.—

I wanted to go to him and comfort him. I wanted to hold him in my arms. I felt my heart breaking. I knew this had to be killing him. I wanted to make it better, yet that wasn't possible this time.

Chapter Twenty

I didn't know the location of Jackson's house. Otherwise, I would've gone there to see him. It didn't seem appropriate to search for directions, since he had never taken me there. Since I didn't know how to get to him, I decided to stick around the office until he came in for the files that he had asked me to put on his desk.

Finally, around seven-thirty, he came rambling through the door. He wore jeans, a T-shirt, and a baseball cap. He looked like he hadn't shaved all week. He looked broken and hollow. He moved through, heading toward his office. When he realized I was sitting at my desk, he stopped in his tracks, pausing for a second with a confused look before he continued his stride.

"Hey! What are you still doing here?" he asked.

"Waiting for you."

He put his hands on his hips. "Hmm. Okay. Well, I'm here now, so you can go ahead and go."

"Are you okay?"

He sucked on his lips. His answer came honest, without any pretense. "No. Not really."

I stood and walked around my desk to hug him. He quickly ducked past me to go into his office. As he passed, my arms hung in the air, in an effort to embrace him. I followed him as he sat in his chair behind his desk.

"Can I hold you?" I asked.

"Uh, I have a lot to do, but if you had a hug, I'd probably take a quick one of those." He pressed his lips together and nodded.

I went to him, pulling his head to my stomach. He leaned over the side of his chair, loosely hugging his arms around me. He patted my back and started to pull away.

"I can't, Lizzy. I'm going to start crying like a bitch," he said.

"So! I don't care," I said, refusing to release his head.

After a few seconds, he turned his chair to face me, and hugged both of his arms around my waist. He put his ear to my stomach as I cradled his head in my arms. He lifted his head and removed his cap before putting his head back against my abdomen. He let me hold him for a few minutes as I stroked his hair. I felt the wetness from his tears seeping through my shirt and dripping on my arm. His body trembled as he let his emotions go. After a few minutes, he cleared his throat and turned away from me, trying to keep me from seeing him. He reached for his cap and put it on his head, rounding the bill, dragging the heel of his hand under his eyes.

He sighed. "Okay. I'm good. Thanks. I have to get this done."

"I'll help you. What are we doing?"

"I don't even know. Uh… Bill Ireland's account is past due. Crendale needs a materials list for what's left to buy to finish the project. They also want to know what's already been bought."

"So, I'll call Ireland tomorrow. I'll ask Lisa to get all of the information Crendale needs. You need to sleep."

"I don't want to be home. I can do this. It'll be good for me. Go home. I've got this." He faked a smile.

"You're faking that smile. You shouldn't have to fake anything," I teased. "Come to my apartment. You can sleep there. I'll sleep on the couch, and you can have my bed."

He chuckled. "You're cute. I'm not kicking you out of your bed, but thank you."

"I'm not taking no for an answer. Just make it easier on yourself and let's go."

"I appreciate what you're trying to do. I really do, but I won't be able to sleep."

"What happened? How did she die?"

"I don't know. Something with her heart. I left to come in here. At some point, she called for an ambulance, but she passed before they could get to her." His voice cracked. "Dammit, huh?"

"I'm sorry! I know you loved her. I'm sure she knew that, too."

"Now, what do I do? Ya know? She's not there when I go… I don't want to talk about it. I just need to work."

"You just need to sleep. You look exhausted."

"I am. I don't sleep. I don't want sympathy. I just want to do this for now. I'll be okay. Go home," he urged with a smile.

"Come with me."

He stared at my face for a second before he let a sigh escape. He seemed too tired to argue with me. I could see it. I was winning.

"To your place?"

"Let's go! You can sleep and try this all again

tomorrow."

"Okay."

He dropped his head back on his chair as though it were too heavy for him to hold up. He slid his hand down into his pocket and took his keys out. He stood and nodded. As we walked out of the office, Jackson flipped light switches, shutting them off behind us.

When we stepped out of the building, I heard a familiar chirp. To my surprise, Lucy sat in a parking stall on the other side of the parking lot from where I had parked. I pointed and smiled.

"She's back!"

"Yep," he nodded. "So, I'll follow you, since I have no idea where we're going."

"Okay."

I kept watching over him as he walked farther away from me. I didn't care if I hated myself later. He needed me now. I had won a small victory, at least in this moment.

When we parked outside my apartment, I got out of my car and waited. Jackson sat in his seat with his head back against the headrest. I walked over to the driver's side door and opened it. I held my hand out, but he didn't take it. He just sat there. I knelt down beside him.

"Are you coming?"

He sighed a heavy sigh. "What are we doing?" he asked as though we were planning an outing.

"We're going to go sleep."

"In there?" he asked, raising his hand, pointing to my apartment building.

"Yes. Is that okay?"

"You tell me. That's *your* home."

"Get out of the car. Let's go sleep."

He kicked his legs out and stared into my eyes. "I can't get dirty with you tonight."

"I didn't bring you here to get dirty. I brought you here so you can sleep. You need to sleep." I brushed my fingers over his cheeks.

My heart melted. My wild, crazy lover with a heart of stone had become more vulnerable than I had ever seen him. He looked so pitiful and sleepy that I just wanted to hold him and protect him from the world.

Jackson got out of the car, pressing the button to lock it. He followed me to my apartment. After I unlocked the door, he followed me inside. He smiled as he looked around.

"This place feels like you."

"What does that mean?"

"Everything about this apartment feels like your personality. It's soft, pretty, sweet. It's nice. It's comfortable."

"Think you can sleep here?"

"Thank you," he said as he smiled down at me. "I appreciate this. I don't want to be at home. Winnie's not there, and I don't want to remember that."

I hugged him, pulling his head down to my shoulder. For just a little bit, he let me be his strength. For just a little bit, he let me *love* him.

"Come on. I'll show you where the sweet dreams happen." I smiled.

I took his hand and led him to my bedroom. I pointed to my bed with my billowy bedding and fluffy pillows. He looked at the bed and looked back at me.

"How do you find your way out of there every day? It looks like you brought the clouds right out of the sky. Fit for an angel." He smiled and winked.

He stepped to the edge and sat down, falling back into the bed. He sighed, interlacing his fingers across his waist. I wanted to fall beside him and cuddle him. I just didn't get a feeling from him that he wanted that.

"Okay, you make yourself at home. The bathroom is over there," I said, pointing to a door across from the bedroom door. "I'm going to let you sleep. If you need me, I'll be…watching television…or something."

He groaned, sounding discontent. He folded his arm over his eyes as his otherwise lifeless body lay on my bed. I pulled the door shut, flipping the light switch as I left the man of my dreams in my room.

I changed into my comfortable clothes and got a bottle of water out of the refrigerator. I made my way to the sofa, picking up the remote. I flipped through a few channels before I settled into some "made for TV" movie, the kind that has a predictable ending from the start, but somewhere along the line, it draws you in, and you can't quit watching.

About an hour and a half had passed. I felt relaxed, lying on the couch when I saw movement out of the corner of my eye. This looming, shadowy figure came stumbling through the darkness. It startled me until I remembered Jackson's sleepwalking habit. He walked over to the coffee table, kicking at it. He bent his knees, dropping to the floor in front of the sofa.

"Jackson, wake up. Let's get you back to bed," I whispered, shaking the body on the floor in front of me. "Come on. You're sleepwalking."

"No, I'm not. I just wanted to be close to you," he said.

"Get off the floor. I'll sit up. You can lie up here."

"No." He breathed, reaching up, looping his arm

around me and pulling me to the floor with him. "We can both lie down here."

He hugged my body to his, holding me on top of him. He tried to be playful, but at the same time, he seemed broken and reminded me of a man who wanted something but had no idea what.

"Why the floor?"

"Because you weren't coming to bed."

"Did you want me to?"

"Mmmhmm." He hummed his answer, closing his eyes. "I could sleep by myself anywhere. You told me to come here. I want to sleep with you." His eyes opened, and he looked at me. "Sleep. I promise. Just sleep."

I giggled, lowering my head, planting a soft kiss on his chest. He pulled my body further up his, as he swallowed hard and stared into my eyes. He lifted his head to kiss my lips.

"Okay! Maybe I want to kiss you first, and then sleep."

He held my head in his hands as he kissed my lips. His tongue gently dipped into my mouth. I wasn't fighting him. Not tonight. Maybe never. I felt like my life had been restored, just from his kiss.

His eyes locked on mine, and he muttered, "I've missed you."

"I missed you, too."

"Do you want to come lie on your cloud with me? It's comfortable, and it smells pretty." He smiled.

"My bed smells pretty?"

"Your bed smells like you. It smells unbelievable." He smiled, raising his eyebrows.

He looked so sleepy. I sat up, my legs straddling

his hips. "Come on. Let's go to bed."

I stood up and held my hand out to him. He only took it after he stood, refusing my attempt to let me help him up off the floor. I pressed the power button on the remote to turn the television off, leaving the apartment dark other than the soft honey glow of the streetlights flooding in from outside. We started down the hall to my bedroom. He pulled back on my hand, pulling me into him. He pushed me up against the wall.

I could see our reflection in the mirror in the powder room. The light through the window in my bedroom cast our shadows on the wall beside us. In the mirror, his silhouette kissed my neck. I saw everything his shadow did to mine and loved the way the reality of it felt. It was like art. Mr. Montgomery had it mastered when it came to painting a sexy scene. Yeah! He was exactly like art.

"I think you're going to be upset with me," he said. "I'm thinking I'm going to break that promise about just sleeping.

"Oh really?" I giggled, wrapping my arms around his neck.

His breath rushed over my skin as his lips pressed to mine. "I want to make love to you."

His tongue slid across my lips before he covered my mouth with his. Our tongues danced together before he pressed his into my mouth. His hands moved down my ribcage to my hips as he sucked on my lips. My breath hitched in my chest, and I swallowed the lump in my throat. He held his body against mine as he stared into my eyes.

"I love you so much."

I smiled. "Mm, I love you, too."

I wanted it to be more than just the emotional drain of a weak moment. I wanted to believe him, so I did. I hugged my arms tighter around his neck and pulled his mouth to mine. Loving a man like Jackson Montgomery was not for the weak. It was as up and down as his hips when we had sex. He drove me insane, and sometimes, in the good ways, but tonight, I wasn't pushing anything. He looked pathetically broken, and he needed me.

His fingers traced over my arms with his soft feather touch. His warm lips skimmed over my shoulder, and then as though he could no longer contain himself, his body fell against mine and pinned me to the wall. He slowly started grinding his hips against me.

"Grrr!" he softly growled as he looked down at me, squinting his eyes.

His touch softened again as though he struggled, fighting an internal battle, fucking versus making love. He took control of the bad boy and, whatever deal he had sold within himself, it became enough to quell his internal wild man. Instead of ripping my laundry off my body, he gently removed each piece. Eventually, he held my naked body in his arms, sending his soft kisses, like fluttering caresses all over my shoulders, neck, and chest.

We kissed, swayed, and twirled down the hallway to my bedroom. I knew his body. I had it memorized in my mental pictures that replayed over and over in my head. My fingers knew the way he felt by heart. His toned and defined muscles were some of the sexiest things about him, but when I started taking his clothes off him, it felt different. He wore that week, or week and a half, of physical labor very well. I bit my lip and smiled up at him.

"I almost thought you were the wrong man," I said.

"The wrong man?"

"Under your clothes, you look a little different than the last time I saw you naked. You've always been the sexiest man I've ever seen, but this?" I smiled shyly as my fingers raked down his chest and his stomach. "Mm, Mr. Montgomery!"

He stared at my face, smiling, as my eyes studied his body. When my eyes drifted up and locked on his, he pressed his lips to mine. I slid my hands from his abdomen over his hips and to his sexy ass. I massaged his butt with both of my hands as I pulled him closer to me. I fell backward on my bed, trying to pull him on top of me. He fell on his side beside me.

"Still not that, huh?" I asked. By this point, it had become comical, but he decided to avoid that conversation altogether.

"I missed you," he repeated.

He slid his arm under my head and traced the tip of his nose over my jaw to my neck.

His lips touched me. Then his tongue gently flicked at my neck. He gripped my thigh and pulled it up to his hip. His hand moved over my body and between us. Every nerve in my body danced under his feather-soft touch as his fingers caressed my sex. The more he touched me, the silkier my skin became. He sucked on my lower lip as he put his finger inside me. I felt his hand against my pussy as he shoved his finger in deeper.

He exhaled, forcing all of the air out of his lungs as his finger slowly moved in and out. He pushed his finger deep inside me and moved it back and forth. He slid his left arm under my head, hugging his arm around me as his kiss became more passionate, and his breath became heavier. He took his finger out and guided his cock, slowly penetrating me. As he entered me, my body stretched around him, remembering what it was like, accommodating his size. The way he felt going in had become one of the best feelings ever. He drew a deep breath as he pushed in deeper.

"Oh, baby! You will never understand how good you feel to me," he whispered.

"Mmm…" I hummed as I kissed his lips, raking my fingers up and down his back.

He moved his hips slow, but he pushed his cock in deep every time he drove into me. I pushed him onto his back, and I sat on him. He sat up, sucking on my hard nipples as he pushed his hips upward. I could feel his heart and soul with every thrust. He fell back on the bed, sliding his fingers into mine and pulling my body down onto his. He held me as he drove his hips upward, into me. He took his time, and I could feel the love in every move he made. I put my hands on his chest, raising up, pushing my pussy down on him. I moved my body with his. We moved soft and slow.

"You're so beautiful," he said as he stared at my face.

He interlaced his fingers in mine and held them to his chest. I used the leverage to move with him. I pressed down on him as he pressed up.

"Mm…" he hummed and put my hand to his mouth, kissing my fingers.

The steady rhythm got me closer. Being able to be that close to him in every way had become something different from any time before. He rocked his hips up a couple more times, and I could feel my pussy tightening around his cock. He gripped my face in his hands, staring into my eyes as my orgasm erupted.

"I love you."

"I love you, too!"

I felt the tingly, fiery sensation as my pussy started tightening and squeezing. He moaned his approval as I came. He pressed into me, pressing his cock deep inside me. I felt that familiar thumping, throbbing sensation. He held his breath as he pumped his seed into me. I squeezed his hands as my body experienced complete euphoria. As my orgasm finished, I smiled at the amazing man beneath me. He exhaled and turned his head away from me as he finished. When I felt his body relax under me, I lowered my body on top of his. He wrapped his arms around me, kissing me before his head fell back onto the bed. I saw tears falling from both of his eyes, an apparent emotional release. I kissed them away, but I didn't say anything. I put my palms on either side of his face and kissed him.

"Don't give up on me, Lizzy," his soft voice pleaded.

"I love you too much to give up on you."

He sighed and hugged my body to him. He didn't take his cock out of me until it softened enough to find its own way out. When it slipped out, he chuckled.

"It's a cold, cruel world out here. Let me back in," he said.

I kissed him, giggling. "Anytime you want, you can be inside."

"Right now, can I just sleep with you?"

I raked my fingers through his hair. "Let's sleep!"

Chapter Twenty-One

After we went to sleep, I felt Jackson fighting to pull his arm out from under me. I lifted my head, and he sat up on the side of the bed. I watched him as he tried to find his feet.

"Where are you going?" I asked.

He mumbled a few words, then I understood him to say, "…pick up this mess."

I hugged my arm around his neck. "You're dreaming. You don't have to go anywhere. Lie with me. Don't leave me."

I pulled on him, trying to get him to lie back down. At first, there seemed to be some resistance. Then, he quit fighting and cuddled up to me again. He sighed as he settled back in. I wondered what it must be like for him, to never get to rest. Then, I found myself wondering how many times he had been productive in his sleep. I wondered how many times he had accomplished tasks, waking up to discover his "to-do" list had mysteriously gotten shorter. I wondered how many times Winnie had spent sleepless nights chasing Jackson all over the house, trying to get him to stay in bed. I didn't care if it meant I would never sleep another night in my life, I would gladly take over keeping watch over him.

The next morning, I got ready for work, and I kept looking at the love of my life, sleeping peacefully in my bed. I had let him sleep as late as I could. I brushed my fingers over his back.

“Good morning.”

He groaned. “Not yet,” he protested. “Just a few more minutes.”

“Do you have anywhere to be today?”

He just remained quiet for a second, laying on his stomach with his face buried in the pillow. Then, he sighed and lifted his upper body, turning his head, in an effort to see me. His hand grabbed my thigh.

“Oh, you’re really here,” he chuckled. “I feared it had only been another dream.”

He dropped his head back down on the pillow.

I repeated the question. “Do you have to be anywhere today?”

“I have to go work,” he said. “Bob will be looking for me. I have to go see Ireland’s job today, too.”

“You have to get up. I have to get to work before I’m late. My boss doesn’t need that.”

“No. Come back to bed. I’ll deal with your boss. He’d understand if it’s for a good reason.”

I giggled as I leaned down to kiss his cheek. “Really? Would he understand if someone else came in late because they were having morning sex?”

He chuckled. “Don’t tell anyone, but yes! That’s a damn good reason to be late.” He rolled over onto his back and moved to the edge of the bed, hanging his head over the side. “Come stand right here,” he said pointing where he wanted me.

“Get your ass up!” I giggled.

“No. I have to do something to you real quick,” he insisted, pulling my leg.

The thought of him doing what he wanted to do

instantly turned me on. I could feel my pussy swelling. I stepped to the top of his head and smiled down at him.

"Right here?" I flirted.

"You need to take these off," he said, reaching under my skirt, looping his finger in the crotch of my panties.

As soon as I had pushed the lacy fabric off my hips, he pulled me to him, putting his head under my skirt and shoving his head between my legs. He pulled one of my knees, putting it on his shoulder. I felt his breath rushing over my skin as he started licking and flicking his tongue against my clit. I could feel the stubble on his face as his mouth moved over me. There was something insanely hot about that sensation. I had missed him so much. I had missed what he made me feel. I had missed what he did with his mouth. As I stared at his naked body, his cock swollen and hard, I wanted to make it even more fun.

"I want to taste you, too."

His tongue swirled in circles, teasing my pussy, making me ache.

I couldn't reach him without breaking his neck, so I tried to pull away from him. He grumbled and I felt his teeth gently clamp down on me as though he were punishing me for moving away. He started sucking on my clit and flicking it with his tongue. I wanted him to fill me. I wanted to feel his cock driving into me as he pumped in and out.

He pushed my knee off his shoulder and took his head out from under my skirt. His face had a shimmer from what he had been doing. He quickly sprang up in the bed.

"Where's your toy box?"

"Toy box?"

"Vibrators. Dildos," he chuckled. "I don't know. Whatever you play with."

"Um…" I hesitated.

"You *have* to have something. C'mon! I want to play with you."

I pointed to the drawer in my nightstand. "Don't make fun of me."

I sat on the side of my bed, watching in embarrassment as he opened the drawer and started laughing. "Holy shit! Sorry I asked. Just tell me they're all named after me."

I giggled. "Of course!"

He pulled one of the six-inch dildos out and turned toward me, biting his lip. "Now, you're gonna get it!"

He pushed my legs apart, staring down at my glistening sex. He hummed a throaty, groan of approval. He moved the dildo over my pussy, gently slapping it against my clit, his eyes shifting to mine. His sexy, devious smile spread across his face. He watched my face as he slapped it against me a little harder. He moved the toy and lowered his mouth on me, instantly licking and sucking my throbbing, engorged sex. As his mouth sucked me, his tongue flicked against my clit. Then, he sank the toy inside me.

I exhaled through my mouth as he sucked on me harder.

He pulled the dildo back and pressed it in again. He started pumping his hand back and forth as quickly as he could. It wasn't as good as his cock, but it felt good the way he fucked me with it as he ate my pussy.

"Ooo!" I moaned.

His hand reached up, grabbing my tit, pinching my

nipple between his fingers. He rolled it between his fingers as he squeezed it, sending a tingle all the way down between my legs. He reached up and moved my hips, encouraging me to grind against his mouth.

"I'm gonna come." I breathed as I arched my back and drove my fingers through my hair.

He pumped the dildo into me, faster and harder as my pussy started pulsing. My orgasm kept getting more intense. My response had gotten a little louder, which only seemed to encourage him to do more. Finally, my body became sensitive to his touch, and I flinched, pulling my anatomy away from his mouth. He withdrew the toy and tossed it to the bed beside me.

"Fuck! Turn over."

I flipped over on my stomach, and he reached around my waist, lifting my hips in the air, dragging me closer to him. He slammed his thick cock deep into me. He thrust in and out a few times. He slapped my ass, rubbing the sting, then slapping me again.

"Oh, yeah!" he groaned through his clenched teeth.

He slapped my ass again and rammed his cock into me again. I felt him throbbing hard, deep inside me. He slapped my ass a couple of more times as he came. I flinched from the sting the last time.

He wrapped his arms around my waist and quickly pounded his cock in and out of me again. He pushed so hard and so fast that I felt my orgasm building again. He slammed into me so hard that his balls slapped against my clit. Fuck! Getting dirty with him felt amazing.

"Oh, fuck. Mm! Fuck, yes…" he growled.

He had lost interest in being quiet. He didn't care that I wasn't being real quiet, either. The concern he had previously had for my neighbors was gone now. He slammed into me so hard, that my bed banged into the wall.

"I'm going to come," I said. "Fuck me, baby! Oh, yes!"

"You want to get fucked?" he groaned.

He tangled his hand in my hair, pulling as he slammed his body against mine. He slapped my ass again, and the sting sent my body reeling. My pussy tightened and loosened against him as he pounded me. He could be so rough. I loved it when he played like this. It was fucking hotter than hell.

"Mm… Oh fuck yeah," he blasted.

I had no doubt my neighbors were hearing everything. He pounded me so hard I worried we would end up in my neighbor's bedroom. It felt so fucking good. He let out a throaty growl, as I felt his cock throbbing inside me, again. I reached between my legs and grabbed his balls. He pulled me into him as he thrust forward. After his body calmed, he rested his body on me and gently bit at my shoulder. He massaged my ass as he ebbed his cock out of me. I sat, facing him.

"Good morning," he chuckled. "Holy shit! Today is going to be a great day."

I giggled. "Yep! I'm going to get in trouble. My boss is going to be all over my ass for being late."

"I already worked out my anger about you being late." He smiled.

"You seem so much happier this morning."

"That's because of you." He smiled and kissed my lips. "You make me feel kind of funny."

"You make me feel kind of funny, too."

"Promise?" he asked as he pressed his lips to mine, again.

"You're the one that told me you could tell when I'm faking."

He chuckled. "No, no! I'm not talking about sex. Is this a temporary thing? You and me. Is this pity? Or are you really with me?"

"Temporary? Do you still want this to be temporary?"

"Yes." He nodded as he smirked. "I do. I want what we are now to be very temporary."

"Okay! Let's not talk about it. I was really looking forward to having a good day."

He smiled his devious, ornery smile. "I'm going to marry you one of these days," he blurted out. "So, I want this…what we are right now…to be temporary. I told you I have a problem. I think I want to be your *lifer*."

"Uh… What!?"

"Okay! That's enough. You're going to be really late. People are going to get suspicious," he teased as he kissed my forehead. "I love you, but you gotta go."

I couldn't breathe. My head felt fuzzy. I blinked and closed my gaping mouth.

"Did you really just say that?"

"No. I'm not ready. Don't freak out, just yet. I'm still trying to deal with all of this with Winnie. I need a little time, but I know that I love you. I'm sorry I hurt you. I wanted to say it, that day. I really did. I was just being a dick. Once again, the joke was on me."

"Mr. Montgomery, if you take all of this back and leave me sitting there, cry—"

"Elizabeth, my love, you're late. I need to borrow

your shower. I need to get over to see Bob. If you want to leave me your keys, I'll lock up and bring the keys to you later."

"Um, there's a spare set hanging on a clip on the fridge. You can just take those…if you want."

"Okay! Go! You're making me late." He winked.

As I drove to work, it occurred to me that I had sort of, almost gotten engaged. Not really, but almost. I pretended it was real. I pretended he wouldn't take it back when his next mood swing came rushing through. I pretended that my daddy would walk me down the aisle and give me away to Jackson Montgomery as my sister, Dena and Jan cheered me on. Maybe I would let Lisa be a bride's maid, too! Bitch! Maybe then she'd get the message that *Jackson Montgomery is taken.*

I walked into the office with an extra spring in my step. I looked around, and all of a sudden, I saw the office differently. I saw it as my future husband's empire. I saw it as his legacy. I felt more determined than ever to do the best job I could do. It was a strange sense of pride. The man I loved provided jobs for all of these people. I actually pretended that after I took his name, it *would* be my name on that building, too. Now, I wanted to give one hundred and ten percent. Then, reality came crashing in and it was ugly…and then, maybe not.

I held my orange juice from the café downstairs as I strolled to my desk. Jan magically appeared out of nowhere, following me to my workspace. She ate a frozen yogurt as she planted her butt on the corner of my desk. She had a funny smirk on her face. She shoveled a bite of yogurt into her mouth, trying to talk around the frozen bite on her tongue.

"Sho, I got a quession for ya." She smiled, scandalously.

"Oh, no. Now what?" I asked, sipping my juice through the straw.

She swallowed the bite and giggled. "Dena and I were talking. What do you think Mr. Montgomery is like in bed?"

I choked, spewing orange juice over anything within ten feet of me. I coughed and hacked as Jan laughed hysterically. She kept trying to shush me, not wanting everyone to tune in to our conversation.

I felt like I had orange juice coming out of every orifice in my head, and she worried about me being too loud. She shoved tissues at me and took another bite of her yogurt. As she tried to patiently wait for me to collect myself, Dena came strolling over.

"Did you let her in on it?" Dena asked.

Jan shook her head and started laughing. "Not yet. She just started spouting orange juice all over the place like a damn water sprinkler or something."

"Okay," Dena whispered looking over her shoulders to insure no one was listening. "We're going to send Lisa to find out what Mr. Montgomery is like in bed. She has this massive crush on him, and we want to know. Jan thinks he's probably a dead lay because she says he's too hot to be good at sex, but me? I think he's such a good person that he's got to be good. He's got this big heart. I would imagine he's probably soft and sweet. I think he's probably one of those tender lovers. So, we're sending Lisa to find out. So, you wanna wager a guess? Lisa will tell us."

"Mm-hmm!" I hummed, certain I looked like a deer in headlights. "I see."

Dena smiled. "I don't think Mr. Montgomery would tell her no. I don't think he would hurt anyone like that. Even if it's only for one date, Lisa thinks she can get him on the first date. That should be long enough to find out what he's like."

Jan cackled. "After they have sex, we can tell him that we instigated this whole thing. Maybe we'll get a raise for helping him get laid. So, pony up, Lizzy."

"Um, I really think this is a bad idea."

"We've already thought about the fact that we'll have to work in the office with them both, and that Lisa will probably end up crying. She's so dramatic about every fucking thing," Jan said. "But I really want to know, so what do you say? Do you think he's good in bed, or not so much?"

"I-I-I th-think he would be a little perturbed that he's paying us all while we're standing here, talking about what he's like in bed," I stuttered.

"It's just for fun," Jan said. "I, personally, don't think any good-looking man is good in bed. They don't have to be. Women are more forgiving and overlook that sort of thing. He'll still line them up, but Dena thinks he's probably some kind of *superhero*. A man is a man is a man. Even Mr. Montgomery."

Dena felt the need to defend herself. "He's been to my house. He's spent time with my family. He's a good guy. If Lisa can pull it off, I know he'll be sweet, attentive, and tender to her."

It seemed so unfair! I offered nothing. I tried to act unaffected by their little game, but inside, I was seething. I wanted to tell them to go away and mind their own business. I wanted to tell them neither of them could possibly imagine what Jackson

Montgomery was like in bed.

John came to join the conversation. He had no clue what the current discussion pertained to. He just sort of "happened" at the wrong time. He asked what we were talking about. I didn't answer, then Jan found a roundabout way to include him.

"John, do you think Mr. Montgomery ever goes on a date?"

John scoffed. "What?"

"He just does so much for us. We want to do something nice for him…maybe set him up with someone," Jan said.

"Uh, I wouldn't do that. His girlfriend might not appreciate that a whole lot."

Dena turned toward him, gasping in surprise. "He has a girlfriend? Since when?"

"Yeah! Since when?" I questioned.

"I don't know, but he told me about taking her somewhere… Some Jewish wedding something… I don't know."

"Amish?" I asked.

"Yep!" John responded, pointing a finger gun at me. "That's it. Amish."

"He told you he took his *girlfriend* to do that?"

"Yeah! We were talking about our weekends one time, and he said something about him and his girlfriend going to some Amish wedding or some shit. But anyway, I know for a fact he has a girlfriend."

The chatter continued around me. I was too blown away to participate in the conversation. Girlfriend? He referred to me as his "girlfriend?" He talked about me to people? He told John about our mock wedding? I couldn't quit smiling. I snapped back to reality when the three around my desk started to disperse.

Jan leaned over and whispered, “In case you missed it, all bets are off. Lisa’s going to be so crushed. No one knew Mr. Montgomery had a girlfriend. Did you know?”

I just smiled and shrugged. “Did you know I have a boyfriend? Some people just have a way of keeping their personal affairs personal.”

John called over his shoulder, “Shh! He’s coming!”

That conversation couldn’t end fast enough. It made me smile to have him back in the office. I just felt happy to be alive. He called me his “girlfriend.” That felt like a major step.

Jackson Montgomery strolled through the door, and I swore I heard angels singing. That beautiful man made my heart quiver and my pussy wet. They couldn’t possibly imagine—Dena and Jan. They would never know what the look in his eye meant as he stared at me over the top of the cubicles. But I knew.

Is this bringing back any memories?

Chapter Twenty-Two

So, here we are! Welcome back. Remember when this story started? Remember how Jackson came into the office, pissed off and ready to "pound" out his anger? Remember how I promised we'd get back to the here and now? We've made it back to the here and now—well, sort of! And, it's just going to get better. Remember how Jackson was about to do things to me that had never been done to me before? Remember how I had asked him to go slow? Remember how he was just about to pound my ass? Ah, yes! Ready? Let's do this!

****

Jackson pushed my body off him, pushing me forward. Again, his hands grabbed my ass, spreading my cheeks apart. I felt the head of his dick pushing against my opening, just as his finger had done. He didn't force anything. He rocked his hips, teasing me, making me want to be penetrated there. He raked his fingers through my hair, gathering it on top of my head so he could watch my face when he sank his cock into me. I felt his stiff arm, pushing down on my back as he pressed his cock against my opening again.

"You're so fucking hot!" he said through his clenched teeth as he gently pulled my hair. "I want to fuck your tight little ass so bad."

I swiveled my hips, teasing him.

"You sure you want this?" he asked as he bumped

his hips, driving his cock against my opening. I gasped and stood again, as I reached up behind me, wrapping my arms around his neck. I had a lump in my throat that I swore would choke me. My chest heaved as I fought to catch my breath. I felt scared but aroused by the thought of what I wanted him to do to me.

"You're going to have to tell me," he insisted.

We had played this game before. He was in the mood to own me. He wanted to be big, powerful, and scary. After all, he had angry energy he needed to expel. It didn't matter what mood he was in. I was always in the mood to be owned by Jackson Montgomery.

"I want it. I just want it slow. Remember? I've never…"

"Tell me what you want," he whispered.

"I want your cock," I shyly answered.

"Uh-huh. Where?" his soft voice asked as he bumped his hips putting more pressure against my hole.

My breath rushed in and out of my mouth, as I nervously answered. "I want you to fuck me up the ass."

"Spread your fucking legs and bend over," he softly barked into my ear.

He was being so demanding. It was sexy as hell. I desperately gripped his thighs as I moaned, still leaning against him. His hand slapped my ass.

"What did I say?" he muttered.

I leaned forward again. "You're driving me wild right now," I said. "This bossy act you've got going…it's pretty fucking hot."

"Spread your legs," he repeated as he pushed his knee between my legs, forcing them apart. His hand reached around and began massaging my mound. His tongue flicked at my mouth, but not kissing me, as his hand roved below, pinching my clit between his fingers. Again, the head of his cock teased my opening. The wild look in his eyes was primal and dirty. I wanted him! Now!

Anxiously wanting to be satisfied but wanting to control how slowly he moved into me, I pressed my hips backward, forcing my tight opening against the head of his erection.

"Mm! That a girl! Come get it. Come on, baby!" he said as he stared down, watching me try to force him inside me.

Again, I wiggled, trying to tease him. He spread my ass apart, clenching my cheeks in his hands as he watched me attempt to push back onto him. I could hear him breathing through his teeth. The heavy exhales told me I had figured out exactly what he wanted me to do.

"This fucking view is incredible," he said. "But I want to make you come."

I smiled a sassy smile over my shoulder at him. Then, to my surprise, he quit teasing, and he quit warning. There was no turning back. The slippery head of his erection slowly began to penetrate me as he gently pressed his hips forward. I gasped, reaching behind me, digging my fingertips into his thighs.

I drew a deep breath and released it through my mouth.

"Oh! Oh, oh, oh!" I elongated my spine, apparently feeling like that would help him somehow. I don't know how to explain what I thought in that moment. I had a mix of emotions—pleasure, pain, and surprise.

"Want me to stop?"

"No! I want this. I want to enjoy this with you."

"Your ass is so fucking tight. Enjoy it fast. This isn't going to take long."

He reached around and began massaging my clit as he slowly began rocking his hips. He bit at my shoulder, his breath heavy and rushed. He was being more careful and gentle than he had ever been. He studied my face, searching for any indication of what I wanted. After a few minutes, I moved my body with his, trying to help. Then, I could feel his own arousal driving him. He blasted his hips forward, quickly driving his cock deeper inside me as he stared at my face. I gasped, knowing him well enough to know what that meant. He gripped my nipple between his thumb and forefinger, squeezing as he tugged at it. His other hand reached around, petting my pussy as he drove his cock into me again. Again, I inhaled a deep breath. It was so much! It was so hot, wild, and naughty. He gripped my hips and leaned back so he could watch what he was doing to me. That must have been a hot button. He started pumping his hips harder and faster.

"Mm, Jackson," I moaned.

His tongue twirled against my neck, behind my jaw, just below my ear.

His soft voice filled my ear. "Are we still friends?"

"Mm, yes!"

He pumped his hips, driving his cock deeper inside me. He held on to me ripping me back as he pressed into me. Then, he began moving faster, with less discipline and restraint. I whimpered, loving everything he did to me. His hand pleasured my clit as he worked my ass over. A sound escaped my mouth, as the intensity mounted. He drove me wild and made me crave my orgasm even more. He pressed his thumb against my clit as he slid his finger inside my pussy.

"You're so fucking wet."

I smirked over my shoulder, knowing it would be asking for trouble to taunt him, but that had never stopped me before. "Well, at least I'm doing *my* part."

His mouth fell open, and he clicked his tongue, arching his eyebrows.

"Are you fucking kidding me?"

He grabbed my hips and began pounding his rock, hard cock inside me harder and faster. I felt his body slapping against mine as he drove into me over and over again. He watched his cock as he drove it in and out of me. He reached around and slapped my clit, leaving a stinging sensation. He repeated the action a few times as he thrust into me.

"Fuck! You better come. You better fucking come," he pleaded, desperately trying to keep as quiet as possible. "Come on. Come with me."

He drew a deep breath through his teeth, and he held it in his lungs. I knew what that meant. My bad boy was about to lose it. I felt his cock begin to throb as he thrust into me. He reached around me, again and began massaging my clit. I bounced my body off him, driving back against his cock, feeling my own release so close.

"Oh, yeah! Oh, fuck! Jackson…" I whimpered as I began to teeter over that edge.

"Yeah, baby, come for me." He swiveled his hips in a circle as his own orgasm finished. He sank his cock deep inside, expelling the rest of his seed.

My pussy pulsed as one of the best orgasms of my life flashed through my body. Jackson reached down, lifting my knee to his desk, making his shaft sink in deeper as my climax intensified. He dropped his head between my shoulder blades as he massaged my ass, squeezing and pulling at my cheeks. He thrust deep into me one more time, slapping my ass as he bowed his hips upward against me. As my body began to calm and relax, he rested on my back, panting for air.

"You drive me out of my mind," he said as he exhaled.

He began to withdraw himself from inside me. I clenched his thighs, needing him to move slower. He thrust into me once more before he withdrew himself. He put his mouth to my ear.

"I could do this all over again. You better be careful."

I knew he could. I knew he would. I wasn't ready to do that again…at least not just yet.

I had just had one of the most intense orgasms of my life, but my needy body wasn't ready for it to be over. My pussy desperately craved his cock.

What a demanding bitch my pussy had become! She had no idea that her asshole neighbor had just stolen her "happy." She had no idea that her dick best friend had just gone to play on another playground, but my demanding pussy had become spoiled. She had gotten used to being that playground and when she played nice, she got something good. She had played nice, but she hadn't been rewarded with something good yet. She knew it and missed it, terribly.

In an effort to soothe the ache, I reached down between my legs, petting and rubbing. When Jackson realized what I was doing, he spun me around and lifted me so that I sat on top of his desk. He sat down in front of me, leaning back in his chair, resting his pointer finger along his temple as he stared into my eyes.

"Give me a show. Let me watch you, again." He smiled.

That turned me on even more, for some reason. I modestly began sliding my fingers along my wet, engorged pussy. Jackson smiled sarcastically, rolling his eyes and shaking his head as though I had affronted him in some way. He put his hands on my knees and quickly forced my legs apart. He had a clear view of my pussy, as well as everything I did to myself. He put my feet up on the armrests of his chair, gently licking the inside of my knee and kissing my inner thigh.

"Now"—he smiled—"let me watch."

My fingers rubbed up and down my glistening sex. Jackson encouraged me as he watched. He looked up into my eyes with a devilish grin.

"Come on, baby! Give me a show."

I began petting my pussy and my clit with more vigor. This pleased him. He smiled as he leaned back in his chair, interlacing his fingers. His eyebrows arched at various points of my "performance."

Then he inhaled as he leaned forward in his chair. He took my fingers and put them in his mouth. His tongue traced up and down them, sucking and tasting every bit of me. His touch felt soft and tender, at least for a little bit.

Jackson's gentle demeanor quickly passed. With a sudden movement, he pushed my feet off his chair, looped his arm around my thighs and pulled me to the edge of his desktop. Without teasing or warning, he clenched his teeth and buried two of his fingers in my pussy. As though he couldn't wait another second, he pressed his mouth to my swollen, aching lips. I could feel his tongue brushing over my sex as his fingers moved in and out. His tongue felt so good, soft and warm, as he flicked it against me. I entangled my fingers in his hair, as he wrapped his arms around my thighs, pulling me closer to his mouth. There was something very beautiful about seeing his handsome face between my legs, sucking and licking, knowing he loved doing this to me.

His tongue teased me, playing with my clit, until I became sensitive to his touch. When I flinched, a smile crossed his lips. He flicked his tongue once more before he lowered his head, taking my sex into his mouth. He sucked on my lips, tickling me with his tongue. Then he lifted his head and used his fingers to hold my lips apart. He lowered his mouth on me and began sucking my clit, while teasing it with his tongue.

My hips began thrusting toward him, almost involuntarily. Holy shit! No one on earth could do it better. My legs began closing, again, involuntarily. Jackson pushed them open and rammed his fingers inside me as he sucked me with that beautiful mouth. His tongue twirled over my clit as his mouth devoured me. When his fingers rammed inside me, it was overload. I couldn't stop my next climax from coming. I covered my mouth, trying to keep quiet. He knew how much I liked it when he did this to me. The sound his fingers made as he worked my sopping wet pussy added even more fire. I wanted to scream his name. That was too risky. We both knew we had to keep quiet, but he loved upping the ante and accepting the challenge.

My body tensed, and I held my breath, then my

pussy began pulsing as I started to come. I could feel the wet spot I had created on his desk, my wetness ebbing and flowing along every fold, crease, and crack. I almost felt bad about that. He liked my pussy dripping. He got what he wanted, and he seemed to want to keep me wet and ready. He had every right to be proud of himself in this moment.

As I came, he pulled at my hip, encouraging me to grind against his face. As my body pulsed around his fingers, I panted and thrusted my hips, forcing my clit into his mouth as his fingers pleasured me. When my movement broke his suction, he took his fingers out of me and squeezed my clit between them as he rubbed his hand back and forth. He clenched his jaw and breathed through his teeth as he rubbed me with all the pressure he could afford me.

"Again! Let me have your ass again. I'm about to blow my load all over this fucking room."

I slid off his desk and bent over, exposing my bare ass to him. He separated my cheeks and this time, his need seemed so urgent, he only teased me enough to prime my hole for his cock. With how wet I had become, and the precum dripping off his cock, I was even more ready for him this time, especially since I knew what I had coming. He pressed the slick tip gently against my opening, and slowly sank his erection inside me. I drew a long breath as his cock slid in deeper. I had fallen in love with this new sensation. There was no other feeling that had ever come close to taking his cock in my ass. My pussy throbbed, swollen and aching—jealous and wanting to come.

After a few minutes, his soft, gentle penetration, the tenderness started to become something wilder, then the fun really started. He made no apologies for the way he used my body, and I had no complaints. He pounded me fast and hard. It felt so animalistic, primal and erotic. I never wanted this feeling to end. As his hips moved back and forth, I desperately pressed back against him. My body craved a deeper orgasm—a different orgasm.

"Oh, baby! That feels so good."

"You like it when I fuck you like this?" he asked through his panting breath.

"Yes!" I moaned, trying not to be loud.

He reached down and gripped my legs behind my knees, drawing both of them up to the edge of his desk. He slammed into me so hard that his desk started making noise, sliding with each thrust. He gripped my hips, pulling me into him as he slammed into me again.

"You're so fuckin' dirty!" he said through his clenched teeth. "I'm gonna come so hard. Fuck!"

I quit hearing or feeling his breath, then he buried his cock deep, and I felt it start throbbing. He eased it back and pounded it in again, pressing it into me as he continued to come. He rocked his hips back and pressed into me a few more times until he had finished. His body slumped over on top of me.

"Jackson, my legs are breaking like this," I whimpered.

He backed his body off mine, affording me the space to put my feet back down on the floor. I went from, basically, kneeling on the edge of his desk to feeling like I dangled from his cock. My legs were asleep, and he had some height over me. Maybe in a sense, I was dangling from his cock. The sensation was an odd one.

"Um, if you…wanna lean forward a bit, I'll get that out of your way," he joked.

I put my elbows on his desk as he slowly slid out of me. Just before the head, he gripped my ass with both hands, pulling my cheeks apart as he playfully bit my shoulder and pulled out the rest of the way. I turned to face him.

"You bit me."

"I tried to keep your mind busy so you wouldn't hate me for pulling out. I hate that part."

He fastened his pants as his lips brushed over mine. He kissed me as though he would never get to again. When we broke the kiss, he stepped back and smiled.

"That was un-fucking-believable," he said.

"Tell me why we weren't doing that four months ago?"

"Aren't you a funny girl?" he said, holding his hands out to the side. "So, do I look as obvious as I feel?"

"Not really! Especially considering you're not the one without panties and your bra isn't ripped down the middle."

An ornery smile moved across his face, and he shrugged. "Just take it all off."

I saw my panties on the floor. I picked them up and shoved them in his pocket. I smiled playfully and returned the carefree shrug as I patted his pocket.

"I'll let you keep those." I slid the bra straps off my shoulders and put the torn garment in his hand. "And, you can figure out what to do with that."

"I'm going downstairs to the gym for a little bit." He smiled. "I need to borrow their shower, but I'm not sure that I'm done with you. It is going to drive me crazy, knowing you have no panties on under that pretty little skirt. I'm going to be thinking about how easy it would be to— Mmm! I gotta go."

As he stared into my eyes, I reached down and ran my fingers over my mound. "Yeah! It's still wet, and it wants you."

He pulled my hand to his mouth, taking my fingers in and sucking on them. "You taste so fucking good. I really have to go or we're going to be back at it *again*!"

"And the problem with that is?"

"When you pick door number two, door number one is off limits. Now, I want door number one. I like to see your face when I make you come."

"Go to the gym, then! Hurry back to me."

He reached down and shoved his finger inside me. He swirled it around as he flashed me his devious, bad boy grin. I gripped his arm, rocking my hips back and forth as he twirled his finger faster. He arched his eyebrow, surprised by my reaction.

"I expected to get slapped."

"No. Just don't stop doing that," I said.

"Again? Are you serious?"

He put his thumb on my clit and pressed in as he twirled his finger. I couldn't get enough when I got to be with him. He had turned me into a fucking nympho! I couldn't even be mad at him for it. I had been having the time of my life, and he seemed to be having as much fun as I was with our relationship. I had just never had sex with a man that had it all figured out like Jackson Montgomery did. He knew how, and when, and where…

Chapter Twenty-Three

With Jackson's hand in my crotch, he brought me closer to my next orgasm. I gripped his arm tighter as I felt my swollen pussy tightening around his finger. I laid my head on his shoulder to help steady myself. His thumb pressed against my clit harder than before. His finger circled and slid in and out.

"Ooo! Yeah! You're going to make me come again."

He kissed the top of my head. "Come on, baby. Come for me."

"Oo!" I softly sang.

My hips pressed involuntarily toward the source of my pleasure. He curled his fingers inside me, and they hit that spot that had been begging for attention. My pussy began pulsating, and I heard him chuckle.

"You're fucking amazing! I wish I had my cock in you right now. It feels so good when you do that."

"Mmmhmm." I moaned, unable to say much more.

My body loved everything he did to me, evident by my orgasm. No! Excuse me. My *third* orgasm! Though it wasn't as intense as the previous two, it made another mark for me. As the waves of pleasure began to subside, I sighed and turned my head toward him and laid it back down on his shoulder. He drew his head back to look at my face and smiled sweetly.

"Now will you be all right until I get back?"

"I want to sleep. I'm relaxed and happy. I just want to take a nap."

"Can I tell you something?"

"Of course."

"I know we've never had any kind of formal arrangement, but I don't want to share you with anyone else."

He gazed out his office window, but his tone sounded as though he were genuinely worried. I traced my fingers in a circle on his back as I searched his face. He blinked his eyes and looked down at me. He swallowed hard, as if trying to avoid choking.

I let a giggle escape as I thought back over the past four months.

"You're kidding me, right?"

"Um, no! I'm serious. Just as a favor, if it matters, I'd rather not… I'd rather you didn't… I just want…"

"You're actually serious? Jackson, you've been it for four and a half months!"

He flicked my lips with his tongue before he pressed his lips to mine. "Good! Then my favor shouldn't be asking too much, right?"

"Mm! Right!" I purred.

He kissed me with his loving tenderness. He had been soft and sweet before, but this time, something just felt different. Maybe I saw our relationship in a different way. Did having anal sex change people? Surely not! Like a fairytale, his kiss seemed beautiful and sincere!

Then, just like that, he slapped his hand on my ass as he broke the kiss. His more playful side came out. "I can't believe you have no panties on." He winked. "I'm coming back for that pussy. I want to hit it so hard you'll beg me to stop."

"It won't happen! You're too good for me to ever want you to stop."

He slid his hands under my shirt and cupped my breasts pressing them together. "I want to feel your tits squeezing my cock. I want to sink my tongue in your wet pussy. I want to fuck your pretty mouth, but right now, I have to go." He put his hand under my skirt and cupped my lips in his palm. "No one else gets any of this, okay?"

I gripped his bulge. My sudden movement surprised him, and he flinched. As I squeezed his package, a cocky smile settled on his face. He arched his eyebrows as he looked down at me.

"I'll play by the same rules you do," I said.

Amused by my gesture, he chuckled. "You'll get burned out. This will get old, and you'll be begging me to leave you alone. Then, you'll want me to terrorize someone else."

I squeezed harder, not quite as playfully as before. "Jackson, you're not offering me a lot of comfort and security here."

He gripped my wrists, holding both of my hands to his crotch. "Just hold on to that while I tell you this." He grinned.

I massaged his cock and his balls with both hands. His breath hitched in his throat as my fingers teased and played. His eyes glanced down at my hands. I giggled, waiting on him to collect his thoughts.

"Typical! You're always distracting me," he said as he shook his head. "So, look. When I'm not trying to get on you, I'm thinking about getting in you. When those thoughts make my dick hard, if you're not around, I find a quiet corner somewhere and I jack off, but I do it thinking about you the entire time. I've gone bitch blind, and I—"

"Wait a minute! You jack off?" I flirted as though I couldn't imagine.

"Uh…yeah! Don't tell me I can't do that because you drive me bananas."

I smiled and slid my tongue over my lower lip, biting it between my teeth. "I wanna watch."

He almost choked as he tried not to laugh. "Haven't you seen that enough? You want…you wanna watch me jack off?"

"Kinda! It turns me on," I admitted. "Come on! I like watching you do that."

He sighed and shook his head. He pursed his lips as he stared into my eyes, then he finally shrugged his shoulders. "Okay! I'll try to think of some other entertaining performance for you," he said.

"One of us is joking. One of us is not. I want to watch you."

"What? Now? I need to go get my scrub on," he said as he acted out taking a shower.

"No! Tonight. I have an idea. Maybe tonight?" I smirked.

"You have an *idea*?"

"Tonight, I'm the boss, and we're going to play 'Dance, Puppet, Dance'."

He extended his arm and traced my lip with his finger. His eyes locked on mine. His squinted eyes seemed skeptical of my little game. Then, he pressed his lips together and shrugged one shoulder. "Yeah! Okay! I'll play."

"It's going to be fun," I promised.

Jackson flashed me another skeptical look as he picked up papers from his desk. He scribbled something on some of the pages, drew doodles on others, circled items on other pages and signed the back page. He flipped the papers toward me and flashed his devious grin.

"No one's going to believe we went over a budget if you don't take the papers with you."

"Ooo! Good point!"

As we reached the door, Jackson took a couple of pages from the report he had handed to me. He opened the door and pretended to be reading the paper. As though we had been in the middle of a conversation, he nodded his head.

"Yeah, go ahead and put that in there, just in case. Hopefully, we won't need it to be broken down like that, but it's always better to be safe. Thank you, Elizabeth. Great meeting! It looks good. You're doing a great job."

"Thank you, Mr. Montgomery. Did you need me to call and have lunch delivered? Or were you eating out today?" I smiled a flirty grin.

He flashed me a wink. "I'm still trying to figure out what I'm going to eat, but thank you."

"If I can do something to help you decide, let me know."

With that, he shook his head, turned, and walked out of the office. He had only been gone about two minutes before my cell phone buzzed. I glanced down at the screen.

—Naughty girl! You know *what I want to eat.—*

I smiled to myself and thought of a clever reply.

—Sorry! My boss has been riding my ass all

morning. I'm a little scrambled.—

I didn't hear back from him for a while. The phones had been going nuts since he left. After about an hour, when I picked up one of the lines and heard his voice, my stomach fluttered. He spoke in a soft, sultry tone.

"How's everything going?"

"Better now."

"How can I make it even better?"

I whispered into the phone, "Come sit under my desk for the rest of the day."

"You are going to get fired one of these days. Wait a minute! Does your chair have wheels on it?"

"Yes, it does. Why?"

"I'd have to take those off. I don't want you rolling away while I'm doing dirty things to you under there. Might get interesting trying to explain that one."

"Where are you?"

"I'm trying to figure out what the hell you want for lunch. So, what am I bringing you today?"

"Street tacos."

"Chicken, extra lime?"

"Always!"

"Okay! I love you. See you in about fifteen minutes."

"I appreciate it, and I love you, too."

"Show me. Don't tell me." He chuckled and hung up.

After about ten minutes, I excused myself for lunch. I rode the elevator down to the first floor and exited to the parking lot. Jackson had parked beside my car and handed a brown paper bag out the window. He planned to go into the office, look at his watch, and ask if I had gone to lunch. I doubt any of the employees were as dumb as we liked to pretend they were, but it made our cover up efforts more fun, anyway.

After lunch, I sat at my desk and thought about the fact that I could've answered Dena and Jan's earlier question, but why? Jackson didn't want people to know that side of him. Yet, I got to know. He didn't want people talking about how he behaved in bed, but oh my God! I knew exactly how he behaved. There were not words for what Jackson Montgomery could do to a woman. I felt sorry for anyone that would never get to know, because every woman should know that sort of lover, but I wasn't feeling sorry enough to share my little slice of heaven with anyone. Then, my thoughts were interrupted.

"Miss Elizabeth," I heard him call.

I went into his office, with that ridiculous smile that hurt my cheeks. "Yes, Mr. Montgomery?"

He acted so professional and serious. "I have to go make some rounds before all the guys leave. I need you to…" Then, he stopped himself and sighed, softly blinking. "I'm sorry! How's everything? How are you today?"

"You can't imagine. Truly! It's that great. And *you're* that great. And the sex… Oh, yeah! It's great!"

He lowered his voice and flashed me his devious smile as he bit his lip and shook his head. "You better quit it."

"What did you do with my panties?" I asked as I lifted my skirt.

"Oh…oh no! E-liz-a-beth! I *have* to go to the job sites. I'm going to have to fire you."

I smirked and gave a smart-ass shrug. "You always

say that."

"One of these days, the walls will thunder, and the earth will shake, but I will do it," he promised, nodding confidently.

"I love you."

"I know." He smiled. "But I love you just a little…bit…more."

"Just a little bit?" I giggled.

"I'm wondering, if I came stumbling around your place later, would you let me sleep with you?"

"I would love it if you would do that."

"I'll try to earn my keep." He flirted before his tone became serious. "I still don't want to be at home."

I smiled. "Trading favors? Hmm… Interesting. I'm sure I can come up with something you could do, like letting me watch you…remember?"

"Where are your panties?" He demanded in a whisper through clenched teeth.

I giggled. "I really don't know. Whatever you did with them. I forgot about them."

"Holy shit!" He smirked, shaking his head. "You need a fucking warning label."

"Hey! Your name is on the front of this building. I don't want to miss you, but you should go show them what that name means."

He stared into my eyes and nodded. "I love you!"

"I love you, too."

After Jackson left for the day, that became, by far, the most productive workday of my life. I got the Ireland account taken care of. I had Grendale settled and happy. I actually had the *real* budget report, current and updated. I couldn't wait to get home and have Jackson to myself for the rest of the day.

I left work and started for my apartment. Again, my mind drifted through all the events of the day. Again, I thought about Jan and Dena. Lisa! I wasn't angry. Actually, I had even lost my desire to dislike Lisa. I had him! I wanted him to be mine. Lisa probably had no idea what a blowjob was. She probably felt perfectly content with the missionary position. I giggled to myself.

Fat chance, Lisa, I thought.

Jackson Montgomery wasn't just a wild and crazy lover. He was a responsibility…a liability. He required so much more than most men, but I didn't mind. As he had said of himself, it wasn't like I didn't get something out of it. He made my legs tremble. He could get rough, but I trusted him. Nothing about him scared me. I trusted him to give me what I wanted. Even when I didn't know I wanted it, he taught me.

I turned into the parking lot for my apartment. Parked in one of the stalls sat my favorite car in the world. He had beaten me back to my home. Something about that felt very "real."

I walked into my apartment. A vase of red roses waited for me on the table, and Jackson had fallen asleep on the couch. I went over and kissed his lips. He startled awake, batting at me, until he realized where he was and who was kissing him. He smiled and hugged me.

"Wanna fuck?"

I giggled. "Pervert!"

"I really can't help it. I try to not want it, but I just need you," he said sleepily.

"Oh, yeah! You look cocked and ready to rock," I sarcastically replied.

He sat up and pulled me onto his lap. "You have no panties on. That drives me insane!"

He kissed my neck as though I had pulled his chain and started him up. At first, I giggled. He had gone from sound asleep one minute to practically consuming me the next. His hungry mouth covered mine, flicking his tongue in and out.

"Hi!" I smiled.

His eyes locked on mine.

"We're going to bother the neighbors," he smirked, raising his eyebrows.

He stood up, holding my body to his. His kiss alone could turn me on. All the other stuff just amplified that response. He pushed me up against the wall and fought with his zipper to free himself.

"I've been thinking about this all afternoon," he said. "I used my cock to hammer nails today."

I said, "Sounds like that would hurt."

"You're so beautiful, it hurts."

His tongue passed over my lips, and I hugged his neck tighter as he kissed me. He rocked his hips back and forth, teasing me with his cock. He reached under me, dipping two of his fingers inside my pussy. As his lips pressed to mine, he hummed as his fingers discovered how badly I wanted him.

"You're wet." His lips hovered over mine, nipping at them.

"And you're hard." I smirked.

"We're taking this place off the foundation."

"It's all about proof." I flirted.

"You drive me fucking crazy."

He bent his knees and when he came up the look in his eye reflected that "bad boy, no excuses, no apologies" look that made me hot. The confidence he had in his abilities to please me had always been one of the sexiest things about him. He was every father's nightmare, and every mother's wet dream. He ruled my world—the very epitome of sexy.

I loved the way his body felt under my hands when he rocked my world. I loved how his breath blasted against my skin when he pounded me. The way he clenched his teeth, and the noises he made when he came just fueled my fire. His ability to walk that fine line between pleasure and pain kept me ready for him, and always willing. The way he owned my body when he fucked me, made sex with him so much more than anything I had ever hoped for. Then, the way he could quiet his inner wild child to make love to me made me feel so beautiful. The fact he understood the difference made him so amazingly perfect. Of course, the fact that he had the cock of a porn star, the stamina of an entire football team, and the strength of a saint didn't hurt anything, either.

This man wasn't a knight. He wasn't a prince, either. He couldn't figure out which he wanted to be because he was better than either of those. He was *my* king! He owned my heart, and I loved him with everything I had in me.

After we had been "sloshy" and dirty for quite some time, we were getting ready to go for the second orgasm of the evening and things took an interesting turn. Around four o'clock in the morning, Jackson's phone started ringing and pinging. He looked at me, confused as he verified the time. He shrugged and kept pumping his cock in and out of me. We were really having fun now, but if I could walk the next day, it would be a miracle. He gave it to me so fucking good I couldn't resist. Then, the phone rang again. He looked at me with an apologetic look.

"Something's not right," he said as he squinted his eyes. "I should see what that is about."

Chapter Twenty-Four

Jackson withdrew himself and went to look at his phone as I tried to convince my legs that "closed" really could be an acceptable position. I walked over to him as he listened to his voicemail. He looked at the clock on the wall and scrunched his nose.

"Fucking Bob!" he blasted. "He's saying his security guard just caught my guys loading up stuff from his job into one of our company trucks. He wants me out there…right now!" he said in a mocking tone as he made an incredulous facial expression. "I'm trying to take care of important stuff here." He winked at me.

"If we're really quick…" I smiled.

He hugged me to him as his devious smile spread across his lips. "You want quick?"

I giggled, but then his phone started ringing again.

"Fuck!" he growled, and not in a good way.

"Bob's not going to stop until he gets to talk to you. You may as well talk to him."

He hugged me to him as he reached for his phone. He slid his finger across the screen, answering the call, as he held the phone to his ear with his shoulder. He took his arm off my shoulder and reached down between my legs, rubbing and massaging me as he made lewd gestures with his tongue, trying not to laugh, as he listened to Bob blasting in his ear. His eyes locked on mine as he pushed his finger inside me. He tilted the phone away from his mouth and whispered to me.

"You make talking to Bob so much more fun."

"You're dirty!"

He smiled, arching his eyebrows, and nodding in agreement. Then, his face suddenly became serious. He listened before he scoffed.

"Bob, are you fucking delirious? Why would I put them up to taking anything from your job site?"

He listened for a few seconds and sarcastically laughed.

"Oh, of course, because I need it for other jobs! Yeah! Good thinking! Do you really believe this shit? My guys didn't take anything. You already said your security guy *thinks* it *looked* like one of our trucks. There are a lot of white and green construction trucks, Bob."

He listened again.

"Okay, Bob," he said. "I will be there in just a few minutes. There's not a damn thing I can do right this second, but I'm on my way, and I'm not calling my guys, waking them up so they can all come tell me what I already know…none of them took your shit. That security guy, though, huh? What a bang-up job that guy's doing!"

He rolled his eyes as his finger pressed the little red circle to end the call. He put his hands on his hips, and his eyes locked on mine. He scoffed and shook his head.

"Fucking Bob!"

I traced my fingers over his abs. "I don't like him all that much, but if I weren't standing here with you, you would've been there already. Go! Go do what you need to do."

He kissed me, his tongue gently nudging mine as he sucked on my lips. “We have unfinished business. I’m not going to forget.”

“I wouldn’t let you if you tried.”

“I love you!”

“You better,” I said. “You’re running off on me when I want you like I do.”

He playfully looped his arm around my neck, pulling my mouth to his. “Bob can wait.”

I giggled. “I’m teasing you. Go help that freak before he ends up standing in front of my desk, yelling about me being a gold digger, again.”

“I’ll belt him in his mouth,” he said as he turned to collect his clothes. “Spouting that bullshit… Bob has no manners. He’s just blunt and crass. It doesn’t matter if he’s right or not. He just carries around an invisible shovel, and he digs at people. Since he found out I’m the bastard child of a gypsy, he thinks he’s going to be the father I never had.”

“You have such a way with words.” I rolled my eyes. “But, that’s sweet of him to want to be something for you.”

“Bob is a mess. Bob has daughters, so he thinks I’ll be the son he never had. He thinks we’re destined to be family.”

“Oh! He wants to hook you up with his daughters?”

“Yeah, at one point, I think that’s what he thought he wanted to do, but there’s this pretty little thing that got in his way.” He winked at me.

“I would say I’m sorry, but I’m not.”

“Neither am I,” he said as he fastened his jeans and leaned down to kiss me.

"I love you, Jackson!"

"We'll see what you're saying when I come for what you owe me." He flirted.

The hands of time, relentless in their forward momentum, moved us through the next couple of days. It seemed as though Jackson and I had never spent any time apart, but we had no issues making up for the time we had lost. I could see a difference in him. Whether it happened because he wanted to appease me, or he actually felt it, it seemed like he sincerely wanted to be more than a temporary part of my life. He even let me help him through one of the worst days of his life.

****

Heavy clouds darkened the day. It seemed like it would start pouring rain at any given moment. It was the morning of Winnie's funeral. Jackson had asked me to go with him. His mother hadn't confirmed whether she would be in attendance or not. He wasn't sure what to expect, but he asked me to stand with him, among some of his neighbors and Winnie's friends. It wasn't going to be anything big, since Winnie wouldn't have wanted that.

We left my apartment to go to the funeral home. Jackson pulled into the parking lot in the back. He got out of his seat and came to open my door for me. I stepped out of the car, holding his face in my palms.

"Are you okay?"

"I have to be." He smiled. "But, between you and me, this isn't my favorite day."

I lovingly kissed his cheek. From a distance, I heard an odd sound, but dismissed it. Jackson's eyes got big as he stared at me. I searched his face, trying to understand his expression as I noticed him focusing on listening to the noises I was hearing.

"What?" I asked.

"Do you hear that?"

Then the sound of a horse's whinny cut through the "normal" city noises. It was a familiar sound, but one totally out of the norm, especially for the city. That day, in honor of Winnie, I got to witness one of the most amazing things I had ever seen. I heard the gritty, clomping sound of horse hooves beating, rhythmically, against pavement. There was also the sound of metal jangling right behind me. Jackson's eyes filled with a sentimental look I'd never seen, a look of pride and honor. I turned just as a horse-drawn buggy pulled up in front of the funeral home. Then came another, and another, and another. Pretty soon, the streets all around the funeral home were lined with horse drawn buggies, parked on the sides of the streets. Jackson and I both stood speechless as we watched all of the people dismounting their carriages. The men were dressed in suits, with pants just above their ankles and hats on their heads. The women were wearing black dresses with bonnets.

Jackson swallowed hard as he watched them. A tear fell from his eye. He looked over at me, trying to speak, but choking on his words.

"What are they doing here?" I asked curiously.

His watery eyes looked at me as he nodded. "They're coming to take her home."

"Do we need to do something? Do we need to keep them away?"

His voice grew shaky. "She gave up that world to care for me. This is everything she would have wanted. This would've meant everything in the world to her."

He covered his eyes with his thumb and his finger, trying to hide his tears. I hugged him, moved by everything I witnessed. An elderly gentleman stepped toward us. He had glasses that reminded me of Santa's spectacles. He had a warm smile hiding under his lush beard. Even through his smile, you could feel his sorrow as he approached.

"Are you relation to Sister Winifred Fisher?" the man asked.

Jackson nodded. "I am." He extended his arm. "I'm Jackson Mont… Fisher. Jackson Fisher."

The man refused his hand but hugged him instead. "I'm Joshua Fisher. Winifred was my niece, as is your mother. Sister Winifred has served you well, boy. We would like to take her home…one last journey, and we would like to give her a proper Amish burial."

Jackson's lip quivered, choking down the lump in his throat, as he nodded. "She would have wanted that."

Joshua waved his hand and a number of men filed into the funeral home. Within a few minutes, they came out of the funeral home, carrying "Sister Winifred" to a covered hearse wagon. Jackson turned away, exhaling through his mouth as he wiped his eyes.

"You know our laws," Joshua said. "We cannot welcome you into our world, but we have a nice funeral arranged. We have plenty of food. Sister Winifred would have also wanted you to be part of this day. She turned her back on our ways out of her love for you. We have discussed it and for today, Brother Jackson, you and your wife are welcome in our homes and at our tables."

I couldn't keep it in any longer. My tears flowed as I reached up to wipe my cheeks. I had never seen anything so touching and bittersweet. These people overcame divisive differences for a common cause. If it were an option, I think I would've become Sister Elizabeth Michelle Roundtree right then and there. I had never been more moved by anything in all my life.

Realizing there were people inside expecting a funeral, and probably a little confused, I decided to go explain the situation to them. I dismissed myself from Jackson and Joshua, leaving them to talk. I climbed the steps of the funeral home, rehearsing what I would say.

I felt it went well.

"So, thank you all for coming. As some of you may know, in her earlier years, Winnie lived as an Amish woman. Her Amish family has come to take her for a proper Amish burial. This is what Winnie would have wanted. This day is for her. I apologize for any inconvenience. Um…that's all."

I couldn't ignore the odd humming of voices chattering, trying to figure out what was going on. I'll give it to them. My announcement had been awkward, but you give a bride anything she wants on her wedding day. You cater to a pregnant woman in labor, taking whatever she dishes out and doing it with a smile, and you *always* grant the final wishes of those who have passed on. I believed in that. So, it wasn't so outlandish to me. I trusted the others to reach the same conclusion. I sort of just sulked off out of the funeral home and went back outside, just as the buggies were beginning to pull away from the curb.

Jackson smiled and stretched his arm out to me. "Want to go to go be Amish with me on real Amish land for just a little bit?"

"Of course!"

He opened the passenger side door for me. "Um, are we supposed to be driving?"

"I didn't have time to get my buggy and my horses ready, so this is the best I can do." He smirked sarcastically. "We can't drive inside the community, but we can drive to the community…behind all of these buggies."

I scratched my cheek as I fought back a laugh. "Uh, okay!"

"When we get there, we ride in with Josiah and his family. I don't know. I just know the last buggy is the one we'll be in. Oh, and for today, you're my wife, so you're Sister Elizabeth Fisher or some something."

"But we're not married."

He pursed his lips and nodded. "Joshua knows. He said today, we're married. They planned for me to have been married already, so my wife and my kids were welcome. We don't have kids yet, and I'm not asking you to fake anything, other than being my wife."

"Jackson, I'd be honored to be your mock wife…again!"

He chuckled. "We should probably take the hint, already. Get in the car! Those buggies are super-fast with their two-horsepower. We don't them getting away from us."

So, it was! We attended Winnie's Amish funeral. We were welcomed with open arms, at least for the day. Jackson met some of his family from his mother's side. He enjoyed the day, considering the nature of our visit. There were a lot of dishes that were sent home with us. There were various crafts made by children and cards that the ladies had made. One of Winnie's friends had made a pillow for Jackson. She had stuffed it with some of Winnie's old clothing. She told Jackson he could hug the pillow anytime he wanted to hug his aunt. It had truly been one of the most touching experiences of my life. The sad day of mourning turned out to be a beautiful day with some amazing people. Jackson assured me that it was everything Winnie would've wanted that day to be.

After Winnie's funeral, time really seemed to be flying as the next few days passed. Some things were different for Jackson and I, and some weren't much different at all. He stayed at my apartment, still hiding from his empty house. He just wasn't ready. It wasn't anything permanent. He just needed a little more time to accept that Winnie's absence was still awaiting him.

At work, Jackson spent a lot more time in the field. I spent a lot more time encouraging him to spend more time in the field, because to be honest, damn! It looked good on him! Plus, his clients were happy to have the connection with him, his guys were a little sharper, and he was getting to enjoy the physical, tangible part of creating something from nothing, which was where his true passion for construction came from. He had never genuinely enjoyed being stuck behind his desk.

All of us in the office had gotten used to "Mr. Montgomery" being out in the field, and everyone had found his or her little niche, which kept the corporate side well-oiled and functioning. We were all strengthening our friendship and working as a team—even Lisa and Ginger. Actually, maybe I had just gotten over my jealousy, and I decided to be part of the team that had already been in place. Montgomery Construction was operating as a machine, in every way. We had found the magic formula, and Montgomery

Construction felt more stable than ever. As a team, devoted to the man who created our jobs, we were all dedicated to solidifying our position in the construction world. I felt so proud for my Mr. Jackson Montgomery.

Since the minute I sent that perverted email, so much had changed, so quickly. Maybe I had changed. Maybe the rest of them had always been part of what made Jackson's world go 'round. As I shuffled through my thoughts, I heard the elevator ding from out in the lobby. I looked up, and there he was, sporting that sexy, cocky smirk, and undoubtedly up to no good. I could just see it in his eyes. He was a man with a plan. My stomach flipped and tumbled, just at the thought of what was going on behind that sexy smile and those sultry eyes.

Chapter Twenty-Five

It was just before lunchtime when he came through that door. He had a captivating smirk on his face. He was clean, tidy, and he even shaved his stubbly face. He looked different than when he left my apartment for work, a few hours earlier. He sauntered through the office, and his eyes deadlocked on mine.

Oh hell! My panties were instantly soaked. The look on his face had a provocative element about it. I knew that look. That was the look when he just did whatever he wanted to do…and I loved it. I smiled as he approached my desk.

"Good morning, Mr. Montgomery." I smiled.

He walked around my desk and boldly planted his butt right in the middle of it, pulling my chair in front of him. I nervously giggled as I passed him a questioning glare. I looked around him to see if anyone was watching this. Yeah! They were. It was kind of difficult to miss. He put his feet on the armrests of my chair and raised his eyebrows as he smiled his ornery smile.

My heart pounded with a thundering echo. What…the…hell? He reached for the front of his jeans. Wide-eyed, I nervously shook my head as my breasts rose and fell with my racing breath. I covered my face.

"What are you doing?"

He pulled a little sword from inside his waistband

and handed it to me. “I’m giving you my sword. You can keep it…forever. I only want one dragon, and one princess, and I don’t want you to fake anything ever again.”

“They can see you,” I whispered. “They can hear you.”

He shrugged. “Hand me the phone.”

“The phone?”

“Elizabeth, hand me the phone,” he insisted.

I handed him the receiver.

“Okay, now push the speakerphone button.”

“Oh, my God,” I said, jittery and nervous.

With a trembling finger, I pushed the button, as he had told me to do. He handed the receiver back to me. He had that sexy, cocky look on his face.

“Hold this for me, please.”

I took the phone from him and held it in my lap.

“No,” he chuckled and curled his fingers, wanting me to raise the receiver.

He leaned forward, practically in my face as he rested his elbows on his knees and stared into my eyes. I had started shaking so much from nerves that the receiver looked like a fan. He smiled at me and held my hand to his arm, for stability.

“Good morning,” he said as he stared into my face, his voice radiating across the speakers in the office.

I nodded, swallowing the lump in my throat. I nervously giggled as I tried to speak. Nothing came out. He patiently stared at me for a second.

“Miss Elizabeth, you’re fired.” He smiled and nodded at me. “I know I tell you it’s going to happen all the time, but today is the day. You’re fired.”

I could hear everyone gasping as they stood or

wheeled their chairs out to the aisle between the cubicles. Either way, every eye in that room focused on us. I stared into his eyes, smirking and shaking my head. He winked at me.

"I love you." He smiled. "I want to marry you…but this time I want it to be real." He chuckled. "And maybe not an Amish wedding, but I do want to marry you. I don't care. A knight. A prince. Whatever! I made all of that up, anyway. I'll be whatever you want me to be. I'll be your lifer if you'll let me. Miss Elizabeth, will you marry me?"

He playfully pushed the phone out of my hand and slid a beautiful princess cut diamond solitaire on my finger. It seemed fitting, considering the fairytale he had made up. Forget that, actually! It was perfect considering he asked me to *marry* him! That made it everything! This unruly, wild, maniacal lover wanted to be mine forever!

I pushed the chair out from under me, causing his legs to drop, as he had done mine all those days ago. I stood between his legs, hugging his neck, and kissing him. I raked my fingers through is hair, cradling his head in my hands as I stared into his eyes.

"Yes, I will," I said as I kissed his lips. "But I need you to know. You're not a knight or a prince. You're a lunatic." I laughed, shaking my head. "I see you as so much more than that. You're the king of my dreams. It would be an honor to be your wife."

He exhaled as though he had been holding his breath, as if he'd have anything to worry about. He hugged his arms around me, kissing me as the entire office erupted in claps and cheers. Those people weren't just co-workers. They were Jackson's family…my family…*our* family.

"See, Dena? What did I tell you?" Jan called out. "I knew it."

Dena laughed. "You didn't say they were going to get married. You just said you thought they had something going on."

"I knew they did," John said. "I never told you guys his girlfriend's name. I only told you he had a girlfriend, but he let her name slip when he told me about their Amish wedding weekend."

Jackson chuckled, refusing to take his eyes off of mine. "Shut up, John," he playfully jabbed as he kissed my lips.

Everyone made their way to my desk, celebrating with us. It seemed so perfect. Our relationship had started in the office. It wasn't a fairytale made for everyone, but in my eyes, I couldn't have asked for anything better.

"Wait a minute!" Lisa snapped. "No! No, no, no! You can't just fire her. We want her here. We're family. Elizabeth, tell him you won't marry him unless he lets you stay."

In complete shock, I giggled as Jackson shrugged.

"Yeah! Why does she have to lose her job just because you have feelings?" John said. "Suck it up. If you can't work with her—"

"I've promised her for a long time that I was going to fire her, and since I wear the pants, after she tells me which ones I can wear, of course, I had to make good on my promise," he said as he proudly smiled.

"So, I don't need to make up some bullshit severance package, right?" Jan asked with a snarl.

"I don't care," Jackson said over his shoulder. "I

did my part. If she keeps coming in here every day, then keep paying her."

He smiled at me and put his forehead to mine. "Right now, I'm an easy mark. You can have anything you want. I don't care. I'm not going to fight you. I get to be a *lifer*."

I smiled sweetly and thought about taking him into his office, just because it seemed fitting for what we would typically do. Then a thought occurred to me. Missionary! Maybe *now* he would do it.

He stared at my face and laughed. "Do I even want to know what you're thinking? That look on your face… What *are* you thinking, Miss Elizabeth?"

I whispered, only for his ears. "Sex!"

As though I had snapped my fingers and woke him from a trance, he pulled his head back, blinking rapidly, obviously confused.

"What? What about it?"

"Let's go," I softly said, smiling my best seductive smile.

"Uh…o-kay!" He smiled, shaking his head as though I had gone crazy.

I pulled his hand, pulling him toward the door. By that point, everyone around us had gotten involved in his or her own conversations. I announced that we were going to "lunch" as I dragged him through the office. Being the amazing people that they are, they took it in stride and congratulated us as I dragged my future husband out the door.

He followed me, laughing. "Seriously? If you're that stirred up, we have options, here."

"I want you in *my* bed," I smiled.

"Well, okay! Yes, ma'am," he said as he made a

cute, bratty-type face at me.

I felt like a cave woman, dragging my man to my cave to violate him. I didn't have to club him, thankfully, and oddly enough, he wasn't fighting me on the idea too much. In fact, he seemed willing to be violated, curious to see what thoughts I had running through my head.

We got into my apartment and I turned and started kissing him like a fiend. My tongue traced over the pulse in his neck. He hugged me to him, trying to keep up with what I wanted from him. I'll admit that I started being a little…demanding. I wanted him in a whole new way. I wanted him in a way that I had wanted him for a long time. I had hope that it would happen this time. Maybe now, I would finally get to feel his body on top of mine. Oh, yes! I had a brand-new drive coursing through me.

I clenched his shirt in my hands as I walked backward toward my bedroom. He played along, pulling me to him as he pushed me backward. He knew my desired destination, obviously.

We stood beside my bed, and I smiled my flirty smile. I bit my lip as he stared down at me. He wanted to read me, now more than ever. He couldn't quite figure out what had inspired my demanding, needy want for him. He leaned down to kiss me and suddenly froze. He opened his eyes and stared into mine.

He took a couple of steps back and pursed his lips for a second. His tongue slid across his lower lip, and his smile widened. He bobbed his head. He had me figured out.

"Mmmhmm!" he hummed with a knowing grin.

I giggled. "What?"

"I read you, remember? I know what you're doing," he winked.

"Oh really?"

"Uh-huh!" He slowly blinked as he smirked confidently. "Come here," he said as he curled his fingers at me.

I stepped closer to him. He held my face in his hands, and he leaned down to kiss me. His tongue softly swept through my mouth. As our lips pressed together and he drew a deep breath and released it. He reached down, gripping my thighs, wrapping my legs around his hips. He turned toward my bed and put his knee on the mattress, moving our bodies to middle of the bed as he fell forward onto his arms, hovering us above the mattress. He smiled at me and gently lowered our bodies. He kissed me as I felt the weight of his body slowly settling onto mine, for the first time. He did it! He wasn't fighting me this time. He just did it.

I inhaled deeply, hugging his head to me. I felt his lips softly grazing my neck as he kissed his way back to my mouth. He slid his fingers into mine, pulling my hands up over my head as he lifted his head, staring into my eyes. He started grinding his erection against my crotch, firmly, but slowly. In that moment, we were completely clothed, but it didn't matter. Oh, my God, it didn't matter.

His lips brushed over mine, as he stared into my eyes. He didn't kiss me at first, just teased. One of his hands released my hand, and his fingers gently trailed down my body, caressing me with his feather soft touch as his hips pressed into me, driving upward. He lowered his mouth to my ear, and I heard his staggered breath as he focused on rubbing his hard cock against me.

"I don't want to come yet, but I love this so much."

"What?" I asked, pushing up on his shoulders so I could see his face, preparing to pick on him. "I thought you would rather watch golf?"

He shrugged as he smirked at me. "Never! I've never done this. Not even once, until now, so it's kind of getting to me," he shyly admitted.

I smiled at up at him, as I pulled his shirt over his head and tossed it to the floor. My fingers floated over his back as our lips connected. He lowered his mouth on mine as he sucked on my lips. The weight of his body shifted, pressing against me, reminding me that he really did do it.

I rubbed my leg up and down his as he pulled at my shirt. He slid his fingers up my arms as he raised the fabric over my head. He lifted his body off me, but only enough to push my pants off my hips. He pressed his tongue against his back teeth, and he chuckled.

"Fuck it!" He raised his body up over mine and slid off the end of the bed.

He reached up my body, gripping my pants and playfully ripping them the rest of the way off my legs, then he unfastened his jeans and pushed them to the floor. He kissed my body as he climbed up from the foot of the bed. He lowered himself on top of me, again, as his tongue pressed into my mouth.

"Mm!" I said, feeling his naked body on top of mine.

He raised his upper body to look at me, planting his elbows on either side of my head. My fingers traced over his toned muscles, kissing every part that my mouth could reach all the way up to his shoulder. I dragged my leg up his, wrapping it around his hip. He dipped his other hip, gently nudging my other leg out of his way.

He lifted his hips and as he slowly brought them down, he tilted them, driving his cock into my pussy. As he pressed into me, he exhaled and closed his eyes, putting his forehead to mine. He lifted his hips and pressed into me again, slowly going deeper. I wrapped my arms around him, digging my fingertips into his back as tears fell from my eyes. I didn't mean to be an emotional dork, but I had wanted this for so long and feeling him move inside me this way felt entirely different. The fact that he took his time just made it mean even more. Jackson Montgomery wasn't just fucking me. Not this time. He hugged my leg to his hip as he pressed into me. He kissed me as though nothing else mattered.

"I either need to calm down, or you need to catch up." He smiled as he brushed his lips over mine.

"I want to feel you. Come for me."

He smiled as he slid his hands into mine. He pressed them against the bed as he lifted his hips, then he tilted his hips in as he lowered his body again. He slowly rocked his cock back and forth, pressing into me, then he started moving side to side as he moved in and out of me. Something about feeling his heart in every move he made this the most beautiful experience of my life. Everything about it felt fucking amazing! He squeezed my hands and I started moving my body with his. I lifted my head as I felt my body getting ready to tumble over that edge. As my pussy surged, tensing and releasing, Jackson exhaled, and I felt him throbbing inside me. He pressed in deeper, holding his cock deep inside me, then pulling back a little and thrusting in again and again.

"I love you."

"I love you, too."

He released my fingers, scooping his hands under my ass, pulling me into him as he pressed into me one more time. I hugged him, holding his body against mine as he finished. His fingers traced up and down my leg as his other hand still had a grip on my ass. We just held each other as his body melted onto mine.

After a few minutes, he put his elbow beside my head, propping his head up so he could look at me. He brushed his finger down my nose. His smile widened as he stared into my eyes.

"Do you want me to put the television in here so you can watch golf?" I asked.

"Not yet. Hold off on that golf thing for a little bit. I'll let you know," he teased as he kissed my forehead.

After a few minutes, the good times had come to an end for the time being. He lifted his body off mine to go to the bathroom. I heard water slapping against the bathtub floor, then the air filled with a familiar tropical scent. The bathroom door opened, and Jackson came to the end of the bed and stretched his hand out.

"What are we doing?"

"Just come with me." He proudly smiled.

He led me to the bathroom where thick rich bubbles were billowing in the tub as it filled. I laughed as I turned to face him. He smiled down at me.

"What?"

"Too bad we don't have any bonbons," I teased.

He pressed his lips together and jutted his chin out. "So? There's still a nice, bubble bath calling your name."

He waited for me to get into the water. Then he disappeared around the corner. When he returned, he had a tray with two glasses of champagne, along with chocolate dipped strawberries, and truffles.

"Truffles are kind of like bonbons, right? Sort of, maybe?"

He sat beside me with a cocky smile on his face.

"No! I never wanted you to lower yourself to this level of servitude," I teased.

"Good! Because I kind of hoped you'd feed me truffles and strawberries while you sit in your nice bubble bath," he teased. He picked a strawberry from the tray and held it to my lips. "We'll take turns."

Chapter Twenty-Six

For the next few months, we planned a beautiful wedding. With each milestone, I kept checking to make sure Jackson still wanted to get married. He had been so adamant about how he would never get married, but once he had made his mind up, he didn't waver or flinch one little bit. He committed himself to the idea and no matter how many "outs" I gave him, he insisted he knew what he was doing, and that he couldn't be happier about it.

We spent those months before the wedding playing with the missionary position and my wild man's need to make every sexual situation an *event*. Don't get me wrong. That wasn't the only position we played with, but it had become one that seemed to be gaining popularity—leg up, legs around his waist, legs over his shoulder, flat—you get the idea. Anyway, I was perfectly happy and content, enjoying that I had finally convinced him that I needed his body over mine. We flirted and teased each other so much. We had the kind of fun that you hope never fades. He made me feel beautiful and sexy. He had me, but he didn't want to stop chasing me. It didn't bother me in the least.

Since our engagement, his on again, off again emotions seemed to have leveled out. He quit fighting me, and I didn't feel like I had to force anything. I had him. I had won his heart and that was all I ever wanted from him…well, not *all* that I wanted, but that was the most important part. Okay! Who am I kidding? It was *all* important.

Months of wedding planning, shopping, and dress fittings had paid off. We were going to have one of the most beautiful weddings in the world, then we needed to set a time to do the cake tasting appointments. That had always been a point of protest for my Mr. Montgomery, so I presented the idea to him gently…during a blowjob.

I kept moving my mouth up and down on him until he'd get close, then I'd stop sucking him and switch to licking. He'd stare down at me with that desperate look in his eyes.

"Mm! You almost had me," he said at one point.

I giggled. "Oh really? I couldn't tell."

I licked his shaft, kissing him and tickling the head of his cock with my tongue. His breath would hitch in his throat. His hips would tilt upward, wanting me to make him come. When he would calm down, I would slap his cock against my tongue. When he groaned and tangled his fingers in my hair, I started licking him again.

"You're driving me insane." He chuckled, his patience wearing thin.

I kissed his shaft.

"Fuck!" he groaned in frustration.

"I have an idea," I said, and then dragged my tongue up his shaft to the head, drawing soft circles around the top.

"Baby, you're killing me."

"Let's do a cake tasting," I said, and took him into my mouth again.

"Oh, shit. Um…"

I took him out of my mouth, licking him softly.

He chuckled. "You're so mean."

"Cake!" I snapped and lowered my mouth on him again.

He held my head so I couldn't pull away again. He stared down at me, his eyes begging me to make him lose it. I slid my mouth up and down on him a couple more time times, rippling my tongue against him.

"Cake tasting," I said around his cock.

"Yeah! Whatever you want to do," he agreed.

I lowered my mouth on him, and I sucked him as my head bobbed up and down on him for a few minutes until he came. He pulled my hair back so he could watch as he pumped his hips up, driving his cock deeper into my mouth. I loved how vulnerable he could be when he wanted to come. I cheated and used it against him, but he cheated by withholding important information until after I had satisfied him.

When he was done, he leaned closer to me, kissing the top of my head and lifting my hair off my neck. He laughed and looked at me with his sexy, cocky smirk. Then, he shook his head.

"I have a confession." He smiled. "I like your dirty little game. You're a fucking tease, but if you had told me you wanted me to go taste cake, I would've done it. With or without you blowing me. I actually like cake."

"Okay! I have a confession, too. I just like feeling like I can own your cock like you own my pussy."

"I hate to burst your bubble." He nodded, pressing his lips together. "But you've owned my cock since that first time in my office. That first kiss…that was hot! I want that kiss for the rest of my life. If tasting cake means I get to have that, then fine. I'll taste cake, and oh, sweetie pie, would you like my balls? You can just put those in your cute little purse and carry them around with you. Put them in a pretty, little pocket, now. Pick a good one, so you know right where they are. I don't even care, anymore. I get that kiss…for forever!"

So, we tasted cake, and we picked a DJ, and a photographer, and it all worked out so perfectly. I had no understanding of how wedding planning seemed so stressful for some people. I guess it was a sign. We were so meant for each other that nothing could go wrong.

****

The rehearsal dinner happened to be the first-time Jackson met my family. It wasn't ideal, and we had tried to make something happen sooner. The logistics of it all seemed hopeless.

I grew up in one of those wholesome families. My dad worked as a realtor. My mom? A schoolteacher. My sister and I were a lot alike. The biggest differences were that I had always been closer to our mom while she preferred to be close to our dad. I happened to be the younger of the two and the fact that I would make it down the aisle before Ellery made me feel guilty, but she didn't make an issue of it, so I didn't see a need to, either.

The rehearsal dinner went beautifully. My dad talked Jackson's ear off about properties he had listed. It became obvious, from his hints, that Daddy wanted me to move back home. Jackson just patiently listened, and he nodded from time to time, but amazingly enough, he managed to stroll right across that sacred conversation without any scarring or bruising. Daddy could be brutal to my love interests. I had seen it a number of times. Then again, Jackson Montgomery wouldn't let anyone get over on him, except maybe Bob. It worried me when I saw my dad, Jackson, and Bob standing in a corner of the room. Bob's finger must've jabbed Jackson's chest about thirty times.

My future husband looked at me from across the room at one point. He smiled and winked. His eyes locked on mine, and I knew that flirtatious smile. I shook my head, knowing we wouldn't be together again until after our wedding. He squinted his eyes at me, pursing his lips, and then Bob started jabbing him in the chest again. I giggled as Jackson snapped back to reality and glared at Bob with an entirely different expression on his face.

It turned out to be a beautiful evening. Everyone seemed to get along and enjoy each other's company. My mom and my sister, both, commented about how impressed they were with my Mr. Montgomery. They noticed his good looks, of course. They found him to be a polite, well-mannered gentleman. They were impressed with his ambitious nature. Again, it seemed as though nothing could go wrong. Until—

"I hope he's good in the sack," my mom spouted.

"Mom!"

"Well, Elizabeth, you just don't know until it's too late. Once you're married to them, you're stuck with them."

I bit my lower lip, feeling myself blushing. I could see Ellery's shoulders bouncing out of the corner of my eye. I just had to shake my head and walk away. I couldn't believe my mother honestly thought I had saved myself. In the world we live in, now? She couldn't be serious? But I just didn't care to get into it with her. That was just too much.

As we all prepared to leave from the rehearsal dinner, I stood, facing the man I was set to marry. He looped his pointer finger around my thumb and gently swung our hands. We were being lit up with flashes as my mom and my sister snapped pictures of us.

"So." I smiled shyly at him.

He sucked on his upper lip, making a smacking sound as he bobbed his head. He sighed and looked toward my family. His eyes cut back to me.

"I'm going to miss you." He smiled.

"Just until eleven o'clock in the morning."

He scoffed and wrinkled his forehead. "That's a long time!"

I giggled and hugged him. "I love you, and if you'll come marry me tomorrow, I'll let you eat some cake."

"The last time we got married, I only went along with it because I wanted to kiss you. Do I get to kiss you this time?"

"You better." I smiled.

"Then, I'll be there," he said as he leaned down and sweetly kissed my lips. "I love you, too. You better go get some sleep."

He opened the car doors for my mom and myself. Then, he closed us in. I watched him walk across the parking lot toward Lucy. He must've been a glutton for this punishment because I saw the smile on his face. It wasn't one of those fake smiles.

It was real.

****

The next morning, I stood in my bridal suite in

front of the mirror, curling my hair. My sister kept fluttering around like a butterfly that needed to be whacked with a newspaper. She looked excited and anxious. I understood that, but good grief, someone needed to peel her off the ceiling.

I started to curl the next strand of hair, and my phone pinged.

—Hey! I might be a little bit late. Lucy is really dirty. I wanted to wash her for you really quick.—

My jaw hit the floor. I wanted to break his neck! The day of our wedding, the groom would be needing emergency medical attention if the bride decided to follow through with her plan to hurt him.

Late?

Washing his car?

He couldn't just be *late* because he was washing the damn car!

—No. You can't be late. This isn't a thing you can be late for.—

A few moments passed. I started to panic. He had lost his mind! Surely, he knew better than to think he could be late because he felt he needed to wash his car? Then my phone pinged again.

—Well, then you're just going to have to deal with Lucy looking like this.—

He sent a picture of Lucy, parked in the parking lot of the wedding venue. People had already started decorating that beautiful car. They had scribbled some writing on the windows. Flowers were strung together and draped from the antenna. There were cans and ribbons tied to the bumper. There were balloons tied to different parts. I couldn't help but smile. I replied.

—She looks beautiful!—

—So, you don't want me to wash all of that off before we do this?—

—You scared me! That was mean.—

—I get to kiss you this time, right?—

—Yes!—

—Okay. Hurry up! We're all waiting on you.—

—I love you!—

—I love you, too! See you in a little bit.—

About an hour later, I watched our wedding party saunter down the aisle. Bob and Ellery went walking down, blazing the trail for me. I gripped my daddy's arm, and we got ready to walk through the doors. I got a peek of the king of my dreams. He had his hands clasped in front of him, holding his wrist. I got to marry the most stunning man I had ever seen in my life. He looked so handsome in his tux. I watched him as he smiled at Bob. And when the music started, he turned his head toward the door.

As my dad and I stepped to the top of the aisle, my Mr. Montgomery's hand covered his heart, and his eyebrows arched as his eyes locked on mine. He shook his head as though he saw me as the most beautiful woman in the world. He winked at me and smiled the sweetest smile. I saw him quickly brush the heel of his hand under his eye. His eyes stared into mine, and he smiled sweetly. No…proudly.

We went through the ceremony, and when the pastor said, "You may kiss the bride."

Jackson smiled at me and whispered, "Finally!"

He pressed his lips to mine. His tongue swept past my lips, but in a tasteful, appropriate, sweet kind of way. It was beautiful. I felt beyond "in love" with him.

When we were introduced as Mr. and Mrs. Jackson

Montgomery, everyone cheered and clapped. We led everyone out to the reception hall. It seemed fitting, for reasons of my own, to decorate everything with the king and queen of hearts. It meant something to him, and it meant something to me. Bob seemed a little upset that there were no poker tables set up, but you just can't please everyone.

When Jackson and I went up to do our first dance, I cradled his face in my hands and kissed his lips. We danced to the song he dedicated to me. He held me to him and snaked his body as he moved us around the floor. He lowered his mouth to my ear.

"You know what I'm thinking?' he smirked.

"What?"

"You're beautiful and you make that dress so pretty, but it's going to be a little difficult to make you come without all of these people knowing what I'm doing," he said.

I hugged him as I said to him. "You're so bad!"

"Tell me you don't want it, and I won't do it," he teased, winking at me.

He hugged me tighter, lowering his mouth to kiss my shoulder.

When it came time to do the garter toss, I sat in a chair and Jackson put his head up under my dress to get the garter with his teeth. I slightly opened my legs. He put his hands on the inside and outside of my thigh. His mouth felt soft and gentle. He kissed my leg, and slid his hand up to my pussy, petting me through my panties, then he gripped the garter with his teeth, dragging it down my leg, and he came out from under my dress. He got the garter off, commenting about it being hotter than hell under there, and then he offered his hand to help me up from the chair.

He hugged me to him and whispered in my ear. "My wife is wearing crotchless panties under her dress."

I drew my shoulder up to my chin and smiled at him.

"You're unbelievable." He smiled as he kissed me and turned to shoot the garter for the single guys.

The DJ played one of Jackson's favorite songs. It was the raspy voice, singing about preferring old rock and roll and how today's music is missing soul. My husband slid his jacket off his shoulders, laying it over the back of one of the chairs. He smiled at me.

"I'm going to go get your mom and your sister to tear it up with me." He smiled.

I watched him as he sauntered over to Mom and Ellery's table. He held his hands out to both of them, curling his fingers, encouraging them to take his hands. They both laughed as they each latched on to a hand. He pulled them onto the floor, and he spun my sister as he hugged my mom to him, rocking her back and forth. I laughed, watching him win them over. I don't know how the man did it, but he managed to dance with them both fairly well. He would spin one, while he held onto the other one. I didn't even want to think about how he had been able to sharpen those skills. I just wanted to adore my stunningly handsome husband. I enjoyed seeing my mom and my sister having so much fun.

What I loved most was every time he held his left hand out, now, a newly placed gold band reflected the light. I smiled to myself, happy that I got to be the one to put that ring on his finger. That sexy man had become my husband!

"Where's my wife?" he asked as he turned to look for me. He rolled his shirtsleeves up and motioned for me to join them.

"He thinks he can handle three of us at one time." My mom laughed as I got closer. "He's really good. We'll see if he's got it in him. Let's get him, girls!"

I knew what my mother meant, but it was an inside joke for Jackson and me. I rolled my eyes and playfully glared at him. He reached for my hand and pulled me to him. He smiled his ornery smile as he leaned down to kiss my lips. Then, he whispered in my ear.

"I got the only one I want." He confidently nodded and kissed me again.

We looked more like a huddle than anything that resembled any kind of dance, but we were all laughing and having fun, dancing with my Mr. Montgomery. It had to be the most beautiful wedding in human existence. It was an incredible, happy celebration!

****

While I know that's what you were here for, I'd leave you with this one final thought as this beautiful story comes to a close:

Our last guest just left the reception. You know my husband, sort of. We have a hotel room for this week. There are lots of windows, a private Jacuzzi, and some sort of "really great surprise" that my husband has waiting for me. You know what I'm wearing under my dress—more importantly, he knows what I'm wearing under my dress. You know that this man runs hot, quite a bit, which makes me run hot quite a bit. He's staring into my eyes, and he's got that cocky smirk all over his face. His jacket's thrown over his arm, his bowtie is loosened, his sleeves are rolled up, and his top two buttons are unbuttoned And this king of my dream is sauntering his sexy self right straight for me.

So, if you'll excuse me, I'm going to make sure my Mr. Montgomery is one, very happy man.

About the Author

Nadlee Thims is an American author with a passion for the stories she creates. Nadlee has two sons and loves to travel. Thims has two cats, but would have her own zoo, if she could find a way to make that happen. When this author is not traveling, playing with animals, or writing, she can be found walking the edges of some body of water, dreaming of her next story.

~*~

Visit Nadlee at

http://Facebook.com/naughtynadlee

Also Available
from The Wild Rose Press, Inc.
and major retailers.

Hot Bayou Fire

By Elizabeth Shore

Mega-talented glass sculptor Chase Durand just scored the commission of a lifetime. The southern bayou's poshest new hotel is about to open with his art the star feature. His motorcycle-riding, bad-boy reputation perfectly fits the hotel's modern, edgy look. And when a drop-dead gorgeous IT engineer hard wires his high-tech art, her luscious curves ignite a fire in him that's hotter than molten glass. Between them, he sees a perfect pairing of minds…and bodies.

What Autumn Rivette sees is danger. The minute she lays eyes on the sexy artist, her unruly desire screams for satisfaction. His arresting good looks and mammoth muscles make every nerve sizzle. Yet years in foster care taught her two lessons–trust no one and never get attached. Physical pleasure is one thing, but her heart is off limits. When her past threatens both their careers, it's time to learn to embrace the fire or to douse it forever…

Also Available
from The Wild Rose Press, Inc.
and major retailers.

Royal Snapshot

By Anya Sharpe

Gia Perrone is hired to fill in as famous photographer Scott Wainwright's assistant. The job entails documenting the life of Santoria's royal family and the prince's wedding. All work, no play, right? Wrong. Scott lives up to his reputation as an insulting bully of a boss until he makes his off-the-clock interest in Gia clear. Meanwhile, Prince Roman can't stop flirting with her, despite being engaged. Add in non-committal ex-boyfriend Jason Fortin begging for a fifth chance, and good grief, life in Santoria isn't just a job anymore. It's a conundrum of royal proportions.

Which one will win her heart? One she doesn't want. One she can't have. One she can have—maybe—but does she want him?

Thank you for purchasing
this publication of The Wild Rose Press, Inc.

For questions or more
information contact us at
info@thewildrosepress.com.

The Wild Rose Press, Inc.
www.thewildrosepress.com